BOOKS BY JASON SEGEL
AND KIRSTEN MILLER

Otherworld

OtherEarth

OTHEREARTH

JASON SEGEL
KIRSTEN MILLER

DELACORTE PRESS

Copyright © 2018 by The Jason Segel Company
Jacket art copyright © 2018 by The Jason Segel Company

Visit us on the Web! GetUnderlined.com

Educators and librarians, for a variety of teaching tools, visit us at
RHTeachersLibrarians.com

Library of Congress Cataloging-in-Publication Data
Names: Segel, Jason, author. | Miller, Kirsten, author.
Title: Otherearth / Jason Segel, Kirsten Miller.
Description: New York : Delacorte Press, [2018] | Series: Last reality ; 2 |
Summary: "After discovering terrifying information about Otherworld,
the Company's high-tech VR gaming experience, Simon and his friends are on the run,
searching for Simon's old roommate. He may just be the key to shutting the
Company down, although if they don't find him in time, it may be too late
for not only them, but for all of humanity"—Provided by publisher.
Identifiers: LCCN 2018022930 (print) | LCCN 2018029060 (ebook) |
ISBN 978-1-101-93938-3 (el) | ISBN 978-1-101-93936-9 (hardback) |
ISBN 978-0-525-70794-3 (intl. tr. pbk.)
Subjects: | CYAC: Virtual reality—Fiction. | Internet games—Fiction. | Best friends—Fiction. |
Friendship—Fiction. | Conduct of life—Fiction. | Science fiction.
Classification: LCC PZ7.S4533 (ebook) | LCC PZ7.S4533 Otd 2018 (print) | DDC [Fic]—dc23

The text of this book is set in 11-point Minion Pro.
Interior design by Stephanie Moss

Printed in the United States of America
10 9 8 7 6 5 4 3 2 1
First Edition

OTHEREARTH

PROLOGUE

None of this is happening.

I'm standing in the morgue at the Company's facility. I should see my own image in the gleaming metal cabinets where they store all the bodies, but I have no reflection. I don't know if I'm real.

There are corpses laid out on the autopsy tables, crisp white sheets pulled up to their chins. On the far side of the room are Brian and West, two guys from my high school who were victims of an accident that the Company orchestrated. In front of me lies Carole, the soccer mom turned fearless warrior who sacrificed her own life to save mine. Blood seeps through the section of sheet that covers her abdomen. That's where the sword that killed her went in.

She thought I was the one who could save the others. All it takes is a look around the morgue to know Carole was tragically wrong. There are at least a dozen bodies here; most of their faces I don't recognize from the real world. Who knows how many cadavers are tucked away in the morgue's metal drawers? The dead here come in all sizes and shapes and colors. But they all died as guinea pigs, their brains tinkered with and their bodies broken. All to beta test the Company's new virtual reality technology. All to debug a goddamn video game.

The man who started it all is on the table next to Carole's. Milo Yolkin, the Company's boyish CEO and the inventor of Otherworld. Now he's just another shriveled-up corpse. The mind that was hailed as one of the century's greatest turned out to be no match for its own creation. Otherworld may have given Milo everything he'd been missing, but in the end, the game killed him.

I pass a computer monitor on my way to the door. I can see the room reflected in its screen, and I'm still not there. I glance at the floor behind me—I don't even cast a shadow. Whatever this is—dream, hallucination or memory—I know only one thing for certain: Kat's here somewhere, and I have to find her.

I don't know who needs to be rescued. Maybe it's her—but it might be me. The panic keeps building. It's pushing me forward. I rush out of the morgue and into the main part of the facility, then skid to a stop. Ahead of me is a wall of boxes with hexagonal windows. These are the life-support capsules where the Company stores the people whose minds they've imprisoned in Otherworld. It looks like the corporation has expanded its operation since the last time I was here. There must be hundreds of thousands of capsules by now, stacked on top of each other and rising up into the sky.

In the center of the wall is an opening—the entrance to a maze. There's a middle-aged man lying on the floor in front of it, blood gushing from a bullet wound in his arm. As I close in on him, I notice that his eyes remain open. The man doesn't see me, but he might not be dead. He works for the Company, though I have no idea what he does. All I know is that his name is Wayne Gibson. He's Kat's stepfather. And I was the one who shot him.

I step over Wayne's body, resisting the urge to give it a kick, and enter the maze. Walls of stacked capsules tower over me on either side. Inside each capsule is a human being. I glance into one as I pass by and recognize the swollen, purple carcass of a guy my age. The car accident the Company arranged for Marlow Holm and his mother must have been brutal. Mrs. Holm's corpse is probably back at the morgue. Somehow Marlow survived. Now they have his mind trapped in Otherworld. I wonder which of the Holms was the lucky one.

I pick up my pace and try not to look into any more of the capsules. The path in front of me keeps branching in different directions. I don't know where I'm going, so I stick to the left. After a while, I start to think the maze might be unsolvable. Every new bit looks the same as the last. I'm about to collapse from exhaustion when I turn a corner and find myself at a juncture. The path ahead has split again, but this time there's a statue blocking the left side. The tall Clay Man has a Bedouin scarf wrapped around his head and a glowing amulet dangling against his chest. One of his arms is raised, with a finger pointing toward the passage on the right.

"It's you," I gasp. The Clay Man is Busara Ogubu's Otherworld avatar. I'm so relieved to find her that I almost forget that she can't be trusted. Busara was the one who got me into this mess.

She risked my life and others for her own selfish reasons. Still, it's impossible to hate her. If it weren't for Busara's scheming, there's little doubt Kat would already be dead.

"Busara," I say. If her avatar can hear me, he shows no desire to communicate. Then it dawns on me that the finger may be the only message I need.

I choose the path to the right.

I try not to think morbid thoughts while I run. I try not to imagine what might be happening to Kat. I try not to envision my life without her.

Then, all at once, I find myself at the center of the maze. There's a wide-open space here, and it's packed with remarkable beings. Some are giants, others tiny and delicate. A few look almost human, but most can only be described as hideous. No two of them are exactly alike. These are the Children, the creations of Otherworld, the digital offspring of parents whose DNA wasn't meant to mix. When they first appeared, Milo tried to get rid of them—until he realized the Children were every bit as alive as he was.

Above, thousands of captive humans are looking down from the capsules, their faces pressed up against the glass. I came here to find Kat; now I won't be able to leave without helping them, too. There are now thousands of people and an entire species depending on Simon Eaton, fuckup extraordinaire, to rescue them.

And yet no one notices that I'm here. They're all staring at a spot on one of the walls. Somehow I know that whatever is there is what I've been looking for. I weave through the crowd, and when I reach the front I see guards standing on either side of one of the capsules. Their faces are blandly handsome, their bodies buff, and both of them are armed to the teeth. They look a lot like the non-player characters in Otherworld.

No one in the crowd dares to challenge them. It's clear they'll die if they do. The guards can't see me, though. If Kat's in there, this is my chance to save her.

As I walk up to the glass, I pray I'm not too late. It's not until I'm standing between the two guards that I realize everything is all wrong. The person inside the capsule isn't Kat. The body doesn't even belong to a female. Lying on the stainless steel shelf is a tall, pasty kid with a giant nose. I suppose I'm still not used to seeing him with no hair. It takes me a moment to recognize myself.

I spin around to face the Children who are staring straight through me. I see why they're all here. They came for me. I was supposed to help them. But now that they've found me, I'm just a huge disappointment. They're all going to die. I won't be saving anyone.

"Why are you so upset?" A man wearing a garish 1960s suit and a brown fedora steps forward. He's the only one here who can see me. It makes sense, I suppose. I'm the only one who ever sees him. "Don't tell me you're surprised," my dead grandfather snorts. "You always said you weren't the One."

I'm about to respond when something whizzes through the air past my ear. I hear an *oof* and a thud. One of the NPC guards just hit the ground. I'm looking straight at the second guy when an arrow gets him right through the temple.

I catch sight of Kat's hair in the crowd. Her camouflage bodysuit leaves the rest of her little more than a blur.

"Kat!" I call out to her, but she must not hear me.

She rushes past me to the capsule and yanks open the door. Kat slides out the shelf with my body on top. I stand by and watch as the girl I've loved since I was eight years old bends over my motionless body.

"Simon," she whispers. "Remember who you are."

I see my body twitch as if it's coming back to life.

"Simon," Kat says. "It's time. Open your eyes."

I open my eyes. I'm in a hotel room in Texas. Kat is asleep beside me.

BADLANDS

I zip my fly and look up from the weeds I've been watering. The sun has risen over the hills in the distance, and there's nothing but sand and scrub as far as the eye can see. I could be anywhere. There's no way to tell what century I'm in—or what planet I'm on. If I've traveled back in time, I'd never know the difference. And though I'd rather not think about it, there's a chance I'm being held captive in a capsule somewhere, with a disk attached to the back of my skull and my brain imprisoned in a computer-generated world.

My eyes detect movement in a patch of dead brush. A scorpion emerges, and I watch it scuttle across the sand toward my shoe. The thing is a monster—at least six inches long—but I don't even flinch. My startle reflex has been dialed down to zero. I've seen much worse in recent days. There's one thing that worries me, though. It's the color. I didn't know real-world scorpions came in iridescent green. If I had a phone, I'd look it up. I'm starting to wonder if I'll ever have a phone again.

I send the creature flying with a kick and head back toward the car. Kat's there soaking up some early-morning sun. The sight of her pulls my thoughts back from the darkness. She's wearing a Budweiser T-shirt and a pair of hot-pink jogging pants with the word DIVA printed across the butt. She picked up the ensemble at a Walmart in West Virginia, and somehow she makes it look amazing.

Kat's reading a large sheet of paper that's spread out on the hood in front of her. "Is that a *newspaper*?" I ask as I approach. I can't even remember the last time I saw a print edition.

"Nicked it from the hotel before we left," she tells me. "Says here there's a pig-picking in Darwin next week. And Charlie Jones was arrested for stealing three chickens and a pregnant goat. I guess that's what passes for front-page news here in southwest Texas."

"Nothing about Milo? Or the Company?"

She looks up from the paper and snorts. "Are you kidding? Darwin, Texas, hasn't made it out of the twentieth century," she says.

A gust of wind sends Kat's copper curls flying. I feel a twinge as she pulls her hair back and twists it into a bun. It suddenly occurs to me that the two of us may be alone. "Where's Busara?" I ask.

Kat folds the newspaper and points to an identical stretch of desert on the other side of the road. There's a tall, dark figure strolling through the brush. From a distance, she looks just like her Otherworld avatar. I'm an idiot for never noticing the resemblance.

While Busara's communing with nature, I grab Kat and draw

her toward me. We've only had a few minutes to ourselves since we sped out of Brockenhurst two days ago. We were officially a couple by the time we hit I-95.

Being on the run would be so much more fun if we didn't have a chaperone along for the ride. Instead I've had to make do with furtive kisses. When I slide my hand around the back of Kat's neck, I feel the shaved patch at the base of her skull. Her hair is beginning to grow back in. She wraps her arms around me, and my head spins. I pull her closer and she loses her balance, sliding off the hood and landing on her injured leg.

"Awwww, *man*," she groans.

"Shit, I'm so sorry, Kat." I pick her up and gently put her back on the hood. She tries to smile but her face is ashen. She says her leg is getting better, but it still can't bear her full weight. She was injured in Otherworld right before we made our escape from the facility, and her real-world body suffered the effects. I've been trying to convince her to see a doctor, but she won't run the risk. I suppose it's a moot point anyway. We don't have the money to pay one.

"It's okay." I know the pain must be fading when Kat plants a kiss on my lips. Then she gazes over my shoulder at the wasteland I was just contemplating. "What were you thinking about out there?"

"You were watching me urinate?" I lift an eyebrow. "I had no idea you were into that sort of thing."

Kat rolls her eyes. "I was just making sure you didn't step on a snake."

The green scorpion scuttles back through my thoughts. This time it's my turn to wince. Since I returned from my last trip to

Otherworld, I've been having trouble believing that everything I see here is real. This world and the other keep blending together. Maybe it's just my way of avoiding reality. It's still hard for me to accept the fact that, less than two days ago, I shot my girlfriend's stepfather. And it wasn't in a video game.

"Do you think Wayne is dead?" I ask Kat. It's the first time either of us have uttered her stepfather's name since we left New Jersey. As I wait for Kat's answer, I realize I honestly don't know what I want it to be.

"No," Kat replies with conviction.

"How can you be so sure?"

"Because we're not that lucky." I was hoping for more of a medical opinion, but Kat's definitely got a point there. Our luck hasn't exactly been stellar.

We shouldn't be hanging out on the side of a road. It's time to get going again. The paranoia hits us both, and we look for Busara. She's headed back in our direction, as if the same alarm just went off in her head.

"How many miles until we get to New Mexico?" Kat asks.

"Hard to tell," I say. "Three or four hundred, maybe? This is the first time I've ever used a fold-up, paper map. They don't make it easy to judge distances."

"And you're absolutely sure we'll find Elvis when we get there?"

I laugh—and remind myself that Kat never had the pleasure of meeting my former boarding school roommate. "Oh, that part's going to be easy," I tell her. "I doubt we'll be able to miss him."

. . .

It's illegal for me to be driving. My license was taken away last year after my brush with the law. But the odds of being stopped by a cop here seem pretty slim. We haven't passed a human on the road for at least two hours. The only living being I've seen in that time was a monstrous hog standing by the side of the road. I picked up speed to get past it. My companions didn't spot it, and I didn't point it out. The beast's tusks brought back memories I'd rather not share with them. And if I'm being completely honest, I'm not a hundred percent sure it was really there.

I've read that feral hogs are a serious problem here in Texas, and I've come across some crazy-ass pictures online. But I always figured that those Internet Hogzillas were at least eighty percent Photoshop. I guess I didn't expect the real animals to be so god-damn *big*. Judging by the size of the thing I saw, it's only a matter of time before the hogs take over. And to think it probably started with a couple of little pink porkers that escaped from a farm. In the wild, they must have returned to their natural state. Tusks sprouted, snouts lengthened and fur grew. And there weren't any humans around telling them when to breed. Soon all of Texas was filled with monsters like the one I just saw. The feral hogs are what the Clay Man called *unintended consequences*. They're proof that Otherworld isn't the only world that's spun out of control.

Kat's napping in the back while Busara sits in the passenger's seat, quietly tinkering with two small machines. One's a metal sphere the size of a softball. The other is a banged-up, partially flattened version of an otherwise identical device. I'm watching out of the corner of my eye when Busara hits a spot on the intact sphere. Suddenly there's a guy wearing workout gear crouching on top of her lap. I yelp and the car swerves as my head jerks around in his direction.

"Yes!" Busara exclaims.

"What the hell?" I recognize the guy. It's Marlow Holm, who's probably dead by now. My nerves are already on edge. He's not who I need to see.

Thankfully, there's not much to hit on the side of the road. The guy in Busara's lap vanishes and she's cackling hysterically. I don't think I've seen her bust a gut like this. It's definitely the first time she's laughed since we left New Jersey. Or maybe ever.

"Oh my God," she gasps when she finally stops. She marvels at the device in her hands, turning it over and over. "Wasn't that *amazing*? Its sensors must tell it how much empty air is surrounding it. The hologram contorts to fit the available space."

I'd probably take a lot more pleasure in Busara's holographic experiments if I didn't know what happened to Marlow in real life. I told Busara and Kat where he is—the Company has him. I didn't tell them what he looked like the last time I saw him. His entire body was a purple, swollen bruise.

"Hey, what's going on?" Kat murmurs sleepily from the backseat. My eyes flick up to the rearview mirror. Kat's sitting up and rubbing her eyes. When her hands fall from her face, my heart skips a beat.

"I just figured out how to turn the projector on," Busara says.

"That's awesome," Kat says. "Now can you figure out how to

hack an ATM so we can get some food? I'd kill for a pack of Fun-yuns."

They both laugh. I'm not sure what they find so funny. We had to throw away all our credit cards. Busara's smartphone is at the bottom of a trash can, too. Everything good about the twenty-first century leaves a trail, and when you're on the run from a tech corporation, you can't afford to be tracked. So we're back in the Dark Ages, with fifty-four dollars in cash, which we'll use to fill up our car with dead-dinosaur juice. Meanwhile, we're smuggling some of the most advanced technology on earth. The projectors on Busara's lap are the first to generate opaque, three-dimensional holograms. Tucked away in the glove compartment are a pair of visors and two flesh-colored disks. Slap a disk on the back of your skull and place a visor over your eyes, and you'll be transported to Otherworld—a virtual world you can experience with all five of your senses. In Otherworld, anything you desire can be yours, but the disks are flawed. They'll kill you if you make a wrong move. Dozens of people have already died while the Company tries to work out the bugs.

Still, flawed or not, humankind has never produced technol-ogy like these disks. The ones we have are probably worth bil-lions. The Company won't let a pair of them just disappear. If they catch the three of us, there's no doubt we'll be the next to die.

Marlow Holm's hologram reappears on Busara's lap, and this time I lose it.

"Can you stop screwing around with those projectors until we get to Elvis's house?" I bark at her. I sound far more hostile than I'd like. The rage spills out so easily these days. I try to adopt a more civilized tone. "*Please.* We can't be more than six hours away now."

The image disappears. Fortunately, Busara isn't easily cowed. Most people find my size and fluctuating levels of insanity intimidating. But Busara doesn't seem to care. "You want me to stop?" she replies. "You think we have an extra six hours to spare? You think the Company is sitting around twiddling its thumbs and waiting for us to get settled in New Mexico?"

She's right, and she knows it. I sit back and wait for her to finish. Unfortunately, she's on a roll.

"We haven't seen a news report in over twenty-four hours. We don't have a clue what's going on. Who knows how the Company explained Milo Yolkin's death to the world? They could have pinned the murder on you, Simon. You could be the most famous person in the United States right now and we'd never even know it. So you want me to stop trying to figure out how to use this projector? 'Cause last I checked, it's our life insurance policy."

It's true. The Company used one of the projectors to murder four kids back in New Jersey. If we can prove it, we'll have something we can take to the authorities. But that's never going to happen unless we know how the things actually work.

"Okay, okay," I groan. "Do whatever you want. Just shut the hell up."

"I'm sorry, what did you just—" Busara starts.

"Ignore him," Kat advises from the backseat. "Simon hasn't eaten more than a Snickers bar in the past twelve hours, and that giant body of his needs regular fuel or it gets hangry."

"Hey—whose side are you on?" I ask the girl in the backseat.

"Hers," Kat says bluntly. I check her out in the rearview mirror.

She winks at me and I lose the will to fight. I've been in love with Kat since I was eight years old. I almost lost her once. Now that I have her back, I'm going to do my best not to screw things up.

"Besides, Simon," Busara adds. Apparently there's a last word that she needs to have. "You promised me we'd find my father. And for all we know, six hours could make all the difference."

Once again, Busara is right.

THE PHANTOM

I've been staring at the gas gauge for over an hour. The needle is now *below* empty and the red light on the dashboard has burned itself onto my retinas. For the last thirty minutes, the three of us have been sitting in silence, focusing all of our energy on keeping the car on the road.

Kat crawls up between the two front seats. "You sure there's no way to reactivate this?" she asks Busara, tracing a finger across a blue OnStar button on the rearview mirror. "They could send help if we run out of gas."

"If the Company didn't get to us first," I point out.

Kat huffs with annoyance. "Simon, this is a desert. If we end up stranded out here, the Company will be the least of our worries. We have no food and our water is almost gone."

"Then maybe we should have stolen a few bottles at the last place like I suggested," I say.

"And maybe *you* should have filled up the gas tank."

"I thought we should keep some money on hand just in case!"

"This argument is pointless," Busara says. "Even if we wanted to reactivate the OnStar, we couldn't do it without a phone. And besides, there's a gas station ahead of us."

I squint in the bright sunlight that's pouring in through the windshield. Sure enough, there's a sign in the distance. I lean back against the headrest as my whole body relaxes. I feel Kat kiss my ear. "Sorry," she whispers. "I think I'm getting hangry too."

I pull into the station. "You pump, I'll pay," I tell Busara as I roll to a stop. She hands me our last two twenty-dollar bills.

"I'll come in too," Kat says.

"No," I tell her. "You stay. We need to make this fast." She won't approve of what I'm going to do. I'm not thrilled that I'll soon be adding theft to my long list of crimes. But there's no way in hell I'm going to let us starve to death before we reach New Mexico.

I step into the little store and realize it's my lucky day. There's no one behind the counter. I grab a plastic bag and rush down the first of three aisles, filling my bag with anything edible I can see. When I reach the final aisle, I discover I've had company the entire time.

"Get enough for the girls, too?" There's an old man standing by the Cheetos. He's gotta be at least eighty-five, but he's still a dapper dresser. His sunglasses have amber lenses and thick tortoiseshell frames. They go well with his Brooklyn accent, which is like something out of a Scorsese film.

"Huh?" I reply.

An eyebrow rises above the frames of his sunglasses. "You

know, I thought you'd be smarter," he says. I guess I should be offended, but I'm too busy taking him in. There are hipsters who'd kill for the straw hat and guayabera he's rocking. But I doubt they'd try, thanks to the giant gun the guy's got propped against his shoulder. Thinking back to my *Call of Duty* days, I'd say it's a WWII-era sniper's rifle.

"Are you from the Company?" I ask. It seems odd that they'd hire a geriatric assassin with an antique firearm, but you never know.

"What?" One corner of his mouth rises in a sneer. "Fuck no. Irene Diamond sent me." It's so weird to hear a guy his age cursing that I almost miss the name.

"You mean my *mother*?" That is literally the very last thing I expected him to say.

"The fact that Irene Diamond is your mother makes very little difference to me. The fact that she's the Kishka's daughter—that's what's relevant here. You can thank *him* for saving your ass."

My grandfather has been dead for forty years. A small-time Brooklyn gangster nicknamed the Kishka on account of his giant nose, he's been at the bottom of the Gowanus Canal since the 1970s. But that doesn't keep him from popping up every once in a while. I wasn't aware that my ass needed saving at this particular juncture. I wonder what the Kishka knows that I don't.

"Wait—how did you just . . ."

"Find you?" the old man shakes his head at my stupidity. "You got the nose, but you didn't get the brains, did ya? You ever heard of OnStar? It's a goddamn surveillance system. Your friend's car has been spying on you the whole time you've been gone."

I glance out the front window at the car. It seems perfectly harmless. "That's not possible," I argue pointlessly. "The service is disabled."

"So the hell what? You really think that means they stopped tracking the car? God, you're an idiot. You've been leaving a trail of digital bread crumbs behind you. Lucky for you, your mother has a few friends in the law enforcement community. They told her what direction you were heading, and she called me."

"Why *you*?" I ask, hoping the question doesn't sound too rude.

"I'm familiar with the terrain. Been down here for years. Nobody knows the border like I do." I think he's telling me he hasn't retired. I wonder what he's been bringing across the border. Drugs? People? Huaraches? Who'd have guessed that my prim, proper mother was buddies with an octogenarian smuggler? Maybe I owe Irene Diamond a bit more respect.

"So does that mean the Company knows where we are too?"

"Oh, there's no doubt that they do," says the old guy.

My heart picks up speed. "Then why haven't they stopped us?"

" 'Cause they wanted to find out where you're going!" He's clearly exasperated with my ignorance. "Why bother killing a few measly rats when there's a chance to set the whole nest on fire?"

I feel a bit wobbly. I've been leading them straight to Elvis.

"What should we do?" I ask.

"Get your friends in here," the man orders. "If there's anything essential in the car, tell them to bring it." I hesitate. "You got a better idea?" he snaps.

I don't, so I lean out the door. Busara's just putting the cap back on the gas tank. "Kat, Busara. Come here, please. Grab the disks and the projectors, too."

"Simon?" Kat asks. There's a worried look on her face. She

knows something's up. The *please* definitely tipped her off. I've never been known for my manners.

"Don't worry," I tell her. "But *please* hurry up."

A few seconds later, the two of them barge through the door. Kat's limping, with one of her arms slung around Busara's shoulder.

"What's going on?" Busara asks warily.

"Oh my God." Kat's eyes have landed on the old man's gun.

"It's okay," I assure her. "Really." I hope to hell I'm right.

The man offers the two girls the kind of smile you'd see on the Wikipedia entry for *dirty old bastard*. "So which one of these beauties is the girlfriend?" he asks.

I point to Kat and he nods appreciatively. "You may be a bit slow on the uptake, but you're related to the Kishka, no doubt. You got the same taste in ladies." He reaches out a hand. "Name's Leonard D'Ignoto, sweetheart," he says.

"*Lenny* D'Ignoto? You're *the Phantom*?" I don't know why I'm asking. I know it's true. There was an entire chapter on him in *Gangsters of Carroll Gardens*. He was a sharpshooter for the Gallo crime family in Brooklyn, which explains the gun. They say he got his nickname by killing over three dozen made men. He shot them all from a distance, so no one ever saw his face. I gotta admit, I'm a bit dazzled. It's a little like meeting a movie star.

"Wow," Kat says. She remembers too.

"So you really did know my grandfather."

"Yep," he says. "He introduced me to my wife. She just happened to be his girlfriend at the time. Never got a chance to make it up to him." Lenny digs into his pocket and retrieves a large wad of hundred-dollar bills. "This means me and the Kishka are even. Now if you'll excuse me." He walks over to the open window near the register and positions his gun on the ledge. With his sunglasses pushed up on his forehead, he puts his right eye up to the sight. I have no idea what he's trying to hit. The gun seems to be aimed at the sky.

"What is he doing?" Busara whispers. "Who the hell is this guy? How do you guys know him?"

A shot rings out. Before Leonard has time to stand up, an object has fallen from the heavens. Shards of metal and plastic go flying when it hits the ground.

"Holy shit, it's a drone!" Kat gasps, putting words to my fears.

"That's how they've been watching you," Lenny says. "There's a van a few miles back, and I'm pretty sure they just stepped on the gas. So what do you say we swap keys?"

I'm not going to second-guess him at this point. I toss Lenny the keys to Busara's car and he throws his over to me.

"I'm parked behind the station," he tells me. "Hold back and let 'em chase me. Wait until we're long gone before you take off. But whatever happens, don't get on the road again."

"I don't understand. What are we supposed to do?" Busara asks.

"Drive through the desert," Leonard tells us. "Nobody who lives around here uses the *roads*."

After a quick tip of his hat to the ladies, Leonard jogs out to Busara's car, tosses his gun onto the passenger seat and climbs in behind the wheel. Then he's off. Less than a minute after Lenny peels out of the parking lot, a white van races by. It's got to be going at least 130, but if I were betting, I'd put my money on the Phantom winning the race.

We find the vehicle he left parked behind the gas station covered in a beige tarp. I pull it off, revealing a Land Rover painted in desert camo, with a tent tied down to the roof. Busara cups her hands and peeks in through one of the windows. When she turns back to us, she's practically bubbly.

"It's got GPS. And satellite radio." Lenny's border business must be booming if he's giving vehicles like this away.

"Is it safe to use stuff like that?" Kat asks me. "Won't the Company be able to track us again?"

"Why would they try?" I reply. "They think they're already chasing us."

"But what if they run Lenny off the road?" she asks. "What if they find out we're not in the car?"

"I'm going to go out on a limb and say your friend Lenny is the kind of guy who doesn't leave home without a plan that covers all contingencies," Busara says. She looks up at me. "How do you know him again?"

"Long story," I say.

"Great. It's gonna be a long drive," Busara replies as she climbs into the passenger's seat.

Once we're on the move, Busara uses the GPS to chart a course through the desert; then she switches the satellite radio on and searches for a news channel. She finds one and we listen patiently to reports on the latest scandal to paralyze the government and the riots that have been taking place in Rust Belt cities across the American heartland. It's all big news, of course, but none of it's new. I would have thought the shocking death of Milo Yolkin, the brilliant CEO of the Company, the world's most powerful corporation, would have been the top story of the day. But it isn't until the daily business report that we first hear Milo's name.

The Company announced today that CEO Milo Yolkin will be taking an unforeseen leave of absence from the business he founded over a decade ago. With Yolkin gone, the wide release of his latest project will be shelved indefinitely. A major leap forward in virtual reality, Otherworld was on its way to becoming the most highly anticipated video game of the last forty years. Now it seems that only a small group of people will be able to claim that they've played it.

The Company's stock price took a hit following the news. Shares fell by almost thirty percent yesterday, and the plunge is expected to continue when trading opens today. Meanwhile, the rumor mill has been working overtime as investors speculate about the reason for Yolkin's sudden sabbatical. Theories range from standard burnout to life-threatening illness. Many in the tech community are beginning to wonder what the future of the Company might look like without its boy genius.

It takes a minute for it all to sink in. The Company is lying about Milo Yolkin. They're hiding the fact that the boy genius's "sabbatical" is going to be permanent.

"You're sure Milo was dead the last time you saw him?" Busara asks.

I'll never forget the sight of Milo's emaciated body lying motionless on a sliding steel tray. It was hard to believe that it had functioned as long as it had. The most brilliant man in America looked like a junkie who'd wasted away. I suppose in the end that's exactly what he was. But it wasn't drugs that did Milo in. It was his own game that killed him. He got addicted. Then he played until he died.

"Yeah," I mutter. "I'm sure."

"The Company's already suffering. If news got out that Milo was dead, their stock price would totally crash," Kat says. "We know something that the Company doesn't want the world to know. That means we've got leverage."

"It also means the Company has another reason to kill us," I point out.

Everyone in the car goes quiet. There's nothing left to say.

The GPS screen says we're making progress, but it's hard to believe we'll ever get anywhere. I've been driving all day across the desert, and I doubt the speedometer has ever passed thirty miles per hour. Turns out you need a road to drive fast. Since night fell, twenty has been my maximum speed. The darkness out here is so dense that the Land Rover's headlights barely cut through it. There's no moon out, but I can see the Milky Way, a purple streak of stars like a scar across the heavens. It reminds me that my own little world is just one of billions.

The girls are sleeping in the back. Kat suggested we stop and make camp in the desert, but I didn't think that was wise. I'll keep driving as long as I can. If we're still alive in the morning, I'll let Busara take over.

"I knew a guy once who fell asleep behind the wheel on I-95," says someone to my right. I'd recognize the voice anywhere. I look over to find my grandfather sitting in the passenger's seat, one wing tip–clad foot propped up on the dashboard. I can't see much of his face in the darkness, but I can make out the silhouette of his giant schnoz. He looks just as real as Marlow Holm, but he's not the product of any projector. He's coming straight from my addled mind. "Cop told me they had to use a spatula to get his guts off the road."

"This isn't I-95," I say. "Not much to hit around here."

"Still," says the Kishka. "You shouldn't be taking risks you don't need to take."

I suppose that's true, but there's no point in pulling over. I'd never be able to fall asleep.

"I met your friend Lenny," I tell him.

"Yeah, I know. How about that?" says the Kishka. "Guess I can't hate the bastard for stealing my girl anymore, seeing as how he just rescued the sole heir to my DNA."

"Mom arranged the whole thing."

The Kishka laughs. "You sound shocked."

"I am," I admit. "I wasn't aware that she gave a shit. Plus, it doesn't make sense. Why would she risk her law practice? She could be disbarred if they find out she helped me."

"You think that makes a difference to her?" the Kishka asks.

"I have eighteen years' worth of evidence that suggests I'm not exactly at the top of her priorities list."

"You're working with a limited set of data," says the Kishka. I almost ask what he knows about data when I remember that I'm talking to myself. "And even if you had it all, you'd never be able to predict what Irene's gonna do next."

"You're saying my mom is a wild card?" I ask with a laugh. My grandfather obviously never witnessed what happens when his fancy-pants daughter discovers the maid left a speck of dust in her house. "I think maybe you've been gone too long."

"Yeah well, whatever she's like now, I think it's safe to say she's still human," the Kishka tells me. "And if there's one thing I know about humans, it's this—they don't make any sense. And the minute you start expecting them to, you end up at the bottom of a canal."

"Simon, who are you talking to?" It's Busara in the backseat. I had no idea I was actually speaking out loud.

"My dead grandfather," I say. I told her all about the Kishka earlier. I neglected to mention that he and I have been chatting on a regular basis.

She's quiet for a moment. I think I may have just outed myself as a raving nutcase.

"Does it help?" she asks quietly.

"Yes," I tell her. "Sometimes it does."

But this time I don't feel any better.

MAVERICK

"Hey, Simon, wake up." Kat is gently shaking me. I sit up with a jolt when I realize the car has stopped.

"What's going on?" My eyes are having trouble adjusting to the daylight. For all I know, we're surrounded by Company men.

"The GPS says we're here," Busara tells me. As she comes into focus, I see her leaning forward for a closer look at the screen, as if there's been some mistake.

"This is where your friend lives?" Kat asks me. "This isn't even a town."

I look out the window, blinking furiously until I can see clearly. Dark Skies, New Mexico, consists of a filling station and a Mexican grocery store that looks to be permanently shut. The carcass of a deer lies by the side of the road. Most of the skeleton has been picked perfectly clean. The horns that jut out of its skull are curved like a pair of parentheses. They don't look like they belong to any North American beast. Whatever it is, the animal has obviously been dead for quite some time. The roadkill crews must not make it to this part of the state very often.

I'm pretty sure we're exactly where we need to be.

"Do you think we should stop at the gas station?" Kat wants to know. "Maybe they know Elvis. There can't be more than a handful of people who live in the area."

"No need for that," I say with an exaggerated yawn. "I've already found him. He lives up there."

Ahead of us are bald brown hills. Several domed white structures are perched on top of the tallest. From here they look like a Star Wars set. I've never seen anything like them, but I know they're what I've been searching for—what I knew we wouldn't be able to miss. I point up at them through the glass.

"Simon, that's not a house. I'm pretty sure it's an astronomical observatory." Busara was cool with me talking to my long-dead grandfather, but she's clearly questioning my sanity right now. "Nobody *lives* there."

"Oh, really? You don't say," I respond, closing my eyes and resting my head against the seat. I'm a wee bit tired of her know-it-all attitude. "Why don't we drive up and see if anyone's home? Lemme know when we're getting close."

"Kat?" I hear Busara appeal to my lovely girlfriend in the backseat. The two of them have been known to gang up on me, but this time Kat's on my side.

"I think we should humor him," she says. Not exactly the most passionate support, but it does the trick.

"Thanks," I say, smiling as I savor my victory. Busara sighs and shifts the Land Rover into drive.

Fifteen minutes pass before we reach the road that leads up to the observatory. It looks like something that was built for mountain bikes rather than cars. It takes over half an hour to scale the side of what most people would consider a rather insignificant mountain. We're almost to the top when we come to a halt in front of a tall metal gate. A fence festooned with razor wire circles the perimeter of the property. To the left of our car is an intercom with a speaker and a single button.

"Okay, what now?" Busara asks. I can hear the annoyance in her voice. She thinks this is all just a waste of her time.

"Roll down your window," I say as if instructing a kindergartener. She gives me the stink-eye but complies. "Now press the button on the intercom."

"Simon, be nice!" Kat scolds me from the backseat.

Scowling, Busara presses the button and we hear ringing. It goes on for so long that even I am starting to lose hope when the ringing suddenly stops.

"Yeah?" The person speaking has his mouth full of something, and he's clearly perturbed that he's had to stop chewing.

I'm grinning as I lean over Busara in the driver's seat. "*Vidkryty zhopu!*" I shout into the microphone.

The person on the other side is silent. Then he bursts out laughing, which is quickly followed by the sound of choking. The intercom cuts off, and I'm pretty sure I just killed my friend. Then I hear a buzzer, and I'm relieved to see the gate in front of us begin to open.

"What the hell did you just say?" Kat asks.

"I said '*Open up, asshole*' in Ukrainian." Back at school, those were the passwords to enter our dorm room.

"You know Ukrainian?" Busara asks.

"Just the two most important words," I tell her.

Busara shakes her head and pulls past the gates. She drives the rest of the way to the top of the hill and parks in the shadow of the giant domed observatory that I spotted from the town below. I slip out of the passenger's seat as Elvis comes bounding down the stairs of a nearby building. It takes me a second to recognize him. He's put on fifteen pounds that he badly needed and his skin is no longer the color of glue.

"Whoa. *That's* Elvis?" I hear Kat whisper.

"Yeah. Not what I was expecting *at all*," Busara agrees, sounding far less robotic than usual. The car door closes behind me. I don't need to hear what they're saying. I know exactly what they're thinking. Girls have *such* filthy minds. Maybe I should have given the ladies a heads-up that he's handsome, but to be honest, I wasn't sure what to expect. It's been a while, and Elvis wasn't looking so hot the last time I saw him. I doubt the girls would have been so impressed back then, unless they like their men scrawny and scared shitless.

"Hello, Simon!" Elvis calls as I get out of the car to greet him. "I was so choked up to hear your voice that I had to perform the Heimlich on myself! How did you find me?" His accent seems to have thickened a lot in the last six months. Hot *and* foreign. I'm sure the ladies in the car are practically swooning.

"Remember the last time I saw you?" I ask. "When you told me you were leaving school too? I asked you where you were going, and all you'd say was 'where the skies are dark and the land is enchanted.' New Mexico is the Land of Enchantment, and

I knew your parents are both astrophysicists. I just put two and two together."

I've been keeping that little tidbit to myself for the past few days. Kat and Busara would have murdered me if they'd found out we were traveling across the country on a hunch. But my answer satisfies Elvis. "You are genius, my friend!" He wraps me up in a giant bear hug and then kisses me repeatedly on both cheeks. Perhaps I have my cold, clinical upbringing to thank, but I don't think I'll ever get used to being mauled by an overly affectionate Ukrainian.

"Damn, Elvis," I say, finally shoving him away. "Give it a rest. You're gonna make my girlfriend jealous."

Elvis's eyes widen. The irises are the icy blue of Magna's Otherworld cave. I swear, I never would have expected Elvis to morph into a teenage dreamboat. I'm starting to question the wisdom of introducing him to Kat. "She's here?" he asks.

I gesture to the car, from which the two girls are now emerging.

"Whoa." Elvis's tongue is practically hanging out of his mouth. I'm getting the sense that he hasn't seen a female in a while. "Which one is she?"

"Kat's the one with all the hair," I tell him.

"Good," he says.

When I realize what he means, I laugh. "The other girl is Busara. Go ahead and give it your best shot," I tell him. "But I just spent the last forty-eight hours with her, and I'm still not convinced she's human. And I know how you feel about robots."

"If that girl is a robot, I will reconsider my feelings," Elvis says.

In the year I lived with him, I never knew Elvis to be anything other than angry, sarcastic and excessively paranoid. But then again, I suppose there wasn't much point in turning on the charm in an all-male environment. Elvis didn't see any reason to shower regularly back then either, which was fine by me. The smell kept unwanted guests away. Everything about the kid was a little bit off, including the fact that his parents had sent him to a prestigious East Coast boarding school without a computer. That particular mystery was solved when Elvis borrowed my laptop. He used it to hack into a toy manufacturer and program millions of toy robots to announce to the world's children that "The robot revolution is nigh."

It's hard to believe that that antisocial anarchist is this Casanova rushing to greet Kat and Busara. Maybe all the time he spent in our dorm left him with a debilitating vitamin D deficiency. Or perhaps he was suffering from a rare intestinal disorder brought on by eating nothing but ranch flavor Doritos and Slim Jims. Elvis is still not exactly what I'd call *normal*. But now I know he's got at least one thing in common with other eighteen-year-old males.

"Greetings, ladies. Welcome to the Dark Skies Observatory!" The Ukrainian accent is now thick enough to slice.

"Hi," Kat says. She always plays it cool. For her a pleasant *hi* means she's practically drooling. "I can't believe we're finally meeting. I've heard so much about you."

"And I have heard *much* more about you," Elvis assures her, wiggling his eyebrows suggestively. Now that I think of it, I did have a tendency to go on and on about her back then, though I don't remember saying anything that would justify an eyebrow wiggle. I spin around to admire the scenery in the opposite direction, just in case I've turned beet red.

"Is this where you live?" I hear Busara ask in her usual clinical fashion.

"Yes," Elvis replies. "I chose it for the magnificent views. At night, you can see for millions of miles. If you like, I will give you a personal tour after dark."

Kat laughs, but when I turn back around I see Busara hasn't even cracked a smile at the joke. "May I use your Internet connection?"

"No," says Elvis. He's shaking his handsome head.

"No?" Busara repeats. She glances over at me, as if hoping I can translate.

"There is no Internet today," Elvis says. "My parents traveled to Albuquerque this weekend to purchase home goods and alcoholic beverages. They took my phone and the router. I am sure they put a stop on the Internet service as well."

"What? *Why?*" Busara sounds scandalized. "What if there's an emergency? There's no one around for miles. You could die up here on your own. What if you'd really been choking a few minutes ago?"

"Oh, I was," Elvis informs her. "But a ham sandwich is not what will kill me. I am not so easy to dispose of."

I walk over and join the three of them. "I think Elvis's parents are more worried about what might happen to the rest of the world if he goes online while they're away," I say. "Most of Elvis's hobbies are classified as felonies."

"I have . . . how do you say . . . *issues* with technology," Elvis admits with a sheepish shrug. "And the law is so little-minded. I almost got into very big trouble a few months ago. Am I right, Simon?"

"Oh, yes," I say. *"Almost."* Fortunately for Elvis, it had been convenient for both of us to let me take the fall.

"I can't believe the feds still think Simon hacked into that toy company," Kat says. "He barely knows how to operate a microwave."

"Hey!" I object. "You know that's not true. I practically live on Hot Pockets." Kat gives me a kiss, but she and Elvis both keep laughing at my expense.

"Wait—*you're* the robot revolution guy?" Busara asks Elvis. He's finally captured her attention.

"Yes," Elvis replies. "That is why I live here now. My mother and father thought it would be smart to leave Massachusetts after the unfortunate incident. And that is also why there is currently no Internet service on this mountain."

"Do you have running water?" Kat asks.

"Of course," Elvis says. "We are scientists, not barbarians."

"Then is it okay if I go in and have a shower?"

"Please," Elvis says gallantly. "In the basement. Knock your-self up."

Busara merely smirks, while Kat doubles over and nearly drops to her knees.

"Out," I say. "The phrase is knock yourself *out.*"

Kat wraps an arm around Busara's shoulder. As she limps toward the bathroom, I can still hear her cackling.

Elvis watches them, grinning like a village idiot.

"You've been in this country since you were two years old.

Your English is better than mine," I whisper. "You said that on purpose."

"My accent is gift that brings joy to the world," Elvis replies. Then he drops the act altogether. "You won't stop me from having a little fun, will you?"

"Knock yourself up," I tell him.

"'Preciate it, bro," he says in a comically American accent. Then he punches me in the arm for good measure. "Come on, lemme show you around."

I can't stop thinking that this place is right out of Otherworld. I wish I could. The thought is more than a little unnerving. Five buildings form the observatory's compound. All are painted a blinding white. I feel like I've wandered into a futuristic Greek myth. Four of the buildings house telescopes of various sizes, their giant unblinking eyes trained on the sky. The fifth, I'm told, is the residence. From the parking lot it looked like a simple box-like structure. Seen from the side, however, it's something else altogether. Only half of it is anchored to the mountain. The rest juts out into the air. It reminds me of a diving board. Or the plank on a pirate ship.

"You and your parents are the only people who live up here?" I ask. "Aren't there visiting professors or scientists or anything?"

"No," says Elvis. "Most observatories are run by universities, but this one is private. My parents were hired to oversee it."

"Someone actually *owns* all of this?" I ask. "Who buys a—"

Elvis holds his hand up to stop me. "I don't want to keep any secrets from you," he says dramatically. "So please—don't ask. I've already caused enough trouble for my parents. I promise that while you'd find the answer entertaining, knowing who the owner is wouldn't do you much good."

I'm composing a mental list of possible suspects as Elvis leads me up to a metal platform situated on the highest point on the mountain. We have an almost three-hundred-and-sixty-degree view from where we're standing. The land below is barren aside from a few mangy pine trees, and the Dark Skies gas station is just a speck in the distance. There's a single paved road that cuts through the dirt. Nothing seems to be moving for hundreds of miles. It's like the rest of the world has been put on pause. I feel safe for the moment, though I probably shouldn't. I scan the sky for signs of drones. One could be hiding up there behind one of the puffy white clouds, and I'd probably never see it. Then my heart skips a beat when what I assumed were three black rocks suddenly lift off the ground.

"Hey, Simon, you okay?" Elvis asks.

I have to clear my throat before I can answer. "Do you see those?" I point at the objects, which are flying our way. I don't know what will scare me more—if Elvis says they're drones or if he doesn't see them at all.

He's studying my face. I do my best to look sane. "Of course. They're birds," he says.

I'm relieved. "You sure?" I ask. They're close enough now so I can make out the wings, but they seem unnaturally large.

"Yeah, they're turkey vultures," Elvis tells me. "Ugliest things you've ever seen."

"Right," I say, though he's wrong. I have seen far uglier things.

I try to shake off the uneasiness by changing the subject. "What's it like living out here in the middle of nowhere?"

Elvis takes the hint and lets me change the subject. "If you're asking if I miss school, then the answer is *hell no*. But it does get pretty boring—especially when I'm offline. I had a project that was keeping me busy, but I had to give it up."

"What was the project?" I ask.

Elvis grins. "See, now *there's* an answer that might prove very useful for you. But before we get to it, let's talk about you first. You must be in deep shit if you drove all the way out here," he says casually. He doesn't seem particularly worried. "Does it have something to do with Otherworld?"

My head instantly swivels in his direction. My reaction must give the truth away. "How did you figure it out?"

"Remember when you asked me to help you deal with Gina in Everglades City?" he asks. "I know you're a competitive asshole, and you definitely aren't above cheating. But taking down someone's Internet connection is going a bit far, even for you."

A wave of panic floods my brain. For a moment, it's like I'm back in Mammon, the Otherworld realm where players butchered one another for profit. That's where I met Gina—and where Gina almost made a buck or two off me. "That evil witch was going to sell me to a cannibal."

I wipe my forehead and realize it's damp with sweat. I've been out of the game for at least thirty-six hours, but I'm starting to wonder if I'll ever really leave. Kat once told me that Otherworld changes you. I'm starting to think she was right.

"Just so you know, Gina's a dude," says Elvis. "A butt-*ugly* dude, to be more specific."

The panic starts to recede when I laugh. I think of the buxom, black-clad beauty I met in Mammon. "Of course she is."

"So what's going on? You have me taking out people's Internet and hacking into hospitals to find out where a bunch of coma patients have been sent. What's the connection? I'm guessing it's the Company. They're always up to something."

Elvis has committed more crimes than anyone I've ever met. And the fact that he'll gleefully tell you all about them means his sanity is questionable too. I'm honestly not sure I can correctly pronounce his last name. But there's no one I trust more than Elvis. I don't hesitate to tell him everything I know.

"They've been using Otherworld to beta test something they call the disk. It's a technology that speaks directly to your brain and lets you experience virtual worlds with all five senses. But it's got a giant bug. If you get hurt in the virtual world, the disk tells your brain that your real body has been injured too. That's why Kat's limping right now. Her leg was crushed beneath some ice in Otherworld. The accident happened in the game, but her injury is real. If she'd been hurt badly enough, she could have died."

The three vultures are circling above something on the ground in the distance, and Elvis is tracking the birds with his eyes. "How is the Company beta testing a technology that's potentially lethal?" he asks. "Even if it weren't illegal to experiment on humans, nobody's going to sign up for something like that."

"Not willingly. That's why the Company's been testing it on people who can't say no. They found hospital patients who were unconscious and convinced their families that the Company had invented the disks as a new kind of therapy. They even built special life-support capsules to house the patients' bodies while their minds are sent to Otherworld. Dozens of people have died so that the Company can get rid of the bugs in their disks."

"And Milo Yolkin is letting this happen?" Elvis asks. "I never thought he was a saint like everyone else. If you ask me, he's a creepy little bastard. But this seems totally out of character."

"Milo is dead," I tell him. "The Company's claiming he's gone on sabbatical, but I saw his corpse with my own two eyes. Milo was the first person to use the disk, and he got hooked on the game. It gives you everything you want—even things you never realized you were into. Milo ended up staying in Otherworld too long, and it killed him."

I pause. I never realized how crazy it would all sound. I keep waiting for Elvis's head to explode, but he just nods like nothing surprises him.

"Makes sense," he says.

"You're not shocked?" I am.

Elvis offers a shrug. He's spent his whole life expecting disaster. "What should shock me? That the tech finally exists? That the Company has turned evil? That Milo's a putz who got killed by his own game? Come on, Simon. Don't be naive. It was all just a matter of time before something like this happened. I told you before—the future is going to be bleak as hell. People get so excited that we have all this fun new technology. They never sit back and consider how dangerous it might be. We're just a bunch of monkeys playing with a box of matches."

"The good news is that it sounds like the Company's plans are on hold for the moment," I say. "We heard on the radio that they've shelved Otherworld. The Company must have figured out that they don't have the brainpower to fix the tech without Milo Yolkin or Busara's dad."

Elvis turns to me, and I can see I've managed to surprise him. "Busara's dad? What does he have to do with all of this?"

"His name is James Ogubu. He invented the disk."

"He's one of the bad guys?" Elvis sounds thrilled.

"No, Milo stole Ogubu's tech to build the game. Until two days ago, Busara thought her father had been murdered. Then Kat and I saw his avatar in Otherworld. His real-world body must be stashed away in a capsule somewhere. Milo was keeping Ogubu's Otherworld avatar frozen in ice in case he needed tech support in the future."

Elvis stares dreamily into the distance. "The most beautiful girl in the world has genius in her blood? Our children are going to be superheroes. How did I get so lucky?"

"You haven't yet," I remind him. "And I'd be willing to wager big bucks that you never do."

"Deal," he says, holding out a hand for me to shake. "One hundred US dollars says Busara Ogubu falls madly in love with me."

"You're on," I say, shaking his hand. I don't mind betting money I haven't got because there's no way in hell he's ever going to win. "Can we get back on the subject now? What are all the hacker boards saying about the Company? Have you heard anything through the grapevine that could help us?" Even though he's been exiled to a mountaintop with spotty Internet service, I'm betting Elvis knows a lot more than I do.

"Sure," says Elvis. "You just said the Company is shelving Otherworld? Well, that's not *exactly* true."

I have a very strong hunch that I don't want to hear what's coming next, but I suppose it's my duty to ask. "What do you mean?"

"Remember the headsets that went with the early-access version of Otherworld?"

Remember? Does he think I'd forget? When Milo realized the disks were dangerous, he decided not to sell them to the public. Instead, he made special VR headsets to go with his game. The headsets were considered a huge leap forward for virtual reality technology, despite the fact that they only let players experience Otherworld with two of their senses.

"Sure," I tell Elvis. "I used to have a couple of them."

"Where are they now?" Elvis asks.

"One was destroyed. The other was confiscated."

Elvis sighs dramatically. "You're going to wish you'd held on to them, man. The Company's stopped production of the headsets, but they're planning to keep the Otherworld servers up and running—and charge players a subscription fee."

"But only two thousand of those headsets ever got made," I say. "How are people going to play the game?"

"I guess two thousand lucky players are gonna get Otherworld all to themselves. And a lot of people seem to be into that sort of thing. Right now there are bidding wars all over the Internet. Each of those original headsets is going for serious change."

This is not good. I was hoping to get my hands on a few of those headsets. We'll need to go back to Otherworld to find James Ogubu, and the disks are too dangerous to use.

"How much are we talking about?" I ask.

"Gina got two hundred grand for his yesterday. Should have

held out longer. A headset sold this morning for four hundred and fifty thousand dollars."

"You've got to be kidding." I groan, thinking of the headset that my father smashed to smithereens with his nine iron. "Who spends that kind of cash on a video game?"

"That, my friend, is a fascinating question," says Elvis. "Most of the buyers have preferred to remain anonymous. Saudi princes, I'd guess. Third world warlords. Heirs to hotel fortunes. Tom Cruise."

"Tom Cruise?"

"I was joking!" Elvis chuckles maniacally. "How could you question Maverick? He's always one of the good guys. Naw, the dudes buying the headsets are the usual suspects." In other words, any sociopath with half a million dollars burning a hole in his tacky-ass pockets. Two thousand of them will soon be loose in Otherworld.

I think of the Children who've been battling for control of their world. They won't have millions of guests to worry about now that Otherworld's wide release has been canceled, but the two thousand they *will* have are going to be far worse than the last batch. Anyone who's spent five hundred grand on a headset will be itching to get their money's worth.

"There are a lot of guys guessing online—trying to figure out who might have a headset. Gina's put up his own list of potential headset owners. There was only one name on it that I thought might be right."

"Who is it?"

"A Russian oligarch. Alexei Semenov. He made billions in fertilizer before he screwed with the Kremlin and had to disappear. He keeps a very low profile—must not like polonium in his tea.

But he resurfaced briefly awhile back. Bought a bunch of property in New York." Suddenly Elvis turns to face me, his eyes sparkling and a grin on his lips that makes me wonder if he might be a little unhinged. "But why are we talking about Russians? It's time for the big questions. Why are you here, Simon? What do you need to do?"

"Well, first we need to rescue the two people being held by the Company, along with Busara's dad. Then we need to take down the entire organization."

"That's all?" Elvis laughs. "Any idea how to do that?"

"Nope," I tell him honestly. "I thought you might be able to come up with a plan."

"So you want me to help you fight the Company?"

"Yes. I know it's a lot to ask."

"Meh," Elvis says dismissively. "Someone's got to do it. I knew they were evil, but I didn't know they were so far along with the VR tech. I was figuring their big play would be augmented reality."

"Why?" I ask. He knows something. I can tell. But he's not going to give anything away just yet.

"You say you brought some of the Company's VR gear with you?" he asks.

"Yeah. We have two disks," I tell him. "We also have a crazy hologram projector that the Company used to kill a bunch of people."

"Wonderful!" Elvis slaps the railing with both hands, and his accent is suddenly back. "When the girls are clean we can all show each other our goods."

I groan at his latest joke. "How long is that going to go on?" I ask, and Elvis cracks up.

"Until I get laid or I'm no longer amused!" he says. "Don't be a douche, Simon! I've spent the last six months stuck on a mountain with two angry Ukrainian astrophysicists. The least you can do is let me have some fun."

A black dot has appeared on the horizon, and I hear the sound of a helicopter.

"Yes, I do see that." Suddenly Elvis's voice is deadly serious. "Maybe we should go inside now. That one is definitely *not* a bird."

SHOW-AND-TELL

I grab the equipment out of the car. Then Elvis opens the door to the residence and we both hurry inside. Until this moment, I actually felt bad for the guy—forced to live like a hermit on a New Mexican mountaintop. Now I realize that Elvis hasn't exactly been roughing it. The house makes my parents' faux château look like a maintenance shed. Elvis's living room alone has the square footage of a Costco.

"Your house is insane," I say. And that's putting it mildly. There are no windows, but the space is lit by a series of glass enclosures that are open to the sky. Inside each is a garden filled with plants native to different climates. From where I'm standing, I can see a rain forest, a meadow, and what must be a swamp.

"Thanks, but this place isn't mine," Elvis says. "It's just on loan until the apocalypse. The observatory is a cover. Something big goes down, the owner's going to turn this whole place into his personal fortress. Those gardens?" He points to the glass-enclosed meadow a few feet away. "They're decorative now, but they can grow food if he needs them to. When the time comes, maybe he'll let my family stay on as his gardeners or something. Now follow me," he says. "The ladies should be downstairs."

As we descend the stairs, I assume the basement floor is blue. It's only when we're just a few feet above it that I realize I'm looking down at a massive pool of water. The stairs twist around and deposit us on a walkway.

"You can go for a dip if you like, but it's not really for swimming," Elvis explains as we cross to the other side of the pool. "It's a reservoir. Doesn't matter how fancy your fortress is if you end up running out of water."

At the end of the walkway is a sitting area with plush white lounge chairs. There's a waterfall nearby, and the sound conjures an uncomfortable sensation of déjà vu. Fortunately, my attention is quickly drawn to the framed photos on the walls. They're movie stills, I see. Each shows the same man scaling skyscrapers, dangling from wires or escaping from fiery explosions.

"What the hell?" I say when I realize who I'm looking at. I think I've just discovered the secret identity of the doomsday prepper who built the house. "Elvis, is this place owned by Tom Cruise?"

"Who?" Elvis asks as if he's never heard the name before.

A door opens in the distance, releasing a cloud of steam. Busara and Kat emerge from it dressed in fluffy white robes. Kat has her hair tied up in a terry-cloth turban. I see Busara tighten the belt of her robe as we approach.

"Hey! The facilities down here are amazing. And we found the laundry room, too," Kat tells Elvis. "Our clothes were so dirty they could have gotten up and walked off without us. I hope it's okay that we used your washer and dryer."

"Of course!" Elvis says, looking straight at Busara. "Everything I have can be yours!" He's gifted at making even the most innocent statements sound vaguely dirty.

"All right," says Busara. "I think we've all had enough of the horny Ukrainian goat herder routine." Her voice is as humorless as ever, but the sides of her mouth are twitching like she's struggling to swallow a smile.

"I'm sorry?" I gotta give it to him. Elvis is a much better actor.

"We took a wrong turn and ended up in your parents' room. It's like a shrine to their beloved boy—who, judging by the photos on the wall, has been in this country for at least sixteen years."

"Damn them," Elvis says with a sigh but without an accent. "Even when they're not here those two always find a way to ruin my fun."

I hold up the devices I gathered out of the car. "Oh, I think we're all going to have lots of fun today," I say. "What do you say? Time for some show-and-tell?"

Elvis shrugs. "Sure," he says, settling into one of the plush white chairs. "As long as you guys go first."

"Elvis is going to share his latest project with us," I explain to the girls.

"And I believe in saving the best for last," he adds. Humility was never his strong suit. "I don't want to blow your minds before I get a chance to see what you've brought."

Busara snorts and plops down in a chair opposite Elvis.

"That's okay. As much as we're all dying to see your latest science fair project, I think we can hold out a little bit longer."

"Oooh," says Elvis. "Sassy. I like it."

"Okay, okay," I say, putting an end to their jousting. "Let's start with this." I hand the undamaged steel sphere to Busara and set its flattened twin down on a coffee table. "Want to show him what it does?"

Elvis eyes the object. "It's a hologram projector."

"How did you know that?" Busara asks. She's impressed.

"Just a guess." Elvis shrugs modestly. "If I were going to design one, that's how I'd do it."

Busara presses something on the surface of the sphere and sets the ball down on the table in front of us. Suddenly a life-size Marlow Holm appears, doing squats on the coffee table as if it were the most natural thing in the world.

"Nice." Elvis stands up and walks around the table, admiring the image from all sides. Then he sticks his arm through Marlow's stomach and wiggles his fingers on the other side. "Completely opaque. Pretty impressive. Who's Mr. Sporty?"

"His name is Marlow," I say. "His mother worked for the Company. She invented the technology. Then she found out her bosses were exploring military applications."

"Of course they were," Elvis says. "You Americans all love a good war."

I choose not to take the bait, though I'm tempted to point out that he's officially one of us. "Marlow's mother tried to expose the project. So the Company arranged a car accident. She died and her son was badly injured. Now Marlow is one of the people we need to rescue. They put a disk on him and locked him up in a capsule." *Though there's a very good chance that he's already dead,* I add silently in my mind.

Kat picks up the flattened projector and holds it out for Elvis to see. "The Company used this one to cause an accident that killed four people. It's proof."

Elvis takes it and looks it over. It's clear he isn't impressed. "Proof of what?" he asks. "The thing's kaput."

"Simon said you're a genius. We thought maybe you could—" Busara starts.

"Fix it? No way," Elvis says dismissively. "It's totally useless. The other one, though ... Something like that could come in handy. Maybe I can come up with a few ideas. But all that can wait!" He claps his hands and rubs the palms together. "It's my turn to share!"

Elvis reaches over and grabs an ordinary black leather eyeglasses case off the side table next to him. Then he opens the box and pulls out a pair of chunky black glasses. I notice that the sides appear much thicker than usual, but without them, the frames would seem fairly normal. "Not very fashionable," he admits. Then he hands them to Busara. "But I think they would look lovely on you."

"Hey, why does she get to try them first?" I complain. "I'm the one who saved your life, remember?"

"Yes," says Elvis. "But she is the one who is making it worth living."

Busara snorts as she slides them onto her face. I can tell from her expression that she isn't expecting much. But the instant they're on, she jumps to her feet, turning in a circle as she takes in the room. "Oh my God," she marvels. There's respect in her voice that wasn't there a moment ago. "Do you have any idea how dangerous this is?"

"Yes," replies Elvis gleefully. "Do you see the menu? Choose Security. That's one of my favorites. Sanitation is pretty good too."

"Shit," Busara says appreciatively. Whatever she's seeing must be amazing. I'm not sure I've ever heard her use that particular word before. She's obviously experiencing some form of augmented reality, because the glasses' lenses are clear. I can see Busara's eyes right through them. But she's seeing something I'm not—something that's been overlaid on the environment. Whatever it is, it can't be real, so I don't understand how it could be dangerous.

"Take a look." Busara takes off the glasses and passes them to me.

When I put them on, I see the room I'm sitting in. There's a menu to my right that tells me the glasses are still in SECURITY mode. I look around. Glowing green lines indicate the presence of electrical wires connecting a series of security cameras that are invisible to the naked eye. I use my eyes to toggle down through the menu to SANITATION. I can see all the pipes and plumbing inside the walls and under the floor. ELECTRICAL highlights the house's electrical grid. POSITION shows me exactly where I am in the house. It also shows me the location of two secret rooms nearby, their entrances carefully concealed.

"What's in the two hidden rooms?" I ask Elvis.

"One is a vault where the owner stores his gold. The other is a safe room where the owner can hide in case anyone breaks in looking for his gold."

"Wait—there's really gold down here in the basement?" Kat asks.

"Sure," Elvis says as if it's the most natural thing in the world. "Where do you keep *your* gold?"

Now I know why the tech is so dangerous. The information I'm looking at renders this hilltop fortress about as safe as a cardboard playhouse.

I give the glasses to Kat. "How did you do this?" I ask Elvis.

"It was easy. I located the building plans for the house," he said. "Believe it or not, they weren't hard to find. It's like putting all your valuables in a safe and then leaving a Post-it with the combination on the front."

"But the software," says Busara. "Did you design it yourself?"

"I don't have time for that sort of thing. I'm more of an editor than an engineer," Elvis says modestly. "I borrowed some software from the Company. Then I improved it, of course."

"You *borrowed* it?" Kat asks. "You mean you hacked the Company."

"Why get bogged down in semantics?" says Elvis. "I found it. That's all that matters." And now I understand why he thought the Company's next big play would be augmented reality. "They've got a whole team focused exclusively on maps. Last time I checked in on them, they seemed pretty close to finishing one. If I had to guess, I'd say they'll be using it for something soon."

"What's the map of?" Kat asks.

"New York City," says Elvis. "You can access it with my glasses. Won't do you much good here, though."

"They've made a map like yours of all New York City?" I ask.

"No, of course not!" Elvis says with a laugh. "Just the island of Manhattan."

Just the island of Manhattan, he says. The financial heart of the United States.

"That sounds like a security nightmare," says Kat.

"Oh, come on. The Company's not planning to knock off a bunch of Chase branches. They don't need to *rob* people to get all their money. That's so old-fashioned. I think the Company has something else in mind for the tech. Probably an augmented reality game of some sort. With a good enough map, you could turn the whole city into one giant sandbox." He claps his hands once more and rubs them together greedily. "So! My turn again! When do I get to try Otherworld?"

I knew he'd ask. Elvis may be a genius, but he's never had much common sense. He's the sort of guy who'd find a way to cure cancer and then celebrate by shooting bottle rockets out of his ass. "You don't get to try it," I tell him. "It's too dangerous without a headset."

"Then come with me to Otherworld," he says. He's not going to give up. I can already tell. "You brought two of those disks, didn't you?"

"No way," Kat tells him. "Didn't Simon tell you about them? The disks are deadly. You could die."

"Like I'm living it up right now," Elvis says. "Come on, just a peek! If you guys don't want to go, maybe Busara could join me."

"She can't," I say. "She's sick."

Busara is giving me serious side eye. "Which doesn't prevent me from speaking for myself. I have a heart condition," she explains to Elvis. "With a disk on, the action in Otherworld could kill me."

"You're sick?" Elvis looks stricken.

"Moving on!" Kat announces.

"Thank you," Busara says with a huff.

"Look, here's the deal with Otherworld," I say. "There's no way any of us are wearing disks. I don't even know where we'd end up in Otherworld when we put them on. We might not be together in the same place."

"You'd both enter the game at the gates of Imra," Busara says. "Elvis is a new player, so he'd go straight to setup and then to Imra. You're not a new player, obviously, and the game will recognize you no matter what gear you're wearing. The last time you were in Otherworld, you passed through the exit in the ice cave. So the game will send you back to the beginning too. And don't forget—one of the disks we brought here is the master disk that my dad made. Remember the amulet I wore when I was the Clay Man? Whoever has the master disk would be wearing it in the game. It could send you anywhere you want to go."

I give Busara a dirty look. I don't know why I was expecting her to back me up. The only thing she really gives a damn about is finding her father. Busara was the one who tricked me into putting on a disk in the first place—all so she could punish Milo Yolkin for the things he did to her dad. In the past few days, I'd almost started to trust her again. *Almost.*

"Yeah, the master disk could send *one* of us anywhere he wanted to go. The other person would get screwed. That's how it worked when you were the Clay Man, remember? You got to go wherever you wanted, and I was the one who always ended up fighting for his life."

"I'm sorry," Busara says.

"Yeah, sure you are."

"Come on, Simon! Don't give me a hard time!" she pleads. "It's just that we're safe here for a little while. If you and Elvis go to the ice cave, you guys could find a way to free my dad's avatar from the ice. He could help us figure out what to do to stop the Company. My dad will tell us where to find his body, and who knows—maybe he can help us rescue Marlow and Gorog, too."

"I think we should do this," Elvis announces. "I get to see Otherworld. We both talk to Busara's dad. It's a win-win situation." No, it's a blatant attempt to suck up to Busara.

"No one's going to *win* if you get murdered by some psycho player," Kat points out. "I vote no. We wait until we can buy some headsets."

She doesn't know about the headsets. I watch her face fall as Elvis tells her about the bidding wars. There's no way we'll ever be able to purchase one. If we return to Otherworld, we'll have to use disks.

"We'll have to go back sooner rather than later," Busara says when Elvis is done. "We could use my dad's help. And he needs ours."

I look over at Kat. It hurts to see her look so defeated.

"I gladly volunteer for this mission," Elvis announces.

"He can't go alone," I tell Kat. "I'll have to go with him."

"Elvis shouldn't be going at all," Kat says. "*I'll* go with you."

"Your leg is still injured," I tell her.

"It's getting better!" she insists.

"It's still too much of a risk. Your body needs a few more days to heal."

"Then it's decided!" Elvis claps his hands and rubs them together. "Grab the disks. It's time for Elvis and Simon's big adventure."

"Not tonight," I say. "*Tomorrow.*" If I'm doing this, I'm going to need a good night's sleep—and some time alone with Kat.

It's the first time Kat and I have shared a bed without someone else in the room. I've dreamed about this moment every day for a million years. Now it's finally arrived, and she's lying with her back to me, which manages to be extremely depressing despite the fact that her newly clean sweatpants say DIVA across the ass.

"Kat—" I say.

"What if something happens to you?" she asks.

"I'll be careful," I promise, though we both know it's bullshit. There's no way to be careful in Otherworld.

"We've been a couple for less than ninety-six hours. We deserve more time together," she says.

I couldn't agree more. I finally get the one thing I wanted most in the world—and now I have to leave her. I've experienced my share of disappointments in life, but this is by far the biggest. I'm really hoping the universe gets tired of teaching me lessons. Each one seems to suck more than the last.

"Oh, come on." I try to play cool. "You're acting like I'm already dead! Elvis and I will only be crossing the ice fields. The Children will help us reach the cave."

"And what about the two thousand psychos who've bought all the headsets?"

"We'll just have to avoid them."

"How?" she demands.

"I don't know," I admit, giving up the act. "Listen, Kat, if you think we should wait, we'll wait. But you heard what Elvis said. We won't be getting headsets anytime soon."

Kat doesn't respond.

"Do you want to spend tonight arguing?" I ask her.

"No." When she rolls over, I can feel her heart pounding against my chest. This is our first night together, and both of us know that it may be our last.

Kat is sleeping, but I haven't once closed my eyes. I slide on my jeans and leave the room, shutting the door softly behind me. Outside in the upstairs living area, the glass-enclosed gardens are dimly lit. I make it to the kitchen and manage to locate a glass. I'm filling it with water when I hear something behind me, rolling across tiles. I turn to see Marlow Holm walking toward me, wearing jeans and a T-shirt. He stops right in front of me. His nose is less than a few feet from mine, yet his eyes are staring straight through me. He doesn't seem to realize I'm here. I feel the glass slip out of my hand—and the spray of water on my ankles. Either I've gone completely insane or Marlow must have died in Otherworld and I'm being visited by his ghost. My knees weaken. I'm on the verge of collapse when Marlow vanishes and another figure steps into the room.

Elvis has already shaved his head so he can stick on the disk in the morning, and I probably wouldn't recognize him if it weren't for his shit-eating grin. The smile vanishes as soon as he sees me, and he sets the controls he's fashioned out of old PlayStation gear down on the counter. "Jesus, Simon. I didn't mean to scare you. Are you okay?"

One of my hands finds the fridge handle, which I use to steady myself. The other clenches into a fist that flies through the air but hits nothing.

"Hey! I'm sorry!" Elvis cries. Despite the punch I just threw at him, he lurches forward and grabs me before I rip the handle off the fridge and crash to the ground. "I really thought you'd find it funny."

"How did you do that?" I gasp.

"The projector," he says. Once I'm fully upright, he lets go of me and takes a hesitant step backward. "That's why it's round—it moves. I've been tinkering with it since you guys went to bed."

"Don't you ever sleep?" I ask him.

"Sure. About four hours a night," Elvis tells me. "They've had me on Adderall since the second grade. But seriously, Simon. What the hell has happened to you?"

"You'll see," I tell him. "When we get to Otherworld."

THE PETTING ZOO

I never wanted to see this place again. Yet here I am, standing on top of a dormant volcano with high, gilded gates at my back. The buildings behind me house the workers of Imra, the Otherworld welcome center that lies deep inside the volcano's cone. This is where all new players arrive. In Imra, you can sample the pleasures that the virtual world has to offer—and figure out what suits your tastes best. I have zero desire to set foot inside the city the Company once billed as the Resort of the Future. Elvis and I have a long trek ahead of us—across a wasteland and over the ice fields. There's no telling what we'll encounter along the way.

In the distance, a cloud of red dust is rolling across the otherwise empty landscape. I'm pretty sure it's a herd of buffalo. Like the other animals here, they're much more dangerous than the real-world creatures they were designed to resemble. I was nearly trampled by the buffalo on my first visit to Otherworld. Their stench alone could have killed me. As I watch the stampede, it occurs to me that there's nothing for the beasts to be running to or from. I wonder if they ever rest. They must know as well as I do that it's dangerous to stop moving in Otherworld.

A glowing strip of white lines the horizon beyond the wasteland. It's the edge of the ice fields. The realms here end and begin abruptly. You can literally step out of one and into the next. I'm trying to calculate how long it will take to reach the ice, when I feel a tap on my shoulder.

There's a female avatar standing behind me, a gleaming battle-axe swung over one shoulder. Whoever's controlling the avatar is clearly a developmentally challenged pervert. Her boobs are so massive that if Earth physics applied here, she'd fall over face-forward.

"Yeah?" I ask, my fingers ready to reach for my dagger. I'd be even ruder if it weren't for the battle-axe.

"Simon, it's me."

I groan. "Good God, Elvis. This is pathetic. What are you? Twelve years old?"

"Don't give me a hard time, dickhead," Elvis says, gazing adoringly at his enormous bosoms. He hasn't bothered to change his voice, and the combination is goddamn disturbing. "I've been stuck in the middle of nowhere for six whole months. By the way, this tech is fantastic. My boobs feel amazing. Just like the real things, I bet. They are cumbersome, though. You really have to respect the ladies. How do they manage to run or play sports?"

"Go back right now and get rid of the giant boobs," I order. "And toss the axe, too. I told you to choose fire as your weapon. We'll need it in the ice cave. Go! You have ten seconds."

Elvis gives me an exaggerated once-over. "Maybe you should

come back to setup with me," he snips. "Your avatar could use a little work too. I think you could do a lot better than a farmhand with a fur fetish."

My avatar never changes. Black shirt, black pants, brown cloak. In preparation for the ice fields, I've donned a thick fur coat. The body inside the ensemble is identical to my own.

"I'm a Druid, you moron," I bark. Of all people, I would have expected *him* to recognize the costume. "Just go, would you?"

The avatar rolls her anime-size eyes. "You're not a Druid. You're a petty tyrant," she informs me in Elvis's voice. Then she disappears.

While Elvis is changing into something more appropriate, I hear a shot behind me. I spin around and peer through the gates. The road that leads to the entrance of Imra cuts straight through the workers' town, which is currently eerily quiet. The last time I was here, there were hundreds of non-player characters going about their business. Now the place appears to be empty, though it's pretty clear that the inhabitants didn't wander off. I don't see any bodies, but the brick walls of the buildings look wet with what I'm starting to realize is probably blood. I hear a spray of machine-gun fire, and I suddenly know what's happening. A headset player has gone on a rampage. He's slaughtering the NPCs one by one. I feel the rage begin to swell inside me. What kind of psycho massacres characters that weren't designed to fight back?

The answer appears right in front of me. A muscle-bound avatar with a buzz cut darts across the road from one building and presses his back against another on the opposite side. His bulging biceps strain against the sleeves of a black T-shirt that's neatly tucked into camouflage pants. The guy is GI Joe pumped up on a cocktail of meth and steroids. There's a crazy smile on his face as he waits for someone to round the corner. A few seconds later, a female NPC appears in the intersection. She's a standard model, pretty and bland. GI Joe points the gun to her head. She looks at him in confusion. There's no fear on her face. This is not what is meant to happen. I turn away just as the shot is fired. When I glance back up, there's a bright red stain on the road, but the female's body is already gone.

Of course Elvis chooses this moment to reappear. His avatar is a perfect copy of his real-world body. He's dressed in a long sable coat and matching fur hat. A torch is tucked into his waistband. I grab him by the collar and drag him behind one of the pillars that frame the gates.

"Hey!" he cries. "What the hell, Simon! That hurt!" Then there's a moment of reverent silence. "It hurt. Oh my God, it hurt! This tech is amazing!"

"Shut up," I hiss. "There's a guy killing everyone inside."

Elvis peeks around the pillar. "Well, that's not very nice, is it? Let's go take him out," he says. "Come on. We've got time for a bit of fun, don't we?"

Apparently none of my warnings have managed to make an impression. "This is not a game, dipshit! If that guy shoots us, we'll die!" How many times does he need to be told before it sinks into his head? Would it make any difference if I spoke in Ukrainian?

"Riiiiiiight," Elvis says, pulling his head back from around the corner. "Then I think we may have a problem."

"That dude saw you, didn't he?" I groan.

"Yeah," Elvis says. "Sorry about that. He's coming this way."

We can't make a run in the direction of the ice fields. There's nowhere to take cover—not even a rock large enough to hide one of us. The killer could stand at the top of the mountain and take leisurely shots until both of our avatars are riddled with bullet holes.

"There?" Elvis asks.

He's pointing to the right of the gates, at a dense wall of foliage that I assumed was decorative. But now I can see a wooden roof poking out from the top. There must be something beyond the greenery. We run for cover but find the vegetation impenetrable. Thick green ivy vines have twisted together to form a wall. I pull my dagger out of my boot and start hacking away. But every time I manage to cut through one of the thick stems, a new vine immediately snakes out of the ground and takes its place. These are no ordinary plants. Like everything else in here, they're mutants that have little in common with their Earth-dwelling counterparts.

A bullet whizzes past my ear. "Let me," Elvis insists. His torch ignites and he steps forward, shoving the blaze at the ivy. The vines curl back, desperate to escape the heat, and a narrow passage opens in front of us. We step inside and the wall of foliage closes behind us. We can hear GI Joe spraying the vines with a shower of bullets, but we never get hit. Nature has formed a protective cocoon around our avatars. "See?" Elvis says cockily. "I get us into trouble and I get us right back out again."

His bragging makes me nervous. I'm not convinced we're out of the woods just yet. Some of the vines seem to have scales. The fire is still holding most of them back. But then I feel a flicker against my cheek, then another on my ear. I yank my foot away from a tendril that's trying to creep up my pant leg. The ivy is getting bolder.

Elvis stops. "Do you hear that?" he asks.

I do. The sound is soft enough that I might have mistaken it for the wind. But it's not. It's hissing. "Keep walking," I urge Elvis. "Don't stop again."

"Where was the snake that was making that sound?" he whispers, moving fast with the torch held out in front of him. "Did you see it?"

The snake. What a joke. I'd laugh if I weren't going to die. Elvis is about to get his second lesson in Otherworld survival. Suddenly all the vines around us are writhing. "You mean *snakes*," I say.

The tip of one of the vines whips toward me. I lop it off with my dagger and a fanged head falls at my feet.

"What the—" Elvis starts to say.

"Shut up and run!" I shout.

Elvis leads the way, slicing through the air with his torch like a master swordsman. This is hardly the first game he and I have played together. I knew he was a genius with handheld controls, but this shit is ridiculous. I can smell the burning flesh of snake vines that have gotten too close. It's not an entirely unpleasant odor. I wish I'd eaten a bigger breakfast.

Then the vines suddenly part and we find ourselves standing out in the open, with a wooden cottage in front of us. I turn around in time to see the passageway disappear. All that's left is a solid mass of slithering scales, fangs and muscle.

Elvis is bent over, panting. "What the hell are those?" he asks.

"Unintended consequences," I say. "Digital DNA mixes easily in Otherworld. I've seen a few crazy combinations, but this is my first plant-animal hybrid. I didn't even know it was possible."

"Anything is possible in Otherworld!" A movie-star-handsome NPC appears at the entrance of a tiny Swiss-style cottage with a steeply pitched roof and overflowing flower boxes. The NPC is wearing lederhosen—leather shorts with leather suspenders—along with knee-high socks and boots. He's topped off the outfit with a dorky hat, complete with feather. Then again, who am I to judge? I'm sure Elvis and I look equally ridiculous.

The cottage stands at the entrance to what appears to be some kind of amusement park. The structures behind it have been overtaken by the ivy. Monstrous green forms loom over the three of us. It's impossible to say what any of them might once have been.

"Welcome to Gimmelwald," the big blond NPC says cheerfully with a slight German accent. "My name is Gunter. Are you here for a tour of our child care facilities?"

"Child care facilities? We just walked through a wall of snakes," I say. "I hope you're not expecting a bunch of kids to show up here anytime soon."

"So you're not in need of our services?" Gunter asks.

"We aren't looking for a babysitter, if that's what you're asking," Elvis says.

Gunter appears disappointed by the news, and I wonder if the NPCs ever get bored. "Then may I ask why you are here?"

"Someone was trying to kill us," Elvis tells him. "We came in here to hide."

"You were being chased by another guest just now?" Gunter inquires.

"Yes," I say.

Gunter appears genuinely upset by the situation. "I do apologize. Everything has changed so much. Our realm is no longer what the Creator intended it to be. Some of—"

Elvis puts a hand up. "I'm sorry, can you hold on just one second, Gunter?" he says. "I need a quick word with my colleague." Then he leans over with his lips near my ear. "Isn't this guy an NPC?" he whispers.

I nod.

"But it doesn't seem like he's sticking to a script. He's improvising," Elvis says. "That means—"

"Yeah," I say. There's no doubt that Gunter is the most advanced AI that Elvis has ever encountered. But he hasn't seen anything yet. I'll let him figure that out for himself. "That means it's probably a good idea not to be rude."

When Elvis looks back at Gunter, his avatar's eyes are wide with wonder. "I apologize for interrupting," he says. "You were saying?"

"I was about to say that some of the guests these days can be quite unpleasant. But you're safe with us. There's no need to worry about anyone following you into Gimmelwald. Please," Gunter says, gesturing toward the cottage. "Come inside for some cocoa. You're our first visitors since the incident. How *did* you make it inside, if you don't mind my asking?"

"Fire," I say as we follow Gunter into the little house. I'd ask him about the incident he just mentioned, but we don't have time for a story.

I step into the cottage and have a look around, which takes all of two seconds. The place is the size of a large playhouse, and if I had to guess, I'd say Gunter's interior decorator was a six-year-old Swiss girl.

"It sounds like you got very lucky," says Gunter. "The vines may fear fire, but there are many beasts here who would happily risk being burned for a meal."

"Beasts?" I ask. "What kind of beasts do you have in Gimmelwald?"

"I don't really know," the NPC replies cheerfully. "By now there could be almost anything in our forests. That is why I choose to stay in the cottage." There's a tiny stove in the corner. Gunter turns a burner on low and begins to fill a pot with milk.

"No cocoa for me, please," I tell him.

"Or me, thanks," Elvis chimes in.

"No?" Gunter seems heartbroken for a moment. Then he discovers his cloud's silver lining. "Oh well, more for me!" His life—if that's what you'd call it—must suck. No wonder he was happy to see us.

"So you stay here in this cottage all the time?" Elvis asks.

"It's either that or be eaten by the beasts," Gunter replies.

"Why are there man-eating beasts here in Gimmelwald?" Elvis asks. "I thought you said this realm was meant to be for *kids*?"

"Oh, it was," Gunter says. "The Creator knew many of our adult guests wouldn't feel comfortable leaving their young offspring unattended at home. So he designed several realms that would allow human children to experience the wonders of Otherworld. But the few guests we've greeted here have all been adults. And some of them were *quite* unsavory."

The image of child-size capsules pops into my mind. I wonder if the Company was planning to offer family discount plans.

Mom and Dad could live out their homicidal fantasies while the "offspring" were coddled by NPCs.

"It's a pity. Gimmelwald was meant to be the ultimate petting zoo," Gunter continues, gesturing to the wild world beyond the cottage. "Our beasts were designed to be docile enough to cuddle and ride. There were lambs and goats and ponies, of course. But there were also bears and wolves and wild boars. Unfortunately, none of them have stayed tame. The Children were able to keep them under control, but now that the Children are gone, the beasts have free rein."

"Children?" Elvis looks over at me. "What children? You said no kids ever came here."

He thinks Gunter is talking about little humans. I suppose I should have given him a heads-up about the Children. "Remember what I said about digital DNA? The Children are what happens when you mix beasts—the animals that Milo created for the game—with the Elementals that rule Otherworld's realms."

Elvis's jaw drops. "Wait, are you saying the Elementals and the beasts—" I once got scolded for asking the same question. I'm glad to know I'm not the only one with a dirty mind.

"No," I assure him. "I don't know exactly how it worked, but supposedly there wasn't any sex involved. Before the Company fixed the bug, hybrid babies kept popping up all over the place."

"Our Elemental once had dozens of Children," Gunter announces proudly. "A few of them belonged to the Creator as well."

"The Creator?" Elvis massages his temples as if he's worried his head might explode.

"The Creator was Milo Yolkin's avatar. Milo was in Otherworld before anyone else, and he really got around. He mixed his digital DNA with pretty much everything here," I explain. Then I turn back to Gunter. "So where are the Children of Gimmelwald now?" I ask.

Gunter instantly clams up. Despite the pleasant conversation, we still haven't won his confidence. "They are in a safe place," he says.

"Good." As long as he's sure the Children are safe, I have no interest in digging any further. "Glad to hear it. So how do my friend and I get out of here? We're on a mission and we don't have much time left."

"You're free to leave this realm at any time," Gunter tells us.

"Okay, maybe I should rephrase my friend's question," Elvis says. "How do we get out without getting eaten by some kind of mutant beast?"

"Oh, I'm afraid you will both be consumed shortly after you leave this cottage," Gunter tells us. "It may be unpleasant, but once the kill is registered your avatar will return to setup. If that option does not appeal to you, perhaps suicide would be preferable?"

I can't believe I let Elvis and Busara talk me into this shit. I should have listened to Kat. From now on, no one's coming back to this hellhole with a disk on. "No," I tell Gunter. "We can't let our avatars die. We're not like the other guests. This isn't a game for us."

"Then perhaps you should speak to Volla," the NPC says. "She is the Elemental who rules this realm."

"How the hell are we going to speak to Volla without leaving this house?" I demand.

"Hey." I feel Elvis tapping my shoulder. "Naked lady alert, three o'clock," he whispers.

Outside the window, at the edge of the forest, a woman is rising from the ground. Her skin is the color of rich, dark soil, and the hair that cascades over her shoulders and chest is composed of braided vines. When she finally steps out of the earth, she stands at least seven feet tall, with curves that no earth woman could possibly possess. I'm sure Elvis would love to know if her boobs are equally impressive, but she's holding something against her chest.

Gunter guides us outside and greets the Elemental with a reverent bow.

"These two guests would like to leave, but they don't want their avatars to die. They claim they are not like the others."

"All guests are the same." Volla moves toward us, shedding a fine layer of dirt with each step. Her voice is soft, like a rushing stream or the rustling of leaves. "They come here to kill and torture and abuse. They do not deserve any mercy." She stops and glares down at Elvis and me. "Your kind has inflicted great pain upon the residents of Otherworld, and yet you refuse to suffer a single moment of unpleasantness?"

"Excuse me, ma'am, but I just got here," Elvis says. "I swear I haven't inflicted any pain on anyone yet."

"You burned my ivy," Volla says. "You don't imagine it feels any pain?"

Elvis actually stops for a moment and seems to ponder the idea. "Wow," he replies. "You know, that's actually a really great question. Might end up keeping me awake for a couple of nights. But for now all I can say is I acted in self-defense. I only burned the vines because they were trying to kill me."

"They've seen guests enter my realm and slaughter many of my

Children. They've witnessed the rest of my offspring being taken away for their own protection. The vines were gentle once. They changed into what they've become to repel humans like you."

I wonder if the slaughter is the incident Gunter mentioned earlier. I'm about to ask when Volla shifts and I finally see what's in her arms. It's a tiny creature covered in pale green scales. It looks like a baby, but I must be mistaken. Milo Yolkin fixed the bad code that was responsible for the Children. There shouldn't be any babies here in Otherworld.

"Is that one of your Children?" I ask, moving toward her for a closer look.

"Step back!" Volla bellows, clutching her baby against her chest. The ground shakes and leaves rain down from the trees.

Elvis elbows me in the side. "Come on, Simon! Tell the lady you're sorry!"

I know I should, but I don't. There's something else that needs to come out first. "Is he new? Is that why he's still here in Gimmelwald with you?"

"He is my first since your kind arrived. It is not safe for him here. They will come for him as soon as he's grown and take him to a realm that guests are not allowed to enter."

I suddenly have a really bad feeling about all of this. Children are being born again, and then someone is rounding them up. "Who are *they*?"

"Moloch's soldiers," says Volla. "Since the Creator abandoned us, the Elemental of Imperium has taken over the Creator's role as the protector of the Children."

Oh, shit. That is not good. Not good at *all*. The Creator died when Milo Yolkin did. And two guys who work for the Company control Moloch. He's supposed to be the Elemental of Imperium, but he's nothing more than an avatar whose purpose is to exterminate Otherworld's Children. I can only imagine what Moloch has in store for the ones he's been gathering—and the new ones the Company has been letting the game generate.

"I know Moloch. You can't trust him," I warn her. "Your Children are in terrible danger."

"You are lying!" she roars, and the earth trembles once more. It takes every bit of courage I can summon to stand my ground.

"I swear to you, I'm telling the truth," I assure her. "If you let us leave Gimmelwald without dying, I promise we will do our best to help them."

"No," Volla says. "I will not take the word of a human guest over one of my own kind. You may leave Gimmelwald, but you must do it without my assistance."

"You go, Simon," I hear Elvis insist. "You have the master disk. Use the amulet and get to the ice fields. I'll stay here and wait for you. If I don't die of boredom, I should be safe in the cottage until the girls pull us out. Gunter and I can play cards or something."

"Cards?" Gunter asks, sounding quite intrigued. I think he may be desperate for company.

"No," I tell Elvis. "We stick together. That's how this works. There's no safe place in Otherworld. I'm not going to leave you behind." It feels a bit strange to be bickering in front of an NPC and a giant woman who's recently risen out of the earth, especially since the queen of dirt seems to be hanging on my every word. I wish she'd give us a little privacy, but I'm guessing that's probably too much to ask right now.

"So we're both going to just sit here until the girls peel off our disks?" Elvis complains. "That doesn't even make sense! Why don't you just go ahead and check on the dirt lady's kids and then pop over for a chat with Busara's dad? I'll be fine here, I swear."

"You don't know that!" I'm about to lose it. Why can't he just take me at my word? "I already lost one friend in Otherworld. I got separated from my companions, and she died trying to save me. I'm not going to lose another person I care about. Either we go to the ice fields together or we don't go at all."

"You care about me?" Elvis asks. He looks genuinely touched.

"Oh, Jesus," I groan. "Do we have to do this *now*? Of course I care about you! Do you want a hug, too?"

"Why do you wish to visit the ice fields?" the Elemental interrupts. I suspect she knows what's there.

"We're trying to reach the cave where the Creator once took shelter," I tell her. "There's someone trapped inside that we need to help."

The naked dirt lady isn't buying it. "I have never known your kind to show compassion toward one another."

"Yeah, well, Otherworld doesn't exactly attract the finest specimens that humanity has to offer," I snip. I've given up trying to convince her that I'm not an asshole.

"What my friend is *trying* to say, ma'am, is that we're not all bad," Elvis says, displaying manners I wasn't aware he possessed. "And Simon here happens to be one of the best. I owe him my life."

That's a bit of an exaggeration, I'd say. If I'm the best of humanity, we're all in a ton of trouble. But Elvis sounds sincere. Even I'm starting to believe him—and to my surprise, the Elemental actually seems convinced.

"It is against our rules to send you where you want to go," Volla announces. "The ice fields are a liminal space. But I will help you get there on one condition. You will visit my Children first, and if they are in danger as you say, you must help them, too."

I have no idea what changed her mind, but I'm not going to look this gift horse in the mouth. "We'll do what we can," I say, and I mean it. But I'm well aware that what we *can* do may not be enough.

Volla holds her Child with one arm and reaches deep into her chest with the other. When her hand emerges, it's holding a glowing red stone.

"I will send you to the realm where my Children were taken. Once you have ensured that they're safe, this will take you where you want to go. Use it wisely. It will only work once."

THE GAME

"Hey, this doesn't look so bad," says Elvis.

We're standing by a watering hole in the middle of a golden savannah. A herd of deerlike beasts is drinking at one end. Mutant flamingos that appear more fuchsia than pink are mingling with the mammals. Not far away, the most fabulous tree house ever built sits atop stilts, nestled in the canopy of the alien-looking baobabs that surround it. A wide porch circles a lovely wooden structure. There's no glass in its windows, and white curtains flutter in the wind.

"We'll see," I tell him. The bad feeling I had back in Gimmelwald has just grown considerably worse. We're out in the open, and I feel exposed. An attack could be launched on us from almost any direction.

Together Elvis and I wade through the grass to the building. As we approach, a ladder is lowered from above. We climb up to the porch, where a woman in white is waiting. But before she greets us, she pulls the ladder back up. There seems to be some urgency to her movements.

"Worried the deer are going to climb up behind us?" I joke just to clear the tension. It doesn't work.

"No, sir," she says. Her voice may be subservient, but her expression says I'm an idiot.

Elvis catches my eye. He's still amazed by the AI. "She thought your joke was stupid!" he whispers.

The NPC drops her head. "I'm very sorry, sir," she says.

"No worries. It *was* pretty dumb," Elvis says cheerfully. "What realm is this again?"

This time, the NPC looks confused. "This is Karamojo. Did you not request to come here?"

"I did," I jump in. "I wanted it to be a surprise. It's his birthday."

That seems to be the right answer. "Oh, good," says the NPC. "The last party left about an hour ago. The next will leave after lunch. Would you like to relax while you're waiting? I would be happy to bring refreshments."

"I guess so," I say. What else is there to do? I take a seat on one of the chairs looking out over the savannah. The view is spectacular. The grasslands appear to be ringed by jungle. A herd of elephants is leisurely plucking leaves off the trees. Then there's the sound of a single shot in the distance. Spooked, the elephants stomp into the jungle and disappear in the dense foliage.

"Do guests come here to hunt elephants?" I ask.

"Of course not." The NPC looks perplexed. "Why would they do that?"

"Okay, I think that's enough questions for now," Elvis announces as he claims a seat next to mine. I shoot him a dirty look and he throws his hands up in the air. "What? I'm looking forward to sampling the refreshments that our friend promised to bring us."

The NPC takes that as her cue to leave, and Elvis waits until she's out of earshot before he leans over the side of the chair. "Okay, we gotta talk. I thought Gunter was an impressive piece of AI, but the dirt goddess was on a whole different level. I think she really loved that creepy baby."

"I'm sure she did," I say. The subject isn't one I'd like to linger on at the moment—not until we know where her other Children have gone.

"Holy shit," Elvis gushes. "So she feels real emotions? She's conscious? The Company cracked true AI? Why didn't you tell me?"

"I guess I wanted it to be a surprise. Milo Yolkin designed the Elementals to be conscious. Their Children are conscious too. But like I said earlier, the Children were never part of the plan. Something went wrong in the early days of Otherworld, and Milo was supposed to have fixed it. There shouldn't be any new Children being made."

"And this Moloch guy who's been taking them—isn't he an Elemental? Why are you so worried about what he's done?"

"Moloch isn't really part of the game. He's an avatar that's controlled by two engineers who work at the Company."

Elvis's brow furrows. "So first the Company undoes what Milo fixed and lets new Children get created. And then they have somebody here in Otherworld round them all up?"

"Exactly," I say. I'm about to tell him my hunch when we hear footsteps coming our way. The NPC sets a tray down on a small table in front of us. On it are two glasses of pale green liquid and a bowl filled with something that looks a lot like jerky.

Elvis leans forward, grabs a strip and pops it in his mouth. "Wow, this is amazing," he tells me.

"You can taste it?" the NPC asks. Her face remains blank, but there's no doubt she's surprised.

"Sure," Elvis tells her. "What is this stuff?"

"I believe it's a unique mixture of things," the NPC says. "We don't let anything go to waste."

"You make all the food here?" I ask.

"In the kitchen," she tells me.

"Mind if I take a look?" I ask her.

She meets my eyes for the first time. She's trying to figure me out. "Of course. This is Otherworld," the NPC says. "Your kind may do whatever you like."

"I'll be right back," I tell Elvis. "Go easy on that jerky."

While Elvis enjoys his refreshments, I rise from my seat and head inside the building. The first things I notice are the gun cabinets to my left and my right. Then my eyes land on a wall toward the back that's covered with hunting trophies. From a distance I can see that some of the mounted heads have horns and others have fur. Many have neither. I can also see that no two heads are alike, and I have to force myself to keep breathing as I register what I'm looking at. I don't think I've ever experienced horror quite like this before. I don't want to step forward. In fact, I can't think of anything I'd rather do less. But I know I have to.

Children stare out at me with lifeless eyes. Females and males. Large and small. Some beautiful, others hideous. There are a few that appear almost human. Most look like what they are—*a unique mixture of things.* I've never successfully vomited in Otherworld, but now I know that it's possible. It smells every bit as awful as it does in the real world.

The NPC rushes over to clean the floor and wipe off my shoes. I barely notice her. My eyes have landed on a familiar face. It was one I was hoping I wouldn't see again. It never occurred to me that I might encounter him in a place like this. The pupils in his amber eyes are a thick black dash, and his flat nose is missing a bridge. A sparse beard of white fur covers his chin, and the buds of two horns strain at the skin of his forehead. On my first trip to Otherworld, he tried to eat me. It's quite possible that Elvis is now outside eating *him*.

"What the hell is this place?" I ask the woman, who's still wiping the floor around my feet. I don't really need to be told. This is what happened to the Children Moloch took from Gimmelwald and all the other realms.

"You didn't know?" I glance down to see the NPC peering up at me.

"They're brought here to be hunted for sport," I say. I gesture to the wall. "Are these the only ones?"

She doesn't need to say a word. One shake of her head tells me the trophies on the wall are just the beginning.

I leave her there and rush out to get Elvis. We have our answer. All my worst fears have been confirmed. I find him standing by the porch balcony, looking down at something below. I can tell by the way he's gripping the wood that it's something he'd rather not see.

There are two hunters on horses heading in our direction.

They're dragging three bodies behind them on the ground. One of them is the same color as Volla's baby.

"Are those what I think they are?" Elvis croaks. For the first time since our reunion, there's not a hint of humor in his voice.

"Yes. They're Children," I say. "This is a hunting lodge."

He inhales deeply. "Are there guns in there?" he asks on the exhale.

I nod. Elvis bolts into the lodge and returns with a rifle. He takes aim at one of the hunters and shoots. The bullet hits its mark. The avatar flashes but doesn't disappear, which means one of two things. Either the avatar's lost a life—or the player controlling it has taken off his headset and left the game.

"Hey!" the guy shouts angrily. Seems he hasn't quit. His avatar lost a life, but he could still have up to two lives to spare.

Elvis takes aim at the second. Again, there's a flash, but nothing else happens. "What the hell is going on?" he asks, staring at his gun. "Why isn't this thing working?"

"It is. But they're headset players," I tell him. "Keep shooting them and you might send one back to setup, but they're not going to die."

There's a shot from below and the wooden railing next to Elvis splinters. Both guests have their guns out. We're now the ones being hunted.

"We have to leave," I tell Elvis.

"How can we go?" he shouts. "These assholes are massacring sentient beings!"

"And I promise you, we'll be next to die if we stay," I say.

"We told the dirt lady we'd help her Children!" Elvis cries.

"Which is not something we'll be able to do if those assholes down there kill us!" I pull out the stone Volla gave us and hold it in my open palm. "Put your hand over it."

"No!" Elvis refuses as bullets fly past. The hunters are growing closer, and their aim is getting better.

"I know where to find the leader of the Children," I say. "I'll take us there. Grab your coat. You're going to need it."

There are tears streaming out of Elvis's eyes as he puts his palm on top of mine.

THE WRANGLER

"Fire," I order. Elvis's torch lights up on command.

"Where the hell are we now?" My companion's teeth are chattering as he pulls on his coat and wipes his eyes. The air around us is frigid and still. Our breath turns into icy clouds as it leaves our lungs.

I'm not entirely sure where we are. We're standing just inside the entrance to an underground cavern. It must be the right place, but it doesn't look like it did the last time I visited. Which means something has gone very wrong.

"We're supposed to be under the ice fields," I tell him as I take it all in. The cavern walls are now carpeted in a thick black mold that looks like a shag rug. I brush a finger against it. A million tiny tendrils latch on, and I'm forced to jerk my hand back. I think the stuff might be carnivorous. "This is where the Children used to hide while they waged war against Moloch. Kat and I were here not that long ago. There were thousands of Children living in the caverns."

"Do you think they've all been taken to Karamojo?" Elvis almost whispers. It's a thought so horrible that it can't be spoken at full volume.

I really hope not, but I have to admit that's the most likely answer. "I don't know," I say. "Let's go have a look. Find out if anyone's still around."

We plunge deeper into the cavern. Soon there's no need for Elvis's fire. The path ahead is lit by a pale blue light that comes from what appear to be strands of stars suspended from the ceiling. Like the mold, they're living creatures. When Kat and I were here together, she told me the Children had cultivated them. Now the tiny beings are blinking madly. It's the same pattern, over and over. I get the sense that they're desperately trying to communicate something, though I have no way of knowing what it is.

I stop at the entrance of an enormous circular chamber. There's a figure on the other side, standing guard in front of one of six passages that branch off in different directions. At first I'm relieved to see him, but something prevents me from getting closer. In fact, I take a quick step back.

"What are you doing?" Elvis whispers. "Isn't that one of the Children? Let's talk to him. We didn't come all this way to be shy."

"I know," I admit. "But we need to be careful, too. I can't tell from here if that's a Child. And even if it is—not all of them are friendly."

"So we're just going to stand here?" Elvis demands.

"Will you give it a rest?" I hiss. God he's starting to get on my nerves.

I take a step into the chamber, and the creatures on the ceiling blaze all at once. In the bright light, I can see the figure clearly. He's wearing a black uniform and a helmet with a single word printed across it. MOLOCH. It must be an NPC soldier from Moloch's realm, Imperium. My body takes action before my brain catches up. The dagger is out of my boot and flying across the room. It lands with a thud in the center of the NPC's chest.

"What the—" Elvis starts. I don't hear the rest. I'm across the chamber in an instant. I take the soldier's gun and drag his body out of sight. Then I motion for Elvis to join me. When he does, I thrust the NPC's gun into his hands and point to the opposite side of the door.

"Stay there, and don't do anything until I tell you to," I order. This time he keeps his mouth shut and obeys.

Somewhere below us in the bowels of the cavern, a creature shrieks. The inhuman sound ricochets off the walls like it's desperately searching for a means of escape.

"For God's sake, don't damage them." The voice is barely audible, but I have no trouble recognizing it. It belongs to Todd, one of the Company engineers who control Moloch's avatar. "The guests go nuts for the freakish ones."

Whatever Moloch and his men have caught, it doesn't seem to struggle for long. The screaming stops, and we hear footsteps heading toward us.

"You know, these things remind me of cockroaches. Do you guys have cockroaches here? I can't remember." Each word grows a little louder than the last. "No? Well, they're Earth bugs. Really nasty. Anyway, they're hard to exterminate—just like the Children. Every time I come down here there are a few more of these things tucked away in the crevices. I never seem to get rid of them."

"Perhaps it is not possible," says a second voice. "The Creator always said *life finds a way.*"

"Yeah, and I'm sure you think that's really profound," Moloch sneers. "What you don't know is that the idiot stole that line from *Jurassic Park.*"

"What is *Jurassic Park*?"

"Oh, shut the hell up, would you?" Moloch responds. "I'm so bored with you drones. I don't even know why I bother making small talk. I bet it would be far more interesting to talk to *them.*"

I stand with my back pressed against the wall while two creatures are marched out of the passage at gunpoint. It's immediately clear that they're neither guests nor NPCs. Though they're both vaguely humanoid, one has four arms that end in insect-like pincers. The other is almost completely transparent. I can see its purple heart throbbing inside its chest. Right behind them is a clean-cut, handsome man in his midthirties. His khaki pants, navy blazer and crisp blue shirt would look more appropriate on someone sitting behind a desk at a bank. Only the flak jacket he's wearing over his blazer conveys the dangerous nature of his current mission. As always, his name is printed on the front. It makes me think of his tower in Imperium, with MOLOCH written in blazing gold letters on top.

Elvis points a finger at Moloch. He wants to know if he should take him out. I shake my head. Moloch hasn't come here alone. There will be armed NPCs following right behind him. We need to disable them before we do anything else. I keep my back pressed against the wall, and as soon as the first soldier appears, I pull him to the side and slit his throat. Then Elvis steps into the passage and guns down two more NPCs. Moloch immediately spins around to face us, a pistol in his hand. Before he can shoot, I send my dagger flying in his direction. When it spears him in the forearm, he drops his weapon but shows no sign of pain.

"Simon Eaton!" he exclaims as soon he gets a good look at me. "I thought you were one of the parasites. How the hell are you? How's life on the run?" He pulls my dagger out of his arm and graciously steps forward to hand it to me.

As I take my weapon, I see the two Children scuttle up the side of the cave and cling to the ceiling a safe distance away from us. They could make a break for it, but they're clearly curious to see what happens.

"Hello, Todd," I say. Then I turn to Elvis. "This is Todd. He works for the Company. He started off as an engineer. Then he became a serial killer. Now apparently he's moved on to genocide."

Todd shrugs humbly. "I guess you could say I'm always looking for new challenges," he says. "But just so you know, I haven't really earned the genocide charge. We're not interested in *eliminating* the Children anymore. They're a popular form of amusement for our guests these days. The most dangerous game, you might call them. We're just here to make sure all the old troublemakers have been rounded up."

"You're a monster," Elvis snarls. He looks over at me. "What do you say we kill this guy in the most painful way possible?"

"As much as I would love to, it won't do anyone any good," I tell him. "Todd isn't wearing a disk."

Todd's avatar beams at Elvis and me. "Who's your little pal, Simon?" he asks. "Have you made friends with one of the guests? Is this a budding bromance I'm witnessing?"

One dick comment deserves another. "Speaking of bromances, how's your partner, Martin?"

The avatar's face instantly contorts into a scowl. "Dead, thanks to you. Wayne decided he was a liability."

So Martin's out of the picture, but Kat's evil stepfather is indeed alive.

"Wayne had your buddy killed, did he?" I say. "I don't believe I ever caught Wayne's job title. How far up the Company food chain does someone need to be before he can start ordering murders?"

"The people with real power don't need titles," Todd sneers.

"Which means you're not one of them. So is this what the big boss has got you doing these days? Massacring Children? Seems a little beneath you, if you don't mind my saying so. But I guess there's not much else for you to do now that your precious tech has been shelved."

Todd laughs. He sounds genuinely amused. I'm starting to get a bit worried. "You're still a giant idiot, I see," he says. "I'm just doing a little housekeeping before we turn Otherworld over to our two thousand guests. They're paying a pretty hefty subscription fee to keep the servers running, so Wayne wants to leave things in good shape for them. But after this, I'm out. I've got a ton of work to do getting our new and improved disks ready to roll out."

"Roll out?" I was sure they'd given up on the disks after they closed the facility. How could they sell gear that still has a lethal flaw? "What about the beta test?"

He's enjoying my surprise. "It's over, dude. We're moving forward with minimum viable product. We're just waiting for the new software to be finished."

"You mean the game that needs all the maps?" Elvis asks, and I nearly kick him.

Todd's mood instantly darkens. "Who the hell are *you*?" he demands. "What do you know about the maps?"

"A hell of a lot more than I did until now, thanks to you," Elvis says.

"I wouldn't worry about your next project," I tell Todd. "You aren't going to be launching any new software once people find out about the facility. No one's going to want to buy Company games when they hear you've been locking patients inside capsules and experimenting on their brains."

Todd's avatar tucks his hands into the pockets of his chinos and shakes his head. "Wrong again, my friend," he says. "The facility is no longer open. We couldn't run the risk that you or your girlfriend would tell someone what you'd seen. The whole operation was shut down immediately, and all but two of the patients were released to local hospitals. The only people we kept were Marlow Holm and your little ogre friend."

Gorog. He was the only disk wearer ever to survive his Otherworld avatar's death. The Company thinks his brain holds the secret to fixing the hardware's fatal flaw. God only knows what they've been doing to him—even though in the real world, Gorog is only thirteen years old.

I feel my fingers clench into fists. The rage is bubbling up again. I'm not sure I can keep it under control. "If you hurt Gorog or Marlow, I will hand the disks and the projectors over to the authorities. Then I will come and find you and rip your fucking head off."

Todd laughs. "Keep threatening me, Simon, and not only will I personally dispose of both of your friends, I promise I will enjoy every second of it."

I can't think of a single thing to say in response. I had an ace up my sleeve, but Todd seems to have the rest of the deck.

"Yeah, I thought so," says Todd. "Well, it was nice to see you again, buddy, but I've gotta run."

As his avatar starts to walk toward the cavern's exit, he looks up at the Children who are still watching us all from above. "I'll be back for you soon."

"We're really going to let that guy go?" Elvis complains.

To be honest, there's not much we can do. But I rush forward and grab the back of Todd's flak jacket. "Not so fast," I tell him.

"God you're such a dick," Todd says. His avatar flashes and goes still. Back in the real world, Todd's taken off his headset.

"What should we do with his avatar?" Elvis asks.

"Leave it here," I say. "If we kill it, he'll just get sent back to setup."

"May we have him?" says a voice from above. My skin starts to crawl. I'd almost forgotten the Children were watching.

I scan the ceiling and spot two dark shadows crouched in a corner. "Sure," I say. "Why not."

As the Children crawl closer, I start to question the wisdom of that offer. I've seen some creepy-ass creatures during my time in Otherworld, but these two make the others look like beauty contestants. It's a struggle to keep the shock off my face, but Elvis doesn't seem to be having any trouble at all.

"Hey there!" He greets the two of them as if they were invited guests to his own private party. "Are you guys going to eat this jerk? I really think you should."

"We no longer eat guests," says the one with the extra limbs. "It does us no good, since they provide no nourishment to us and cannot die. Ursus taught us a better way to deal with them."

"Ursus?" I ask.

"Our leader," she replies. At least I'm pretty sure it's a she. "Have you forgotten? He took you and the girl to see the Creator."

She's talking about the giant Child with bear DNA who guided me and Kat across the ice fields. "That's exactly who we came to find," I say. "I guess I didn't catch his name the last time I was here." To be honest, I wasn't even aware that the Children *had* names.

"He thought you would help us. Now Ursus is dead, along with most of our kind."

"Ursus is dead?" I don't know why the news hits me as hard as it does. The bear dude and I were hardly friends. But the last time I saw him, I would have sworn he was invincible.

"Ursus claimed the Creator was the source of our troubles— and he was. But the Creator was our protector as well. Once he was gone, there was nothing to stop Imperium's soldiers. The Children cannot harm Moloch. The most we can do is inconvenience him for a while."

The Child sticks one of her pincers into her mouth and pulls out a glistening strand of silk. Elvis and I watch in amazement as she winds it around Moloch until the avatar is completely encased in a shimmering cocoon. Then she hoists the large package onto her back and carries it up the side of the wall, where she deposits it inside a dark crevice in the cavern's ceiling.

"Moloch's men will come search for him soon," she says, using a strand of silk to lower herself back to the floor. "Let us hope that the search does not end quickly."

"Now," says a different voice. "Perhaps you will tell us why *you* are here." I look around for the creature that's speaking. Its translucent body has vanished. All I can see is the purple heart and the blood rushing through its veins.

"We're here to help you," Elvis announces in what I can only imagine is his best superhero voice. Then his avatar's head jerks back in agony.

I'm about to rush to his side when I feel the sensation of daggers being jammed into both of my eyes.

BACK TO REALITY

"Damn, that hurt! And why the hell am I soaking wet!" The first thing I hear is Elvis shouting.

My eyes are still adjusting to the light. I'm blind as a bat and completely freaked out, but I can't help but snicker. I made sure to relieve my bladder before I went under, so my pants are still perfectly dry. I didn't bother to warn Elvis.

"Hey," Kat says. "Welcome back."

The most amazing girl in the world slowly appears in front of me. I lift up my head and kiss her. I wasn't sure I'd ever see her again. "I'm sorry," I tell her as soon I'm done. "You were right all along. We shouldn't have gone to Otherworld wearing disks."

"What are you talking about?" Elvis demands angrily. "We've got to go back! I just told them we'd help them! We promised Volla!"

It's hard to be angry with someone who's sporting a giant wet patch on the front of his jeans, but somehow I manage. "How many times did we almost get killed?" I bite back. "We can't help anyone if we're dead! None of us are going back until we get our hands on a headset."

"Okay, okay, everybody calm down," Busara orders.

"Just tell us what happened," Kat says. I'd rather not go into it, but she must be able to read my expression. She knows it was bad. I never could hide anything from her.

Busara, on the other hand, doesn't appear to share Kat's powers of perception. "Did you see my father?" she asks eagerly. "Do we know where his body is?"

"We didn't make it to the ice cave," I confess.

"But you were there for four full hours! What were you doing the whole time?"

That's it? Somehow it felt longer.

"Simon!" Busara cries when I don't answer immediately.

She's getting on my nerves now, and I don't try to hide it. This is the same shit Busara used to pull when she was the Clay Man—criticizing my performance from the safety of the sidelines. "Oh, let's see," I say. "We were dodging bullets, nearly getting eaten by vines, watching the Children be hunted, having a pleasant chat with our old buddy Moloch."

"Wait." Kat puts up a hand to stop me. Her face is ashen. "Back up. What was that you said about the Children?"

I take a moment before I answer. I'm not looking forward to this. The Children are Kat's special cause. She'll be devastated when I tell her what's been done to them. "Do you remember the story you told me about the time you came across Children being rounded up to be killed for sport?"

I don't think she's able to speak. All she does is nod.

"Without the Creator, there's no one left to protect them."

"What about Ursus?" she croaks.

"Dead. Moloch's been taking all the Children to a realm called Karamojo where the new guests hunt them like wild game." Kat gasps, and I grab her hand. "That's not the worst part. I guess it's gotten so popular that they've rewritten the code. The Company is letting new Children be created again so they have an endless supply for the hunt."

"Oh my God!" Kat cries, burying her face in her hands.

"That's why we've got to go back," Elvis announces. "Right away. Our number one priority should be saving the Children."

"You're being an idiot!" I tell him. "We can't go back without headsets. It's too dangerous!"

"What choice do we have? I don't have half a million dollars to buy a headset—do you?" Busara seems to be firmly on Elvis's side now. I wonder what *that* means.

"We'll find one," I say, though I have no idea where to start looking.

"By the time we do, thousands of Children could be gone. And my dad might be dead," Busara shoots back.

"Wait." When Kat lifts her head, there's a determined expression on her face. "I think I have an idea." She picks up a remote and switches on the giant television screen that's mounted on the wall. "While you guys were in Otherworld, Busara and I caught up on current events."

Kat punches in the number of a cable news channel. The segment playing was filmed across the street from a humble suburban home. The lawn of the house is filled with reporters and camerapeople. There's something about the building itself that seems oddly familiar. I'm just about to ask what we're looking at when a chyron scrolls across the screen.

MILO YOLKIN STILL HOUSEBOUND AFTER FIVE DAYS

I've heard countless stories about the house I'm looking at. It's part of Milo Yolkin's legend. Everyone in America knew that one of the richest, most powerful men in the country lived in a modest home somewhere in the middle of New Jersey. But no one seemed to know exactly where it was. Now the entire world has found it.

"You think Milo's got extra headsets in his house?" Busara asks Kat.

"Of course he does!" Elvis's mood has brightened considerably. "And even if he doesn't, there's gotta be *something* worth five hundred grand in there. And who knows, Busara? Maybe that's where he hid your dad's body."

Busara snorts. "Why would Milo have my dad's body in his *house*?"

"Where else would he put it?" Elvis asks.

"Actually, he's got a point," I say. "Moloch told us the Company closed the facility. And he didn't seem to have any idea that your dad is still alive. I don't think Milo ever told anyone what he did to your father."

Busara still isn't convinced. "So you're saying Milo Yolkin hid everything we're looking for in a house that looks like it belongs to some little old lady?"

Elvis laughs and gestures at the screen. "You think Milo Yolkin would be satisfied in a shithole like that? I happen to know a lot about crazy rich dudes, and I'd be willing to bet that shack is just the tip of the iceberg. There's probably a bunker the size of Detroit underneath it."

"Yeah, well, whatever Milo had in there, the Company's already got it," Busara says. "I'm sure they cleaned out the place the first chance they got."

"How'd they get stuff out with everyone watching?" Elvis asks. "The building's been surrounded by reporters for the past five days." I should never underestimate him. The guy is a goddamned genius.

"If the Company can't take things out, how are we supposed to get in?" Busara counters.

"Trust me, beautiful," Elvis says. "Someone in the neighborhood will know how to get inside."

"Don't call me beautiful," Busara snaps, but she's in. I can tell.

We stayed in New Mexico less than a day. Now we're headed back to New Jersey. I can't decide whether this is a good idea—or the worst thing we could do. I suppose the Company won't be expecting us to return so soon. Or will they?

Each of us will take eight-hour shifts at the wheel. If we drive through the night, we'll be at Milo's house in thirty-two hours. Busara took the first shift, and we're already somewhere in Kansas. I should probably be sleeping. I drew a night shift. But I can't take my eyes off the landscape outside the windows. Tall green wheat lines both sides of the road. It changes color as the wind pushes it in different directions. We still have most of the money the Phantom gave us. We don't need to worry about gas anymore.

But I can't stop thinking about what might happen if the car broke down. At least in Texas you could see what was coming. Anything could be hiding out here in the fields, waiting to spring on us. I'll take the desert any day.

I feel the car slow to a stop. After thirty-two hours of almost perpetual motion, it's a strange enough sensation to wake me up.

"This is it?" Kat asks, studying the car's GPS. "It's not showing up on the map. It's like it doesn't even exist."

Elvis is in the passenger's seat. "Yep," he says. "This is it. Sunset Heights."

Two brick pillars stand on either side of a small paved road. A wooden sign spans the gap between them, forming an arch over the entrance to a private community. A blazing orange sun descends behind purple mountains. SUNSET HEIGHTS is written in fancy yellow script at the bottom.

"Yeah, but there have to be a million places with the same name," Kat says.

"I'm sure there are," Elvis says. "I'm also sure that the others would show up on our maps. This is the Sunset Heights where Milo Yolkin lived."

Kat steers the car into the drive, and we enter Milo's secret realm. Both sides of the street are lined with houses of modest size. There seem to be only four or five styles of home and four or five shades of paint. The lawns are perfectly tended—they're all the exact same color of green. Parked in every sixth driveway is a pickup truck, with a landscaping crew nearby pruning hedges or weeding the flower beds. After a while, I start to worry that we're seeing the same guys over and over again. It's disorienting, like we're stuck in some kind of loop.

"There are no street numbers that I can see. Not even on the mailboxes," Busara points out. "How are we ever going to find this place?"

"Look for the television crews," Elvis says.

"Why would one of the richest men in the world live somewhere like this?" I ask. "I've seen retirement villages with more personality."

"Maybe Milo had other priorities," Elvis replies. "Not everyone cares about fancy houses and home décor."

"I don't think this is about Milo's taste in architecture. I think this is camouflage," Kat says. "It was Milo's way of blending in."

"Yeah, if you think about it, it's a pretty good security system," Busara adds. "It's a private community with no street signs or address numbers. And it doesn't show up on any maps. If anyone ever came looking for Milo, they'd end up driving around for days."

I'm pretty sure they're right. I'm suddenly struck by the genius of it, and I start to wonder if Elvis might be onto something. There's got to be more to Milo's strange suburban world than meets the eye.

Then we round a corner and nearly rear-end a television van that's parked at least three feet from the curb. Just as Elvis predicted, we've found Milo's house. The curtains are drawn and the lawn appears to be a few weeks overgrown. Weeds have conquered the landscaping and the grass is shin-high. Knowing New Jersey, I'm sure there are ticks stationed on every blade. But that hasn't stopped several reporters from wading through the vegetation and up to the house. One is attempting to peer through the windows.

Kat pulls over up the street. As we walk back toward the house, we pass a reporter sitting on a folding chair, applying a fresh mask of makeup.

"This is such a joke. What do you want to bet the little bastard's in Bali?" she asks the cameraman, who's eating a cruller as he waits for her to get ready for her close-up.

"Neighbors say he's inside," the guy responds, sending little flecks of pastry sailing through the air.

"If he's inside, he's gotta be dead. No one's seen him in days. There haven't even been any deliveries. I bet he slipped in the bathtub and broke his neck."

"Even better," says the cameraman. "Milo Yolkin dead in a bathtub is the story of the year."

If only they knew how Milo really died. That would be the story of the century.

"Speaking of bathrooms—did you hear about that guy in the city? The one they found dead in the stall at Bryant Park? He was some kind of bigwig—"

The cameraman's phone beeps. He checks it and immediately chucks the rest of his cruller into the gutter. "Save your story for later," he tells the reporter. "They want you on in five."

Closer to the house, a boy on a bike is watching the action from the sidewalk across the street. He's about thirteen, I'd guess. His shaggy black hair needs a good cut. He keeps blowing his bangs out of his eyes. But after every puff, the same disgusted smirk returns to his face.

"That's the person we need to talk to," Elvis says.

"That kid?" Busara asks skeptically.

"Trust me, hot stuff," Elvis tells her. "You may see a ninth-grade outcast, but I see Milo Yolkin's best friend."

It's hard to argue with that logic. "Fine," Busara huffs. "But if you call me hot stuff one more time, I'm seriously going to kick your ass."

"Okay, gorgeous," Elvis says.

The kid eyes us as we approach. "Get lost," he says. "I'm supposed to call the cops if any of you parasites bothers me."

"Parasites?" Kat asks with a friendly laugh. "Do we look like reporters to you?"

"Did I say I thought you were reporters?" the kid shoots back. "I know who you work for."

I have a hunch that the boy thinks the Company sent us here. I guess Elvis hit that nail on the head. Not only did this kid know Milo Yolkin, he must have known him well.

"Did Magna ever give you a tour of Otherworld?" I ask.

The kid stares at me in silence. He's been there. I can tell. And I don't think he liked what he saw. "So what if you know about Magna. It doesn't prove anything. I'm still not answering any questions," he tells me.

"Milo must have sworn you to secrecy," I say. I hear one of my friends gasp in the background. They weren't expecting me to come right out with it.

The kid's jaw clenches, like he's trying to keep the truth from spilling out.

"Milo is dead," I tell him. "That's why we're here."

"Simon!" Busara whispers.

Does she have to second-guess everything? "This boy was his friend. He deserves to know."

The kid sighs and nods stoically. "I figured Milo was dead," he says. "He hasn't come back in a while. Thanks for telling me. I got stuff to do." He wheels his bike around and hops on. Whatever the stuff is, it suddenly seems pretty urgent.

"Milo gave you instructions to follow if something ever happened to him, didn't he?" Kat asks.

The boy takes his feet off the pedals and looks up at her.

"We're trying to save other people from ending up like him," she says. "He may have something in his house that can help us."

"How do you know all this stuff?" the kid whispers.

I nudge Kat. "Show him," I tell her.

Kat takes her hair out of its ponytail and turns around. A wide strip of her scalp is still visible where they shaved the back of her head for the disk.

"We escaped from Otherworld. Milo didn't," she says.

The boy's face crumples for a moment. Then he wipes his eyes. "I'm Kenji," he says.

"Simon," I tell him. "And that's Elvis, Busara and Kat."

"*Elvis?*" he sneers. A bubble of snot appears briefly in one nostril. "You're kidding me, right?"

Elvis shrugs. "My parents are Ukrainian. It's still a super-cool name there. Do you know how to get inside Milo's house?" he asks, gesturing toward the building across the street. "I'm betting there's a secret entrance."

"Sure," says Kenji. "But that's not his house."

. . .

It turns out that Milo owned the whole suburb, and he handpicked all his neighbors. Kenji's family moved in five years ago, shortly after they'd been featured in a story in the *New York Times*. Medical bills had driven his parents into bankruptcy, and they were living out of the family SUV. One morning, there was a knock on the passenger-side window, and a lawyer handed them a deed to a new house and a check. The family's current neighbors arrived in much the same way. Most of the people in Sunset Heights must have known that Milo was their benefactor, but none of them would have uttered a word. In return for his kindness, they acted as his personal security team. When the reporters showed up looking for Milo's house, his neighbors directed them to the home of an elderly man who'd recently passed away.

"This is it." Kenji leads us up a flagstone path to a beige house with no distinguishing features.

"Kenji?" There's a woman standing on the porch of the house next door with a phone in her hands. "Is everything okay?"

"Everything is fine, Mom," Kenji says. "These guys are friends."

The blinds are drawn, but the door is unlocked. Kenji merely turns the knob and lets us all inside.

The air in the house is stale and musty. We step into a living room that could belong to anyone in any town in any state in America. There's a brown couch, an armchair and a particleboard coffee table. The only signs that Milo Yolkin might once have lived there are a giant seventy-five-inch screen mounted on the wall and a heap of video game consoles—from an Atari 2600 to the latest

Steam Machine. Judging by the dust that's accumulated on them, they haven't been touched in ages.

"We used to play a lot," Kenji says simply.

He takes us to the kitchen, which reeks of rotten garbage, and opens the door to the pantry. Inside, the shelves are filled with every imaginable brand of sugary cereal. Elvis grabs a box of Cap'n Crunch and rips the top open.

"What?" I hear him say. "It's not like Milo's going to need it."

Busara must be giving him the evil eye, but I don't turn around for a look. Kenji has pushed back a box of Cocoa Puffs, revealing a palm scanner. We're about to enter Milo's secret lair. He places his hand on the screen, but nothing happens. He leans forward and says, "Knock, knock."

"Who's there?" replies a voice.

"Lettuce."

"Lettuce who?"

"Lettuce in or we'll break the door down."

The pantry door slides to the right, revealing a flight of stairs. The door closes and locks behind us. I'm immediately over-whelmed by the stench of urine. It's so powerful that I no longer smell the trash.

"Somebody went to Otherworld without wearing his Depends," Busara remarks.

"A pair of Depends only last for a day or so," Kenji says, leading us down the stairs. "Then it just all comes out the sides. Milo never bothered to clean his mess up. There's a mattress down here that really needs to be tossed, but I can't drag it out by myself."

When I get to the bottom of the stairs, I almost forget about the smell. I'm suddenly outside, on the balcony of what appears to be a Roman villa. The sky above is a brilliant blue. Statues of two shapely and lightly clad goddesses stand guard at the doors of the building. Inside, two buff, toga-clad servants are fanning a beautiful woman. Out here, an empty daybed waits in the sun. In the fields below, workers are harvesting olives from a vast grove that surrounds the villa. I can see a sparkling blue sea in the distance. Though it's clearly some kind of projection, it's remarkably realistic.

"What is this place?" Elvis asks.

"Milo told me this is what Otherworld used to be like—back in the old days when it was an MMO. He said he used to feel like a god when he was here. Plus, he told me he didn't know what else to do with all this space. He wasn't all that great at decorating."

No one replies. Then Kat clears her throat nervously. "It's lovely," she says.

"Yeah, sure," Kenji sneers. "It's gorgeous."

He punches a code into a panel on the wall, and Milo's beautiful world disappears. In its place is a dank, windowless room. The walls and ceiling are bare concrete, and the floor is decorated with stains whose origin I'd rather not contemplate. The daybed is now just a soiled mattress lying on top of a concrete base, and the corners of the room are thick with spiderwebs. There's a bottle on the floor beside the makeshift bed. Its contents are the color of apple cider. It's like a cell inside some Central American prison. I'm overwhelmed by a mixture of revulsion and pity. This prison cell was Milo Yolkin's reality.

"Oh my God, is that what I think it is?" Busara asks, her eyes on the amber liquid inside the bottle.

"Looks like I missed one," Kenji replies. "There used to be a million piss bottles down here. He'd use them when he ran out of Depends. He'd pause the game, but he didn't like getting up to use the bathroom. He said he was working on something that would make it possible to stay there all the time—some kind of machine that would take care of his body. Replace food and Depends and plastic piss bottles."

He's talking about the capsules.

Busara's eyes light up. "Are there any machines like that here?"

I know what she's thinking. If the facility is closed and her dad is still missing, Milo must have been storing Ogubu's body somewhere else—somewhere the Company didn't know about. If Milo brought capsules here to Sunset Heights, there's a chance her father might be locked up inside one of them.

I totally get it. But Busara's excitement feels out of place and cruel. This boy lost someone he cared about too.

Kenji shrugs. "I haven't seen any machines. Like I said, Milo hasn't been back for a while. Maybe he finally made one. Maybe that's where he's been."

"When was the last time you saw him?" Kat asks gently.

"A few months ago. I found him half dead down here." Kenji pauses. I want to ask the next question, but I know I'll screw it up, so I let Kat take the lead. But she doesn't say anything either. She just puts a hand on the boy's shoulder. His head falls forward and the words come spilling out. "I was away visiting my grandparents and I couldn't check in on him for a few days. When I got back, I came down here and found him foaming at the mouth with one of those fucking disks on the back of his head. He hadn't eaten or drunk anything the whole time I'd been gone. The doctor said a few more hours and he'd have died of dehydration." He glances up at Kat. "Sorry for using the f-word."

"That's okay," Kat says. "I can't think of a better word to use for what you just described."

"Hey, you guys." Elvis has been examining the electronics hidden about the room. "I know this place is a hellhole, but this is some pretty amazing stuff Milo's got rigged up in here. Far as I know, no one's invented a VR environment like it yet. Is this what your buddy wanted you to destroy?" he asks Kenji.

I catch his eye and shake my head in disgust. He and Busara belong together. I'm not sure either of them is fully human.

Fortunately, Kenji doesn't seem offended. If anything, I'd say he's relieved by the change of subject. "No," he says, setting off down the hall. "That stuff's all back here."

Busara rushes after the kid, still hoping she'll find her father behind one of the doors. I'm less eager now. I've seen more than enough already, but I still drag myself down the hall.

I find them standing in a large room with a green-screen wall around three sides. There are cameras mounted on the ceiling and on tripods stationed around the room. A table runs along the fourth wall. Aside from the giant computer monitors hooked up to a laptop, I don't recognize most of the equipment sitting on top.

"What's in the other rooms?" Busara asks impatiently. "I saw a bunch of doors down the hall."

"Nothing. They're empty," says Kenji.

"This is it?" Kat seems almost as crestfallen as Busara. "There are no headsets down here? Where's yours? You said you'd been to Otherworld, and I don't think Milo would have let you use a disk."

"Yeah, he gave me a headset. I stuffed it down the garbage compactor," Kenji says.

"Do you have any idea what that thing would be worth right now?" Elvis asks.

"I don't give a shit," Kenji snarls. "I saw what Otherworld did to Milo. You think I'd sell that poison to someone else?"

A lot of people would. Apparently Kenji is different. I can see why Milo trusted him.

"What was Milo filming down here?" I ask Kenji.

"Himself," the boy says.

"What the hell?" I turn around to see Busara holding up a projector just like the ones we have hidden back in the car.

"Yeah, that was part of his project," Kenji tells her.

"What project?" I ask.

"Isn't it obvious?" Elvis says, looking at me as if I'm mentally challenged. "The green screen, the cameras, the hologram projector. Milo was making a digital clone of himself."

I don't get it, but Kenji nods. "He said he wanted a replacement. I don't know how far he got, but it's all on that."

Kenji points at the laptop, and I see inspiration light up Kat's face. "We need to take the computer," she says.

"No," Kenji tells her. "That's the number one thing I'm supposed to destroy. Milo told me it should never end up in the wrong hands."

"I assure you, kid, we are definitely the *right* hands," Elvis tells him.

"It's true," Kat says. "We can use this laptop to make sure what happened to Milo won't happen to anyone else."

"Yeah? And how are you going to do that?" I'm glad Kenji asked. I'm curious to know too.

Before Kat can answer, a fan kicks in. Frigid air pours from a small grate in the wall and surrounds us. In a few seconds, the room is as cold as a meat locker.

"Shit," Kenji says, shivering.

"What's going on?" I ask.

"Someone's trying to get in upstairs," he tells us. "It's a level two alarm. That's what happens when someone doesn't tell the joke right. Milo knew he'd feel the cold—even if he was in Otherworld. I don't know why it's a level *two* alarm, though. That means whoever's up there made it past the palm print, but I know for a fact that the only two prints in the system are mine and Milo's."

I turn toward the door so he can't see my horror. I know how the Company got Milo's palm print.

"Wanna guess who that is?" Elvis asks Kenji. "What do you want to bet it's guys Milo didn't want getting their hands on his computer?"

Why the hell is Elvis still so focused on the laptop? Whoever's upstairs will find their way in eventually. And when they do, we're totally screwed.

"Fine," Kenji huffs. "Take it." He doesn't seem too concerned about the intruders, either.

"Where are we supposed to take it?" I ask Elvis. "We're trapped."

"Oh, come on, Simon," he says as he pulls USB cords out of the computer. "You think Milo didn't design this place with an escape route?"

"Did he?" Kat asks hopefully.

"Follow me," Kenji tells her, and I sigh with relief.

There are no lights at the far end of the bunker, but Kenji seems to know where he's going. The rest of us feel our way along the cold concrete wall. When we reach the end, I hear Kenji straining to move something. Then one by one we're ushered through what must be a hole in the wall. There's a ladder that leads up. Kenji and I are last to climb. As we push the door closed behind us, a loud crash can be heard at the other end of the bunker. They've blown the kitchen entrance open.

"Will they find this exit?" I ask Kenji.

"Not unless they're geniuses," he says.

That thought doesn't bring me much comfort. Even the Company's thugs are probably Mensa members.

I follow Kenji up the ladder. At the top is a shack of some sort. The moon is shining through a plastic window, illuminating a rack of what looks at first to be torture equipment.

"Is this a toolshed?" Busara whispers.

"Yep, we're in my backyard," Kenji confirms.

I suddenly hear the sound of sirens in the distance. The police could be on their way.

Kenji cackles softly. "Bet my mom saw people go inside and called the cops," he says.

"Stay here. I'm going to take a look," I tell the crew.

"Yeah, right," Kat scoffs. "I'm coming with you."

Together we slink across the lawn and peer through the fence. There's a black SUV idling outside Milo's house. The windows are tinted—there's no way to see if anyone's inside.

The sirens are getting closer. I can't wait to see what happens when they arrive. Then Milo's front door opens and two men walk out. Neither is rushing. It's as if they know exactly how much time they have before the cops show up.

I can't get a good look at either of them until they step off Milo's porch onto the path that leads to the curb. Their faces come into view, and Kat gasps and lurches backward, landing on her butt in the grass.

I don't blame her. I almost did the same thing. One of the men is Wayne Gibson.

"Do they know we're here?" Kat whispers. "Is that why they've come?"

I don't know the answer. I do know that our car is going to stay parked right where we left it.

MILO RETURNS

At first I didn't realize how important the laptop could be. But as soon as I saw what was on it, I came to recognize it for what it is—serious leverage. Thanks to Milo's digital clone, we should be able to demand the release of Marlow, Gorog and Busara's dad, James Ogubu. We may even be able to force the Company to kick the headset players out of Otherworld. Whether the contents of the laptop will be enough to take down the entire corporation remains to be seen.

"Ready?" Elvis calls from the bathroom.

Kat looks at me and rolls her eyes. We've been holed up for two days in a Best Western in Brooklyn, not far from my mother's childhood home and the fragrant waters of the Gowanus Canal. We drove straight here from Milo Yolkin's house in New Jersey, and aside from a single excursion, we haven't left the room since we got here. I couldn't possibly be more ready than I am right now.

"Ready?" Elvis asks again when neither of us answers immediately.

"Yes!" Kat shouts back.

The bathroom door opens. A second later, Milo Yolkin strolls out, a small metal sphere trailing behind him. He's wearing his trademark hoodie and gray sneakers. His curly blond hair bounces a bit with each step. Milo stops in front of us, pivots slightly, smiles and waves. Then he walks on. When he reaches the door of the hotel room, he and the sphere both come to a stop. And then Milo Yolkin disappears.

Kat and I break into wild applause, and Elvis and Busara emerge from the bathroom to take a bow. They look remarkably fresh for two people who stayed up all night resurrecting Milo Yolkin.

"That was amazing!" Kat gushes. "What else can he do?"

"That's it for now," Elvis says.

"That's it?" I ask.

I can tell from the frown on Busara's face that it wasn't a smart thing to say.

"Do you have any idea how hard it was to put that together?" Elvis chides me. "Yolkin had just started cloning himself. We didn't have much to work with."

"It's more than enough for now," Kat says unconvincingly. "You guys did great."

"See?" Elvis says to me. "*She* knows how to recognize genius."

"Still—is it going to be enough? We'll need the hologram to do more, won't we?" I ask. "We have to convince the Company that Milo 2.0 is under our control."

If hologram Milo shows up in public, investors will assume the boy genius is alive and well. The price of the Company's stock is bound to soar. But if he happens to get hit by a New York City bus in front of thousands of witnesses, the stock price will tank and never recover. The Company needs to believe that we're capable of destroying them financially—otherwise they'll never meet our demands.

Elvis starts to argue, but Busara puts a hand on his arm. It's the first time I've seen her make such a tender gesture toward anyone. Elvis seems surprised too. He's marveling at the hand like it's the most magical object in the universe. I'm starting to wonder if he's actually made some progress with Busara when she blinks and appears to come to her senses. In a flash, the hand gets snatched away. It all happened so fast that I'd probably doubt my own eyes if Kat hadn't caught it all too. I know because one of her bony fingers is currently poking me in the thigh. It's the private language Kat's used since we were both eight years old.

"It's good enough for today," Busara says. "You and Kat go out and bring Milo back from the dead. Elvis and I will stay here and get back to work."

"Another deranged Milo Yolkin hologram coming up." Elvis is suddenly chipper again.

"By tomorrow?" Kat asks. "That's when we'll need the second hologram if the plan's going to work. So no screwing around."

"Excuse me?" Busara asks as if the idea of screwing around simply does not compute. "Is that supposed to be a joke?"

Kat rolls her eyes. "Never mind," she says.

. . .

It's been a long time since I've been around so many people. Rockefeller Center is packed for the filming of a top-rated morning show. Today the crowd might even be bigger than usual. A teen star is here to promote his latest movie, and the square is filled with squealing ten-year-old girls and their indulgent parents. The adults all look the same to me, like mannequins dressed in slightly different outfits. If I didn't know any better, I'd swear they were NPCs.

The interview they're waiting for will be taking place on the other side of a giant window positioned a few feet above street level. The movie star and the show's host are milling about the studio, chatting while a news segment is filmed. I recognize a publicity photo that flashes up on a monitor. The subject of the news segment is a well-known movie director.

"Who's that?" someone beside me asks.

"Some Hollywood guy. They say he attacked an actress and tried to kill her. She had to hide in a bathroom to get away."

Inside the studio, a picture that must have been taken at the crime scene replaces the first photo. It's the same guy, his shirt wet with sweat and his chunky black glasses askew.

I turn my attention back to the task at hand. "You sure this is going to work?" I ask Kat.

"I keep forgetting that you never watch television," Kat says. "The cameras *always* pan the crowd between segments. Someone watching will spot Milo. That's all we need. The footage will be all over the Internet by noon. You have the projector ready?"

"Yep." I lift the shopping bag in which digital Milo is waiting.

"Don't get caught on camera," Kat says, pulling the bill of my baseball hat down.

"I'll try." I grab her and kiss her. "Let's do this."

There's a roped-off path that cuts through the crowd. I station myself behind a giant dad at one end of the square. Kat's on the other side, crouched behind a lady with a cloud of curly hair. I put the projector down on the ground. All it has to do is roll sixty feet in a straight line. I wait until the people in the crowd throw their arms in the air. Then I turn Milo on.

The small silver ball produces its three-dimensional hologram. As it rolls silently across the concrete, Milo takes his first few steps. A little girl barreling down the path runs straight through him. My heart is pounding and I feel a bit dizzy, but everyone's arms are still in the air and no one else seems to have noticed. Inside the studio, the teen star has come to the window to wave at the crowd. His face is at least sixty percent smile and he can't be more than four feet tall. He doesn't look totally human, if you ask me. Then I see him do a double take and point outside. I can't hear what he says, but his lips seem to form the words *Milo Yolkin*. The television show host rushes to the window for a look. He says something to the crew and the cameras are suddenly up against the window. The timing couldn't be more perfect. At that very moment, Milo stops, pivots and waves. Then he continues walking. Once he's behind a lamppost on the other side of the square, I make him disappear. I see Kat snatch the sphere and vanish into the crowd. I meet her on the corner of Fifty-Sixth and Sixth Avenue as planned, and we catch the subway downtown.

Our next stop is a computer store in another tourist-trap part of Manhattan where we can use the devices on display to check out the news. The employees are all too busy staring at their own phones to pay us any mind. The video of Milo is everywhere. It's trending on every social media outlet. Even the newspapers have already picked up the story and are reporting that the boy genius is alive. In the thirty minutes it took to get here, the Company's stock price has shot through the roof.

"That was fast," Kat notes merrily. "Ready for stage two?"

We picked out the spot yesterday—a café on a side street in lower Manhattan. It met our two big requirements—lots of people inside the café, but not many people on the sidewalk outside. There's also a mailbox in front of the building where we can leave a hidden message for the Company to spot. Today it will be a single word written in Sharpie—*Nemi*.

Kat and I loiter outside for fifteen minutes, waiting for the sidewalk to clear completely. Then, standing out of view, I set the projector down on the sidewalk. Milo Yolkin appears, walking slowly past the café window. Once he's past, the hologram disappears and Kat snatches up the projector on the other side. I'm starting to worry that no one in the café witnessed the show. Then two people rush out the door, their smartphones in their hands. They look both ways, but Milo is gone. They're already typing away as they return to their tables inside.

Success achieved, Kat and I head to another computer store, this one in SoHo. Two pictures of Milo outside the café are already making the rounds on Twitter. One is little more than a blur. But the second is clear as day. Milo Yolkin is already trending on Twitter, just a few places down from the homicidal movie director.

"Do you think they'll notice our message?" Kat asks.

I expand the photo.

"Yeah, they'll notice." The word on the mailbox is perfectly legible. *Nemi* will mean nothing to anyone who doesn't work for the Company. It's a deserted realm Kat traveled through during her time in Otherworld. Wayne and the engineers will be scouring all the images for information. They'll know how to interpret it. We're arranging a meeting. The *where* has been answered. The *when* is yet to come.

Kat and I head back to Brooklyn to drop off the projector with Elvis and Busara. Then we leave them to work their magic in peace. Wandering the nearby streets, Kat and I end up on one of the bridges that span the Gowanus Canal. The surrounding neighborhood isn't what I was expecting. It used to be one of the most desolate parts of the city—and the Mob's favorite dumping ground for dead bodies. There are still a few scrap metal yards and a couple of coffin factories, but now luxury apartment buildings are rising up among them. The buildings along the banks of the canal are some of the priciest addresses in Brooklyn. Which is doubly surprising considering the whole place smells like crap.

Kat and I stop on the south side of the Union Street Bridge and peer down at the water. A wave of brown foam is making its way toward New York Harbor, carrying lumps of fecal matter along with it. I feel Kat's hand on the small of my back, and I wonder if she's thinking the same thing I am. Somewhere down there, among the oil spills and chemicals, is my grandfather's final resting place.

"We haven't had much time alone together," Kat says.

I turn my attention to her. Whenever my eyes are on her, I can't imagine ever looking at anything else. "Yeah, when I daydreamed about the two of us, this wasn't exactly what I had in mind," I admit.

"You daydreamed about us?" she teases me.

"Every single day since I was eight years old," I tell her.

"Liar." She laughs.

But it's the honest truth. I can't remember daydreaming about anything else. I lean down and kiss her. Just as our lips make contact, I feel a strange tingling at the base of my skull. I glance up to see that we're being watched. There's another bridge a few blocks down, and a man is standing at the railing looking north at us. He's wearing a plaid suit that belongs to a different era and a fedora cocked at a raffish tilt. I'm too far away to see him clearly, but when he turns to the side, the outline of his giant nose makes him easy to identify.

"Do you see the man watching us from the other bridge?" I ask Kat before it even occurs to me that I shouldn't.

"What man?" she asks. If he were really there, she'd be looking right at him. He hasn't budged an inch.

"Never mind," I tell her. My grandfather wants to speak to me. Until recently, he only appeared in Otherworld or my dreams. But this is broad daylight. There's not even a cloud in the sky.

"Simon?" I feel Kat's fingers slip though mine. She's concerned. She should be. "Are you okay?"

"Yep. Forget it," I say, squeezing her hand and forcing a smile. "I think the stress is starting to get to me."

I finally get time alone with Kat, and my brain betrays me. My luck's never been great, but it keeps getting worse. For the next hour, Kat and I walk in silence around the neighborhood until we turn back toward the motel. We're still a couple of blocks away when we see the building. It rises several stories above the rest of its neighbors. Bland, new and clean, it hardly fits in with the weird, old and grimy. It's like something sculpted out of plastic with a 3-D printer.

Suddenly I lurch backward. Kat's come to a stop and grabbed my arm. "Look." She points up at the roof. There's a figure standing on the edge, staring down at the earth like a gargoyle on a French cathedral. I know what it is, and Kat does too. We don't need to discuss. We both break into a run.

We stop across the street from the motel's lobby. We can see him clearly from here. Milo Yolkin is standing on what must be a ledge that circles the roof. The tips of his sneakers are sticking out over the side and his curly blond hair is dancing in the breeze. It's so brilliant I almost want to applaud. Elvis and Busara have taken the simplest image imaginable—a man standing still, facing the camera—and turned it into someone who's literally on the edge.

A cab pulls up in front of the motel, and a couple of Midwestern tourists wearing the pastel costumes of their native land climb out. They notice Kat staring at the sky and glance up to see what has her so mesmerized. They don't look like the sort who'd be able to identify Milo Yolkin. All they see is a man who's dead set on testing the laws of gravity.

"Oh my God, Justin, dial 911!" the woman screeches at her husband, who's frantically patting down the countless pockets in his cargo shorts in search of his phone.

I don't know whether it's purely coincidence or if Elvis and Busara heard the commotion, but at that very moment, Milo Yolkin disappears. The tourist puts his phone down and looks at his wife. They've been in Brooklyn for less than two minutes and they've already had the shock of their lives.

"Did you see all that?" the woman asks as Kat and I make our way past them into the hotel.

"You mean the pigeon orgy up there on the roof?" Kat asks with a perfectly straight face.

"What? No!" the man says. "The guy about to jump."

"Nope, didn't catch that," Kat tells him.

The woman's hand flies up to her lips and her eyes widen in horror. "Justin," she gasps. "Do you think it could have been a ghost?"

She has no idea how close she is to the truth. Milo Yolkin may have passed away, but he hasn't vanished. He's risen from the grave like a restless spirit with a score to settle.

I'm back on the bridge over the Gowanus Canal. The fancy buildings are gone. Everything is dark and the only sound is that of the sewage lapping against the banks.

"Don't do that again," I tell the man standing next to me. "Don't come to see me when Kat's around."

"You think I wanna show this face in the light of day?" he asks. "I didn't visit on purpose."

That means neither of us is in control. "Shit."

"You said it. She needs to know," the Kishka tells me. "You can't keep it from her."

"Keep what from her?" I demand.

"That something's wrong."

I've been trying to ignore it, but the truth never goes away.

"What is it?" I ask him. "Do you know?"

"All I know is that none of this is right," he says. "I haven't figured out how, but it ain't."

I hear a splash below. My gaze drops to the surface of the water. There's something down there—something white and fleshy.

I wake up in a sweat. Kat's bare arm is lying across my throat, and there's a mattress spring jabbing me in the back. Kat must have opened the window. The smell of the canal always grows stronger at night.

For reasons that are clear to anyone with an ounce of common sense, accessing a Manhattan rooftop is usually no easy feat. But thanks to the Company, Elvis has a blueprint of every building on the island downloaded on his glasses. Not only can the glasses guide you to the access stairs, they'll show you which security wires to snip when you reach the locked door at the top. The four of us together would have drawn attention, so it was decided only one of us could do the job. Aside from the shaved strip on the back of her head, Kat's hair is long enough to cover the AR glasses' unusually large temples. The rest of us are standing across the street, waiting for the show to begin. I don't like this one bit. Now I know how Kat's felt when I've left her for Otherworld. I won't breathe easily until she's completed her mission and returned to me.

Unfortunately, the weather is not cooperating with our plans. The sky has grown dark and the wind is picking up. Powerful gusts race through the city's canyons, and every few minutes, there's a rumble of thunder in the distance. A storm is rolling in. We don't have phones anymore, so none of us checked the weather. There are thousands of people on the street, but none of them are looking up. Everyone is rushing to get inside before the rain arrives.

There's a clap of thunder overhead, and a drop splatters against my forehead. Milo Yolkin appears on the ledge of the roof, holding his sign. No one down below notices. I'm starting to think it's all a lost cause. Then Busara steps forward, points a finger in the air and screams.

The sidewalk traffic immediately comes to a halt. Within seconds, a crowd of people gathers, all staring up at the man about to jump. Dozens of phones are filming the scene. I only hear one person dial 911. No one else wants to miss a second of the action. It makes me want to pack up and leave them all at the mercy of the Company. I'm not sure any of these jerks deserve to be saved.

A guy next to me is zooming in on the figure, hoping for a close-up. "Oh, *daaamn,*" he says. "Is that Milo Yolkin?"

"Milo Yolkin!" someone else repeats, and the news spreads through the crowd. Cars on the street have come to a stop, and people are climbing on top of taxis for a better view.

"What's he holding?"

"A sign that says *noon.*"

"What the hell does that mean?"

"Don't jump!" a woman shouts. "We all love you!"

"Release Otherworld!"

"The end is near!"

"Hey," says someone nearby. "I'm in Midtown, and Milo Yolkin is about to jump off a roof. . . . What? Yeah, I'm serious!

So short the Company stock.... Hell yes, I'm sure. Just do it!"
He ends the call and lifts his phone back up in the air and hits
Record. "Go ahead and jump, you little idiot," he says.

Then the clouds break and the rain pours down. Within seconds, the witnesses are drenched and their phones rendered useless. The devices are quickly tucked away, but otherwise no one
budges.

"Hey—why isn't he getting wet?" a girl asks.

She's right. Milo Yolkin is standing in the middle of a thunder-
storm, but he and his sign are still perfectly dry. Thankfully, no
one has caught it on camera.

There are sirens heading our way. I'm about to lose it when
Milo Yolkin takes a step back from the edge and vanishes from
view.

The four of us are back at the hotel by ten a.m., soaked to the
bone by the storm that refuses to stop. For the next two hours,
we listen to the rain pound the neighborhood while we watch
the cable news coverage of Milo Yolkin's bizarre appearance on a
Manhattan rooftop. The Company's share price has plummeted.
The red line on the stock chart in the right-hand corner of the
screen looks set to drill through the bottom of the television and
down into the center of the Earth.

An ad comes on and like a bunch of addicts, we all reach for
the remote at once. Whoever gets it switches the television to the
next news channel. The screen is split. On one side of the line
is a woman dressed like she's on her way to a cocktail party. On
the other is a handsome man with a scruffy chin and thick black

glasses. It's a carefully cultivated look that's supposed to tell us he's both exceptionally brilliant and devastatingly cool. The costume doesn't quite suit him.

"I'm here with Ryan Booncock, CMO of the Company and a personal friend of Milo Yolkin," says the woman. "Ryan, were Milo's actions this morning a cry for help?"

Ryan laughs, taking the anchor by surprise. I lean in closer to the television. Maybe it's just the studio makeup, but if I didn't know better, I'd say that Ryan was one of the Company's less convincing robots. Everything about him is uncanny valley. "A cry for help?" he echoes. "Of course not. It was an *announcement*. Milo wanted to make it himself, and as we all know, he's always had a flair for the dramatic. Perhaps he took it a little too far, but you gotta admit—he certainly got everyone's attention."

"An announcement?" the woman asks.

"We're releasing the first trailer for our latest software. We were planning to post it to the Company website at noon." Okay, I'm officially impressed. This is some serious jujitsu. We come at them, and they use the attack to their own advantage. If the Company pulls this one off, maybe they deserve to be humanity's evil overlords after all.

"How exciting!" The tone of the interview has instantly gone from gloomy to giddy. "Can you tell us more?"

"How 'bout we just give you a sneak peek at the trailer?" Ryan asks. He's running the show now.

They cut to the video, which opens on an image of Earth from space. "For thousands of years, this little blue planet has been our home," says a man's voice.

"Holy shit," I gasp. "Is that Tom Cruise?"

Elvis has gone sheet white. "Could be," he admits. I can practically see his mind spinning as he tries to figure out if it's just a coincidence—and what it could mean if it's not.

"Shhhh!" Busara orders.

The camera is now hurtling toward Earth, closing in on North America, then the northeast US, then an island off the coast of New York State. It plunges past the Empire State Building in the middle of Manhattan and comes to a stop at street level. It's a sunny summer day. People stream past, taxis honk, and we hear a faint rumble as a subway train passes beneath us. A beautiful woman in a red dress gives the camera a wink. "Man has long yearned to escape—to explore other worlds."

Suddenly a shadow darkens the street. "But soon we'll discover there's no place like home."

The camera pans up. We see the underbelly of a giant winged creature that's sailing between skyscrapers.

"OtherEarth," says maybe Tom Cruise. "*Your* world. Only better."

Someone hits Mute and we all sit in silence.

"God that looked awesome," Elvis finally says.

THE DINNER PARTY

I have no idea where I am. My eyes are covered and my hands and legs are bound. I can't move an inch in any direction. Even my chest is wrapped so tightly that my avatar's lungs can barely expand enough to breathe. I feel the material against my fingertips. It's a silk as fine as my mother's scarves. I curse out loud when I realize what's happened. The last place I visited in Otherworld was the cave beneath the ice fields. When I was pulled out of the game unexpectedly, the spider Child I met there must have wrapped up my avatar and hidden it along with Moloch's. Elvis is probably keeping us company. I guess that's the thanks we get for saving Spider Lady's butt. I get that she doesn't like guests. But what do you have to do these days to prove you're not a psychopath?

There's a pain in the center of my chest where something hard is pressing into my flesh. The Children let me keep the amulet, which seems like an improbable bit of good luck. A pale blue light filters through my silk blindfold. The stone knows I'm eager to go, and it's ready. I can't move my lips, but I don't need to. I think of the place I need to travel, and suddenly I'm outside Imra. I'd rather be anywhere else, but there's one last trip Kat and I have to make before we say goodbye to this place forever. Kat's arranged a meeting with her stepfather. After we see Wayne, I don't intend to ever come back.

Kat is waiting for me at the gates. She's wearing her camouflage bodysuit, which blends in so well that most of her appears to be a smudge on the graphics. But her head is uncovered and her copper-colored curls flow freely. In Otherworld, the shaved strip on the back of her head is gone.

"What the heck happened here?" she asks.

I peer through the gates. The suburbs of Imra are deserted. Weeds have grown through cracks in the pavement. Red sand from the neighboring wastelands has blown in on the winds and formed small dunes against the sides of the buildings. I was here not that long ago, yet Otherworld's nature is already reclaiming realms. I'm starting to think time might be speeding up here.

"One of the guests killed all the NPCs," I say. "Elvis and I watched him shoot one—then he came after us."

"The game didn't regenerate the NPCs after they died?" Kat asks skeptically.

"I guess not," I realize. It *is* strange. When the Children die, they're gone for good. But NPCs are just part of the game. They should have regenerated, but it looks as though they haven't. I wonder what Imra's like now that its NPC workers are gone. And I wonder what the headset players will do when there's nothing in Otherworld left to shoot.

I start walking before I even know where I'm going. Kat doesn't ask. She just stays beside me. Soon we're standing in front of the green wall of ivy that once protected Gimmelwald. A wide hole has been burned through the center. Most of the vines surrounding the passage are dead. A few scorched tendrils are twitching. I can't imagine a torch like the one Elvis used ever causing this much damage. This required a much more powerful weapon.

With Kat right behind me, I enter Volla's realm. There is nothing left of it. The land is black and empty. The fire spared nothing. The mutant vegetation is gone, and the structures that once resembled green monsters have all burned to the ground. Whatever fierce beasts lived here have been massacred. There's no sign of Gunter or the cottage that he lived in. I feel a sudden pain, as if someone has reached deep inside my chest and yanked out my heart. Elvis and I probably showed the murderer how to get inside.

"Volla!" I shout, though I know I shouldn't. The guest responsible for all this destruction might not be far away. "Volla!" I shout again.

There's no answer.

"Who is Volla?" Kat asks.

"The Elemental of Gimmelwald," I remind her. I can't bear to say more. I can't find the words to tell Kat about the little green baby—or the promise I failed to keep.

"I don't think guests can kill Elementals." Kat tries to soothe me, though neither of us really knows the truth. Maybe Volla fled with her child, but the chances are just as good that she's dead.

The rage takes me by surprise. It's more potent than anything I've felt since my trip to Nastrond. I manage to push it down deep in my belly. But as I stomp back through the hole in the vines, I can feel it burning and boiling—like the molten rock inside Imra's volcano. It's only a matter of time before I explode.

Imra and Nemi are separated by a swamp—one of the countless wastelands that separate the realms. It's unbearably hot and humid, but Kat and I are forced to keep our sleeves down and our hoods up. The insects here are large and hungry. I've seen mosquitolike creatures that could drain a man dry. We wade through rancid-smelling muck that reaches well past our knees. It's hard to believe that anyone would willingly spend time in this hellhole, but we're barely a mile in when we hear the first shot. It's followed by at least a dozen more. The spaces in between are filled with hooting and hollering.

I glance over at Kat. She shakes her head and points in the opposite direction. We should do our best to avoid other guests, it's true. But there's a chance that one of these assholes may have destroyed Gimmelwald. There may be no judgments in Other-world, but if I find the person responsible, he's going to pay for his sins.

"Stay here," I whisper to Kat. "I'll be right back."

"Stop saying crap like that!" She huffs in annoyance and read-ies her bow. "If you're going somewhere, I'm going too. We stick together, no matter what."

Moving slowly and silently, we make our way toward the gun-shots. Soon buildings appear in front of us. They're bayou-style wooden shacks that sit perched atop stilts that rise four feet out of the swamp. They look hand-built and weathered—not the sort of place that headset players would seek out. Yet there are three guests here. Their avatars are standing on a porch that surrounds one of the houses. Two of the guests are burly camo-wearing types. The third is slender, with neatly combed dark hair. He's dressed in simple gray coveralls, like a mechanic at a fancy car dealership. He watches passively, hands in his pockets, while the other two men shoot at something in the water. Whatever it is, they've hit it multiple times. The water is red and thick with blood, and there's a metallic stench in the air. Standing by the gray man's side is a Child. I have no idea what two beings might have blended to produce the creature. It's human in appearance, though its waxy skin is as pale as a corpse and its thick black hair has a bluish sheen. The creature's crisp navy outfit appears military in style, with a kilt that ends just above its knees. The legs sticking out of the skirt are rather ordinary, but the Child's feet are bare and it's rocking a massive tail.

"What are they shooting at?" Kat whispers. She gets her answer almost immediately. A giant beast surfaces from the deep water around the building and lunges up at the avatars on the deck. It has the scales and snout of a crocodile, and it looks prehistoric. It snatches one of the camo-wearing avatars by the boot and drags him into the water.

The second man in camo lurches backward and falls on his ass. His gun lands a few feet away, discharging a bullet that splinters the bark of a nearby tree. There's silence for a moment as waves lap against the house's stilts. Then the Child begins to laugh. The deafening sound is more dolphin than human. Kat and I both shove our fingers into our ears. The humiliated avatar snarls and reaches for his weapon, but he's not quite fast enough. The man in gray already has a gun to his head.

"Go to hell, Alexei," the man on the ground sneers. "The next time I see your little pet, he's going to Karamojo with the rest of them." He has an Eastern European bad-guy accent, the origins of which I can't quite place.

The gray man doesn't so much as blink. "Set one foot in my swamp, Dimitri, and we will do this again." He fires once and the other avatar flashes. "Over and over"—he fires again—"until you learn your lesson." He pulls the trigger of his gun a third time. The fallen avatar flashes once more and disappears.

The gray man then passes the gun to his companion. "Go," I hear him tell the Child. "Get the ones that were taken. Bring them back."

"Alexei," I mutter. That's what the other man called him. Like the Russian oligarch Elvis mentioned back in New Mexico. I bet they're one and the same.

Kat nudges me with her elbow. "Did you see that?" she whispers. "The guest protected a Child. Do you think we should speak to him? We could probably use some backup." She sounds so hopeful that it almost breaks my heart. Kat probably thinks she's just witnessed proof that humanity isn't complete shit after all. I'm still not so sure. And one thing's for certain—we're not here to make friends.

"We can't trust him," I tell her. I don't know why the gray man is in Otherworld. But I do know that he's not like us. He's one of the two thousand. He's one of *them.*

. . .

The hours we spent trudging through the swamp should have been some of the most miserable of my life, but I'd be lying if I didn't admit it was nice to spend time alone with Kat. She was keen to avoid killing anything on our way to Nemi, but the beasts of Otherworld were determined to test her resolve. They came at us with teeth, claws, beaks and stingers. Despite Kat's best intentions, we left a trail of carnage behind us. Now we've finally reached the edge of the morass, only to find ourselves standing on the shores of what appears to be an inland sea. Deadly beasts are one thing. But I wasn't prepared to face this kind of obstacle.

"How are we going to get across *that*?" I ask Kat.

"We aren't," she says. "This is Nemi."

No sooner has the name left her lips than a massive pleasure barge appears on the horizon, moving swiftly our way. As it draws closer, I can see there's a garden planted on its deck and two luxurious Roman-style structures positioned at either end. The boat crosses the water in mere seconds, without fluttering a frond on the palm trees in its gardens. It stops in front of us and a gangway is lowered to the shore a few feet from where we're standing.

"You didn't mention we'd be heading out to sea. Are you sure this is safe?" I ask Kat.

"Safe? This is Otherworld, remember?" she replies. "But I'm pretty sure we'll be the only guests."

An NPC appears at the top of the gangway. He's wearing a navy blue uniform that's identical to the one worn by the Child we saw in the swamp. He's holding an empty wooden box.

"Your weapons, please," he drones as Kat and I approach.

Kat hands over her bow and arrows, but there's no way I'm giving the guy my dagger.

"Yeah, right." I try to slip around him, but I can't. Some invisible barrier keeps me from stepping onto the ship.

"Your weapons, please," the NPC repeats.

"What's going on?" I ask Kat. "Why do they want our weapons?"

"That's the rule here," she responds. "Nemi is the only realm I passed through where weapons aren't allowed. That's why I chose it for the meeting."

"Are you crazy?" I demand under my breath. "Have you forgotten the two thousand psychopaths who've turned Otherworld into their personal slaughterhouse?"

"Of course not," she replies. "The weapons rule is one of the reasons Nemi stays empty. You're not supposed to kill anything here."

I reluctantly toss my dagger into the box. I feel naked without it. But it turns out Kat's right. Though the boat is lousy with NPCs—all dressed in the same distinctive navy blue uniform— there don't seem to be any other guests.

The weather couldn't be more perfect. The sky is cloudless and the sun golden. A gentle breeze washes over me, and I realize the boat has left the shore. I step over to the starboard railing and peer over the side. The water below is clear and blue, and there's a school of shimmering silver fish swimming past. I doubt they're the only creatures that live in this sea. It makes me nervous to realize that we'll soon be out in the middle of the water, at the mercy of the barge's crew, with no way to get to shore on our own.

"Welcome to Nemi." Another uniformed NPC interrupts my

worries. He's one of the blandest beings I've encountered in Other-world, with a face I'll forget the second he's gone. "Would you care for a tour of the ship or shall I guide you directly to your table?"

"Table?" I'm confused again.

"Nemi is known for its food, sir," the NPC explains. There's the second reason no other guests come here, I guess. If you're wearing a disk, Otherworld food is irresistible, but headset players can't taste a thing.

"We're expecting a visitor," Kat notifies our host.

The NPC nods. "Yes, madam, he's already on board. He's waiting for you both at the table."

A bolt of nervous energy shoots down my spine. "Is he alone?" I ask.

"You three are our only guests at the moment," the NPC confirms.

Kat catches my eye. She looks like she'd rather trudge back through the swamp than sit down with our visitor. "Let's get this over with," she says.

"Very well. This way." The NPC guides us toward the larger of the two buildings on board. Supporting the roof are eight marble columns, and the walls are decorated with naughty murals of Roman-style gods at play. Sheltered from the sun is a square table surrounded on three sides by plush banquettes.

Seated against the far wall is Wayne Gibson. He looks exactly as he does in the real world, right down to his chinos and button-up shirt.

"Well, hello there." Wayne glances down at his watch. "You two are late. I was starting to think I might have misinterpreted your message."

"We had to travel through a swamp to get here," I tell him. "It took longer than we thought."

"I sympathize," he says, as though that were something he was capable of doing. "But you chose the time and place. I've never visited Otherworld, and it took me a while to get here myself. But I managed to be on time. *Please.*" Wayne gestures to the banquette to his right. "Have a seat. I see the food has arrived."

Before we can take our places, the NPC sets a platter down on the table in front of us. Piled on top are hundreds of small beasts that don't resemble anything I've ever seen. Their bodies have been roasted whole and stuffed so full that they're perfectly round. In the real world, the white stuffing that's escaping from their mouths would probably be cheese. In Otherworld, there's no telling what it might be. Yet despite the revolting appearance, the smell wafting off the dish is intoxicating.

Wayne reaches over and picks up one of the stuffed creatures and bites into it like an apple. I hear his teeth break through the skin and then the bones crunching between them. "Boy, I bet this tastes delicious," Wayne says. "You two want to try one? I can't even imagine how amazing it must be with a disk."

The temptation is almost overpowering, but I know better than to fall for the trap. Once you start eating in Otherworld, it can be impossible to stop.

"What's the problem?" Wayne asks with a grin. "You think I got here early just to have the food poisoned?"

"I wouldn't be surprised." Kat fakes a toothy smile. "But I'd be a little more cautious if I were you. If anything happens to us, Milo Yolkin's going to kick the bucket in a truly spectacular way.

The Company managed to pull its stock price out of the toilet with that OtherEarth trailer. But if Milo commits suicide on camera, a new game is not going to save you."

"So you'll have poor Milo jump off a roof, will you?" Wayne asks, popping the final bit of the beast into his mouth. "What will people say when they see there's no body splattered on the sidewalk below?"

"If Milo jumps off a bridge, there won't *be* a body to find," Kat informs him.

Wayne chuckles warmly. "Clever!" he admits. "I always knew you were a smart girl. Maybe if you'd been a little less intelligent you wouldn't be in all this trouble."

Kat smiles again and winks at me. "I had no idea we were in such big trouble. Did you know, Simon?"

"Nope." I play along. "In fact, if anyone's in trouble, I'd say it's Wayne here. When the Company goes belly-up, he'll be out of a job."

Nothing seems able to wipe the smile off this jerk's face. "So what is it exactly that you two want?" Wayne asks.

"We want you, the engineers and the doctors who've worked on the disk project to turn yourselves in to the authorities and confess to your crimes," I say.

Wayne nearly busts a gut laughing. "Nice try, kids."

I knew it wasn't going to happen, but I figured it was worth a shot.

"Fine," I say. "But our next offer is our last offer. We want the Company to destroy all Otherworld disks and kick all the headset players out of the game. And we want you to release Marlow

Holm, James Ogubu, and Declan Andrews, otherwise known as Gorog."

"James Ogubu?" Wayne looks genuinely surprised. "Now there's someone I haven't seen in ages. I can't exactly hand a man over to you if I have no idea where he is. Last I heard, he walked off the job months ago. In fact, if you find him, tell James he's fired."

I'm not sure why, but for once I think Wayne might be telling the truth. Though if no one at the Company knows where James Ogubu is, what the hell did Milo do with him?

"Forget Ogubu, then," Kat says. "The rest is nonnegotiable."

Wayne sits back with his arms crossed. "So you really want us to destroy all the disks—just when we're so close to completely debugging them? It could be a matter of days at this point. People died for that technology. One of them was a friend of Mr. Eaton's, as I recall. Don't you want to respect Carole Elliot's sacrifice?"

The name sends a jolt of rage through my system. Along with Gorog, Carole was one of my companions on my first trip to Otherworld. Without her, I wouldn't be alive. "Carole was murdered." I have to shove my hands under my thighs to avoid strangling him.

"All in the name of progress," Wayne says.

"You must mean *profits*," I correct him.

"More often than not, the two go hand in hand."

I stare at him across the table. The guy looks like a Boy Scout troop leader or a Little League coach. You'd never guess he was evil incarnate. "You're a sick bastard, you know that?"

Wayne smirks and picks up another stuffed creature and pops it in his mouth.

"You guys not gonna have any of this?" he asks once he's

finished chewing. "I'm sure you're really missing out on something special," he says when neither of us responds. He lifts a finger and calls a waiter over. Three identical NPCs arrive at our table.

"Are you finished with the dish, sir?" one of the NPCs asks.

"I sure am," Wayne confirms. "You can take it away. In fact, while you're at it, why don't you go ahead and take these two as well."

I'm still not certain I heard right, when one of the NPCs grabs Kat by the shoulders and drags her out of her seat. Before I can do anything, the other two have my arms pinned behind me. I start to struggle. Then I see a dozen NPC reinforcements arrive.

"What in the hell are you doing?" Kat growls at Wayne. "Didn't you hear? If anything happens to us, our friends will shove Milo Yolkin off a cliff."

"Your *friends*," Wayne repeats. "You mean Busara Ogubu and Elvis Karaszkewycz?" He stops and smirks at what must be the look of pure horror on my face. "Oh, yes, we know who they are. It won't be long before we know *where* they are, too."

I'd ask how he got Elvis's name, but I'd rather not give him the satisfaction. "If you kill us, Elvis and Busara will make sure you're out of a job by the time you get back to the real world," I sneer. "And in jail soon after that."

"Katherine's life isn't in danger," Wayne says, referring to Kat by the full name she's never used. "Her poor crazy mother's suffered enough already. I figure we'll find a way for the two of them to spend more time together. I'm on friendly terms with the man who runs the mental hospital where Linda's staying. He's already agreed to set aside a room for Katherine."

"What about Simon?" Kat asks.

Wayne shrugs. "Well, my dear, what happens to him will depend on you. First we're going to give him a good ass-whupping to punish him for shooting me the night you two escaped from the facility. I figure that's only fair. As soon as his whole body feels as bad as my arm, I'm going to ask *you* to tell me where you and your friends are hiding out in New York. If you're forthcoming, I'll let Mr. Eaton live. If not, he'll die and I'll find your friends anyway."

Wayne claps his hands and two NPCs open up a trapdoor in the barge's deck. Then they disappear into the darkness below. "I bet you two aren't planning to stay in Otherworld forever. Someone back in New York's gonna be taking your disks off soon. So what do you say? Should we get this show on the road?"

The NPCs reemerge with a creature in chains trailing behind them. There's no doubt it's a Child, but I've never seen one this large before. He stands at least seven feet tall, with broad shoulders and giant hands. His thick gray skin sags around his joints, and two tusks lift his upper lip into a permanent snarl. He has elephant DNA, no doubt. But there's something else mixed in as well—something unusual.

"I know you depend on your dagger," Wayne tells me. "But as you've learned, weapons of all sorts are banned in Nemi, so I hope you won't mind a little hand-to-hand combat."

Now I know what this is all about. Wayne Gibson didn't come here to save the Company. I made a mistake thinking he'd ever set aside his desire for revenge. His only goal right now is to make me suffer. "You're saying you want me to fight this guy?" I ask. "Forget it. I refuse."

"Fine by me," Wayne says. "It'll be less entertaining for the rest of us if you don't fight back, but I figure I'll be the winner either way."

As the Child's chains are removed, the ship's NPCs form a circle around us. I could probably break through, but there's nowhere to go. I glance at the railing that rings the deck. I wonder if I could reach shore if I managed to jump over the side.

"I wouldn't even consider that if I were you," Wayne warns me with a yawn. "There are some pretty big beasts down there in the water. All things considered, getting eaten by one seems like a pretty shitty way to go."

"You don't have to fight!" Kat calls out to the Child, who doesn't exactly look thrilled by the situation either.

"Kick his ass, and you'll earn your freedom," Wayne tells the Child. "If you kill him, I'll set your friends free too."

"He's lying!" Kat cries as one of the creature's fists streaks through the air. Guess we just found out where *his* priorities lie. I barely have a chance to dodge the blow. I'm not quick enough to evade the next one. It hits me square in the stomach and sends me flying across the deck until my back hits the railing. While I do my best to suck air into my lungs, I see the Child moving in my direction. He grabs the front of my cloak and lifts me up, only to slam me back down a split second later.

"Katherine, dear," I hear Wayne call out. "Are you ready to tell us where you and your friends are hiding?"

"Don't," I manage to croak. I struggle to my feet and face the Child. I can already taste blood in my mouth, and I don't think I'll be able to withstand another punch. When he comes at me, I make the only move I can. I step to the side. He's too big and moving too quickly to reverse course. As he charges past, I jump onto his back and climb toward his neck. Soon I have the Child in a choke hold. He's flailing about, but he can't reach me with his arms and he can't shake me off. I squeeze until I lose all sensation in my right arm. Finally, he crashes to his knees and then hits the floor, unconscious.

The deck is so silent I can hear the water lapping against the sides of the boat.

"Do it," Wayne orders me. "Finish the Child off."

"Simon's hurt!" Kat shouts. "You got your revenge! What else do you want?"

But Wayne isn't swayed. In fact, he seems almost pleased by this turn of events. He sees the chance to do far more harm to me than a beating could ever deliver. "Kill the Child, Mr. Eaton, or I'll have the men here kill you."

"No." I let go of the Child and rise to my feet. I walk toward Wayne and position myself with my back to the creature. He's awake now. I can hear him moving. He could easily attack, but he doesn't.

"Throw them both over the side," Wayne tells the NPCs.

The men take a step forward and a gunshot rings out. Everyone on the boat looks startled by the sound. There shouldn't be any weapons in Nemi. Something hits the deck with a thud. I'm still breathing, so I assume the Child must be dead. But then I see he's risen to his knees from the deck. One of the NPCs lies on the ground instead, blood spilling out of his body. The form vanishes just as the Child from the swamp appears on deck.

He's almost handsome up close. His skin's still a bit chalky, and his wide-set eyes are pure black, but he has all the right features and they're right where you'd expect them to be. I might even have mistaken him for a guest if the tail hadn't given his origins away. Avatars in Otherworld can be large or small, but they must assume a human form. He seems like he might be around my age, but I don't doubt for a moment that this creature's seen far more than I have.

I expect the other NPCs to attack the moment he appears, but instead they line up as if awaiting new orders. The ones holding Kat have set her free, and she hurries over to join me. We stand shoulder to shoulder, waiting for the shit to hit the fan.

"Go down to the hold," the Child orders the elephantine creature I was just fighting. His voice is calm and firm. "Release your companions and bring them up to the deck."

"What the hell is going on? Why does this freak have a weapon?" I hear Wayne cry out in rage, but the NPCs don't answer. It seems they have a new master now.

"All of you—swim to shore," the Child orders the NPCs. One by one, the men dive over the side and into the shimmering blue water. The loud splashing that follows tells me either the NPCs couldn't swim—or something was waiting down there to greet them.

"Who *are* you?" Wayne demands.

"My name is Fons, and this boat is my home. My father is the Elemental who rules this sea, which is why I'm allowed to carry weapons if I please. My mother is the beast from below," says the Child. The second he says it, I realize that the appendage I'd assumed was a tail is actually a *tentacle*. "Now, if you don't mind my asking, who are *you*?"

"Someone you don't want to mess with." Wayne bares his teeth like a rabid pit bull. For a second I see the evil beneath his bland disguise. "Now give me the gun."

Fons cocks his head and observes Wayne quizzically. He seems intrigued rather than intimidated. "You must be quite important if you feel you have the right to come to my realm and issue orders."

"As far as you and your kind are concerned, I'm God."

"This is Otherworld," Fons replies calmly. "We choose our own gods here." Then he tilts his head back and calls out in a strange, singsong language. I have no idea what's happening until a shadow falls across the deck and I turn to see a giant tentacle rise up from the water. It towers over the ship before it swoops down to snatch Wayne. It squeezes his avatar until its face turns purple and its eyes bulge out like a cartoon character. When the body flashes and goes limp, the tentacle slams it back down on the deck. The avatar flashes once more when it hits, and the tentacle retreats, disappearing beneath the waves.

Fons aims his gun at Wayne's head and pulls the trigger. Three kills in a row. Wayne's avatar is headed back to setup. As soon as the body disappears, the Child turns his gun on me.

"No!" Kat shouts. "Don't hurt him! We're not like the other guests. We don't murder your kind."

"There's only one guest in Otherworld who neither murders nor lies," says Fons. "I've learned not to place any faith in the rest."

"The female is telling the truth." The giant elephant Child steps between Fons and me. He's reappeared topside with a group of other Children who must have been imprisoned in the hold below. "The guest you shot forced the male to fight me. He had the chance to kill me, but he refused."

Fons waves the elephant Child to the side and steps up to where Kat and I stand. His nose twitches as if he's picking up a strange scent. "Why are you here in Otherworld if you don't want to kill?" he asks.

"Why is your friend in the gray coveralls here?" I reply. "He's a guest too, isn't he?"

The Child smiles, and his mouth stretches all the way from one side of his face to the other. It's a rather disturbing sight. "You know Alexei?"

"We've never met him," Kat says. "But we saw him kill the avatar in the swamp to protect you."

I don't think the Child is happy to find out that someone was watching, but I'm almost relieved when his creepy smile disappears. "Why are you here?" he asks again coldly.

"It's complicated," I tell him. I don't have time to recount the whole story.

"You think I cannot understand?" the Child sneers at me. "You imagine your kind is more intelligent than mine?"

"No," I assure him. "We know the Children are our equals. We're here to help them, not kill them. That's what the Creator would have wanted us to do."

"We knew Magna," Kat explains. "The man you just shot is the reason he's dead. His name is Wayne Gibson. He let Magna die so he could take over a company your Creator founded. Now he's responsible for the guests who are destroying your world. We thought we knew how to force him to get rid of them all. But our plan didn't work out the way we expected."

That's putting it mildly. Everything's gone to hell. We might be able to use Milo's hologram to destroy the Company, but it would die a slow death. It could take months for the enterprise to finally go under. In the meantime, the Children could die—along with Marlow, Gorog and James Ogubu. *James Ogubu.* As the name passes through my mind, it gives me a jolt of hope. Ogubu's avatar is still here in Otherworld. If he can tell us where his real body is, we can free him. He was one of the Company's top engineers. Maybe he'll know what we should do.

"We need to get to the ice fields," I tell Kat. "Ogubu's our only hope now."

She nods. She must have figured it out too. "How long do we have left before Busara and Elvis pull us out?" she asks. "We've been here for a while now."

"I don't know," I admit. "I think time is moving faster in here than it used to. We might be able to make it. If not, we can come back."

Fons steps up to us. Something has piqued his curiosity. "What do you hope to find in the ice fields?" he asks.

"A man who might be able to help us," I say.

"One who can rid this world of guests for good," Kat adds.

I hadn't thought of it like that, but it's certainly possible. Milo stole James Ogubu's software to make Otherworld. Who knows what Ogubu will be able to do?

"Then we'll go to the ice fields," Fons announces. "You." He points at Elephant Boy. "And you two." He chooses two of the Children who were brought up from belowdeck. Small and wiry, with silvery skin that shimmers in the sunlight, they're clearly related, perhaps even twins. "The four of us will escort these guests." I can see why Fons would choose the big dude for an expedition. The other two Children look like underfed seventh graders. They'll only be liabilities.

"Thanks for the offer," I tell Fons. "Kat and I can make it to the ice fields on our own. We've been there before. We know the way."

"Our company is not optional," says Fons. "I would like to meet this man for myself."

THE MASTERMIND

Fons isn't much of a talker. He leads us back through the swamp, around the city of Imra and down the side of the mountain—all without saying more than half a dozen words. I get the sense that the three other Children in our expedition would be far more personable if he weren't around. But anyone who speaks out of turn gets knocked to the ground by the guy's giant tentacle. Fons either hates guests or mistrusts us, or both. I don't blame him. I'd just love to know why he thinks this Alexei guy is different from the rest of us.

We stop for a break in the wastelands between Imra and the ice fields. Kat and I collapse beside a rocky outcropping surrounded on all sides by sand and scrub.

Fons pokes me with the tip of his tentacle. "How are your energy levels?" he inquires.

"Low," I admit. The truth is, they're almost depleted. I can't even remember the last time my avatar ate. Kat seems just as exhausted. With her forehead resting on her knees, she's all but invisible in her camouflage suit. All you can see is the bow strapped across her back. I reach out to her and Fons's eyes widen for a fraction of a second before he quickly looks away. He's probably not used to witnessing affection between guests.

"You'll need food before we begin our trek across the ice," he says. And just so I don't think he's developing a soft spot for us, he makes sure to add, "None of us wants to carry you."

I hold out my arms as if to embrace the emptiness all around us. "Thanks for the nutritional advice. Could you point us in the direction of the nearest 7-Eleven? I could really use a hot dog and a Slurpee right about now."

"Make mine a blue raspberry," Kat adds, her voice seeming to come out of nowhere. I swear the girl never lets me down.

Fons doesn't dignify the quip with a response. "Stay here and make a fire," he orders Elephant Boy. "You." He signals to one of the twins, who both seem as fresh and energetic as they were when we left, which makes me think I may have underestimated their usefulness. "Come with me."

The twin who's been left behind immediately gets to work gathering scrub for the fire, while Elephant Boy arranges it in a meticulous pile in the center of a circle of rocks. I wait until Fons has disappeared over the horizon before I lean forward and speak.

"My name is Simon," I tell him. "That's Kat."

"Hey," says Kat. Her face becomes visible for a moment as she lifts her head from her knees.

"Probo," he grunts back without taking his eyes off his work.

"Where did Fons go? Is there really food around here?" I ask.

"If there is food, Fons will find it," Probo says. "He's traveled everywhere in Otherworld. He's seen things the rest of us have not."

"So you know him?" Kat asks.

"Everyone knows Fons," Probo responds.

The lithe little Child who's been gathering scrub scampers back in our direction with more fuel for the fire. "You're not allowed to talk to them!" she hisses at Probo when she arrives.

"Screw off," Probo replies. The small creature drops what she's gathered into his lap and darts away again.

"You speak like one of us," Kat notes with amusement.

"I know your kind well," Probo replies bluntly. I'm pretty sure that's not a good thing, but his answer doesn't seem to faze Kat.

"What were you doing on the boat in Nemi?" she asks.

"Waiting to be taken back to Karamojo," he says.

"Back?" I ask. I wasn't aware that Children ever made it out. "You escaped?"

"While I was at Karamojo I heard a rumor that there were colonies of Children living free in the wastelands. The day I was chosen for the hunt, I made a run for it. A few of the other prisoners begged to come with me, and I led the party into the swamp. We were free for a few hours. It was my fault we were captured. I'm too big to hide. Two bounty hunters spotted us and rounded us up. They took us to Nemi, where we were being held until Moloch's soldiers could transport us back to Karamojo."

The small creature is back with another load of scrub. "I'll tell Fons you've been speaking to the guests!" she hisses.

"Do as you will," Probo says. I can't tell if he's given up hope or just doesn't care. I suspect it's a bit of both.

"Why is she so scared of Fons?" Kat whispers when the other creature is gone once more. "He rescued you both, didn't he?"

"The Children know that if you're rescued by Fons, you're expected to live by his rules. You trade your life for your freedom."

"What kind of rules?" I ask.

"The first rule is no talking to guests. Ever."

"What's going to happen if that little snake over there rats you out?" I want to know.

Probo shrugs. "We'll find out soon." He finishes shaping the scrub into a mound and sets it on fire.

I like this guy. Fons can go to hell as far as I'm concerned. I've got Probo's back. I catch Kat's eye and I can tell she feels the same way. I never doubted she would. We've both always had a healthy disrespect for authority.

"Why does Fons think he gets to call all the shots?" Kat asks.

"He's the favorite companion of the guest who saves Children," says Probo. "The Creator is gone and Ursus is dead. Some say the man is a tyrant, but he is all we have."

I have a million more questions for Probo, but there won't be time to ask them. A scream draws my attention to the left. A tiny figure is racing toward us with a giant pink monster hot on its heels.

"*No.*" Probo's single word is filled with more horror and disbelief than any I've ever heard. He can't believe what he's seeing. I still have no idea what it is.

Kat jumps to her feet, her bow in her hands. Three arrows

pierce the air. Two fall short of the mark, while one hits the larger creature in the flank. The wound does nothing to slow it down. With my dagger clenched in my fist, I break into a sprint. I can't risk throwing as I run. If I don't land a hit, I'll lose my one and only chance. The Child and I will both be dead.

The beast gets clearer as I get closer. I can see it's a mutant bear from the ice fields, its snowy white fur died pink by blood. *Whose* blood is anyone's guess. Most guests still avoid the ice fields, for good reason. Three more arrows fly past me and embed themselves in the beast. One of them is lodged six inches deep in the creature's rib cage. The wound should have been fatal, but the beast doesn't stumble.

This isn't right. An ice bear shouldn't be here in the wastelands. An ordinary beast—even an Otherworld monster—should have died by now. The small Child whizzes past me and an instant later, I make contact with the bear. It knocks me backward as my dagger sinks into its skull. The beast roars in pain. But it doesn't fall. My knife is still sticking out of its temple. Eleven inches of steel have entered the beast's brain and yet it continues to go for the kill.

I hear a gunshot and part of the beast's head explodes in a shower of blood and tissue. A second shot follows shortly afterward, and what was left of the bear's head is blown away. The decapitated corpse falls on top of me. I'm crushed beneath it, unable to breathe.

"Simon!" I hear Kat's voice and the sound of her feet as she runs my way.

Soon the bear's carcass rolls off me, and I marvel at Kat's strength. She's like one of those parents you hear about who lift cars off their kids. Then I see Probo beside her. Kat drops to her knees and brushes the hair off my face.

"Is he alive?" It's Fons's voice, as emotionless as ever.

"Yeah, I'm alive," I groan. "I appreciate the concern."

Now he's looking down at me as if he sees something that interests him. "Go get dinner started," he orders Probo, and the elephant Child disappears from view. "You are really hurt," he notes, keeping his voice low. "How is that possible?"

"We told you, we're not like the other guests," Kat says. "When we get injured, we feel it. And when we die, we're gone for good."

With Kat's assistance, I manage to sit up. Fons kneels down so the three of us are face-to-face. He's staring at us as if he's discovered a whole new species. I suppose in some ways he has.

"Why did the bear attack you?" he asks. "What did you do?"

"Nothing!" Kat's justifiably annoyed by the question. "The thing came out of nowhere. It was chasing the twin who'd been gathering firewood. Simon and I tried to stop it."

"Something was wrong with it," I add. I glance over at the beast. Without its head, it's impossible to offer a diagnosis.

"You're telling me you risked your lives to defend one of our kind?" Fons asks. I have no idea if he's happy about it or not. "Why would you do that?"

"What else were we supposed to do?" I ask. "We couldn't stand there and watch someone get eaten."

"*Someone*," Fons repeats skeptically.

"Oh, give me a break. Your friend saves Children," I say. "Why is it so hard to believe that we would too?"

"It's hard to know what to believe anymore," Fons tells us. He looks up at the sky and then around at the wasteland. "Everything is changing. Nothing is how it was meant to be. Beasts never attack Otherworld Children. This is the first time I've had to kill one."

I know how he feels about everything changing, but this time I don't say a word. Maybe someday we'll swap stories over beers, but Fons doesn't seem like the sort of guy who's interested in having a shoulder to cry on.

"Are you able to stand?" he asks me.

"I think so," I tell him. Kat hops up first and offers a hand. I'm a bit wobbly, but I'm on my feet.

"Good," Fons says. This time he actually sounds like he means it. "Come to the fire. I found food."

The three other Children are already seated in a circle around the fire, using sticks to make kebobs out of something that still appears to be wriggling.

"I am Ita," says the Child Kat and I saved. She points to the identical Child sitting beside her. "That is my sister, Ino."

"All rules still apply," Fons grumbles, and both mouths instantly seal. But no one got whacked by his tentacle. And our little companion has managed to make one thing perfectly clear—she won't be ratting out Probo for speaking to the guests.

My eyes dart in his direction, and for the first time I get a good look at the meal he's making. A dozen large scorpions impaled on sticks are waiting to be roasted. My knees buckle at the sight of their iridescent green exoskeletons glinting in the firelight. The scorpion back in Texas looked just like them. Kat manages to catch me before I fall all the way to the ground.

"Simon, what's wrong?" she asks, her voice a worried whisper. "Are you okay?"

"No," I tell her honestly. I am not okay at all. I wish I could say more, but this is neither the time nor the place.

"Sit him down," Fons orders. "He needs food."

The two smaller Children hop up and help Kat guide me to a seat. A leather bag gets moved to make a place for me at the fire. A giant green scorpion scuttles out from inside it and scampers over my shoe before it vanishes into the scrub.

I think I need a lot more than food.

Nothing is how it was meant to be. The whole way to the ice fields, that thought has been bouncing around in my head. Milo Yolkin's world is falling apart, and it's taking mine down with it. Things that belong only in this world have been showing up in the real world. Characters who belong in neither place have been making cameos too. Today we passed through a snowstorm on the way to the glacier. Though it could have been my imagination, I thought I saw a figure standing in the distance. It was nothing but a gray blur in the middle of all that white. But for a moment I could have sworn it was the Kishka. Kat must have seen me staring into the snow. She's been quite attentive for the past few hours, which tells me she must be concerned. I wish I could say I'll be all right, but I'm no longer sure I will be.

We've arrived at Magna's ice cave and found it crumbling. It's a good thing we decided to come when we did, because I'm not sure how much longer this place will last. Fons orders Probo and Ita to stand guard outside as the rest of us enter. Inside the tunnel, there are cracks in the ceiling that are wide enough to shove my whole arm into. As we walk down the path, we can hear the ice creaking and groaning above us.

At the end of the path lies the empty throne room. I remember Magna, Milo's avatar, sitting in the center, the heat from his burning red body carving this chamber out of the glacier. Most traces of Magna are gone now—even the door that once served as Milo Yolkin's personal exit from Otherworld. The Company must have removed it. But thankfully they left what we've come to find. They must not have realized it's here, buried deep inside the cave's wall. You'd have to look closely to see that the hazy silhouette belongs to a man trapped in the ice. We're here to take him out.

Fons lights a torch and holds the flame to the wall. I can feel the heat of the blaze on my cheeks. Slowly, the ice begins to recede, and the figure becomes darker and more distinct. Then Fons pulls the torch away from the ice and gestures for Ino to come closer.

"Who's in there?" she asks Fons. She doesn't dare direct the question to us.

I answer anyway. "An avatar. It belongs to the man who's responsible for your world."

"The Creator?" she asks.

"No," I tell her. "Before the Creator."

"How could there be someone before the Creator?" she asks.

"That's enough," Fons snaps. "No more talking." I shoot him a look. I'm not one of his kind. I don't have to take orders from jerks with tentacles for tails.

Ino places her hands on the dripping wall. Her silver skin turns pink and then a blazing red, and what's left of the ice melts away and the face of a handsome man begins to emerge. There's no doubt the guy is Busara's father. They share the same prominent cheekbones and regal nose. Next Ino melts the ice around his chest and arms. As soon as his first hand is freed, it rises to his face, where his fingers wipe the moisture away from his eyes. When they open, they land right on me.

"A Druid," he says, and I swear I almost give the dude a hug. Apparently, he's the only person in Otherworld who knows a kick-ass avatar when he sees one. He glances down at the amulet around my neck. "A Druid who's wearing a disk. To what do I owe the pleasure?"

God, where should I start? I guess I didn't think through the introductions. Kat notices me struggling to put a sentence together and steps in just as things are about to get awkward.

"We've come to set you free," she tells him.

"Ah," says James Ogubu. There's a smile on his face, but he's hardly jumping for joy. His eyes pass over Kat and move on to our companions. "Such creative avatars."

"We are not guests in Otherworld," Fons informs him. "We are Children."

Ino's finished defrosting the avatar, and James Ogubu steps out of the ice. Tall and slim, he's wearing dad jeans and a pale blue button-down. His shoes look like he bought them from a medical supply shop. I'd love to know what the Children make of his outfit. Even on Earth it would be a little unusual.

Ogubu holds out a hand to Fons, who seems confused. I guess no one's ever attempted to shake his hand before. "I've heard about your kind, but I was never lucky enough to meet any of you," Ogubu says. "May I ask who your parents are?"

"My father is the Elemental of Nemi," Fons responds warily. "My mother is the beast from below. She lives at the bottom of the Nemi Sea."

"You're an aristocrat," Ogubu notes, without sounding the slightest bit smarmy. His daughter may have inherited his looks, but Busara got none of his charm. He glances over at Ino and smiles warmly. "And your father must be the one your kind call the Creator."

How could I have missed it? Of course he was. The burning red hands that she used to melt the ice away from James Ogubu make perfect sense now. That's why Ino and her sister were invited along.

"Where is he?" Ogubu asks, looking around. "This is still Magna's cave, is it not?"

"The Creator has left Otherworld," Fons announces. "He abandoned us all."

"Milo is dead," I explain. "The game killed him. The Company allowed it to happen."

"Milo?" Fons asks. He's never heard the name.

"I'll explain later," I tell him. But James Ogubu doesn't hesitate.

"Milo was the man who used my inventions to build your world," he tells Fons. "His avatar was Magna, otherwise known as the Creator."

"The Creator was a guest?" Fons asks.

"Yes," Ogubu tells him.

While Fons struggles to absorb the information, Ogubu turns to me. "You're certain Milo is dead?" The news doesn't appear to have brought him pleasure.

I grimace at the memory of Milo's withered corpse. "I saw the body with my own eyes."

Ogubu nods sadly. "I knew it would happen eventually. Other-world had already destroyed Milo's mind. There was little doubt that his body was next. The last time I saw him he was skin and bones. But if Milo is dead now, who sent you to free me?"

"Your daughter," Kat tells him. "She's been looking for you."

"Busara?" Ogubu's eyes brighten and fill with tears. It's touching to witness, but I can't help but be struck by the irony of it all. This is the man who invented the disk. The same technology that's killed so many people started with Ogubu's desire to help a daughter with heart problems. It's hard to believe that something as pure and wonderful as his love for his child could have led to a world that's so rotten and wrong. But that's the big lesson I've learned here in Otherworld—you can't predict how things will eventually turn to shit. You can only accept that they will. "How is her heart? Is she well?"

"Busara's fine," Kat assures him. "She's anxious to see you."

"And she'll probably be much easier to live with as soon as we locate you," I add.

It may be my imagination, but James Ogubu's image seems to flicker for a moment. "I don't understand. You *have* located me," he says.

There's something off about this guy, though I'm having trouble putting a finger on what it could be. I suppose he seems far too composed for the situation—like his real-world body has been hooked up to a strong sedative drip. Then again, who knows what's flowing through Ogubu's veins right now?

"We've found you *here*. Now we need to find you in the real world," I explain. "Do you have any idea where your body might be?"

"Yes," says Ogubu with a cryptic smile. "It's in a long, narrow container just large enough to hold it." He's describing a capsule. "That's as specific as I can be at the moment. After all, we've only just met."

"No rush," Kat assures him. "When you're ready to tell us, we'll be happy to listen." I look over at her with a raised eyebrow. I'm glad *she's* feeling confident. If he doesn't spill the beans, we could end up back at square one.

"You're certain that finding my body's the best use of your time?" Ogubu asks her.

This guy is way too cool. "It's not really up for debate," I say. "Your daughter's going to drive me completely insane if we don't get you home soon. And we need your help. As you probably predicted, Otherworld's gotten a wee bit out of control."

"Otherworld was never *under* control," Ogubu replies. "This world should not have been built."

"This is our home," Fons jumps in, sounding pissed. "Without Otherworld the Children would not exist."

"Of course." Ogubu places a hand on the Child's shoulder. "I apologize. I didn't mean to be callous. This subject has grown far more complicated since I last discussed it. There are no easy answers today. Perhaps there never were."

"Otherworld isn't the problem," Fons responds. "Guests like you are the problem."

I see Kat grimace, but Ogubu doesn't react to the insult.

"He's like us," I inform Fons. "He's not wearing a headset. He's not here to kill."

"Headset players are the biggest issue at the moment," Kat tells Ogubu. "There are two thousand in Otherworld, and they've been slaughtering Children for sport. There's an entire realm devoted to the hunt."

Ogubu's head bows forward and his hands rise to his face. A few seconds pass before he speaks. When he does, his voice is filled with grief. "I am so sorry," he tells Fons. "I warned Milo that such atrocities were likely, but he refused to listen. He thought he was powerful enough to control the world he'd created. And he assumed he was brilliant enough to govern his guests. I suppose in the end he was neither.

"When the Children first appeared, Milo set out to exterminate them. Later he realized what terrible acts he'd committed, and he brought me here hoping I'd help find another solution. He told me he'd scrapped the disk. Going forward, only headset players would be allowed into Otherworld. He thought I'd be pleased, but I knew what that would mean for Otherworld's inhabitants. Total annihilation. So I came back here on my own and I brought something with me that would put an end to all of it. But Milo found out, just as I prepared to unleash it. That's why he imprisoned my mind in this cave, and that's why I've been here ever since."

"What were you planning to unleash?" Kat asks.

"A virus," Ogubu says. "One specially designed to destroy the headsets Milo created and spare Otherworld's inhabitants."

My heart skips a beat, but it's too good to be true. The virus is exactly what we need—and it's within our reach. It's like coming across the Holy Grail mixed in with the mugs in your kitchen cabinet.

"Will it destroy the disks?" Kat asks.

"No," Ogubu tells her. "I didn't think destroying them would be necessary. Never in my wildest dreams did I imagine that anyone other than Milo or myself would ever enter this game with a disk."

"What is a virus?" Fons demands. His tone of voice could use an adjustment, but it must be frustrating to keep up a conversation with beings from another world.

"A virus is a piece of code that can replicate itself and destroy software," Kat says. The explanation seems to do nothing for Fons.

"It will kill all the new guests," I say. Then I meet Ogubu's eyes. "And we need it."

"Then bring my daughter to me," James Ogubu says. "I will tell her where to find the virus—and where she can locate my body."

I'm confused. Shouldn't Ogubu, of all people, know why that's not going to happen? His daughter isn't well enough to fight headset players. "This game is too dangerous for Busara now. Even the liminal spaces are filled with psychos and beasts. We have no access to headsets—only disks. If we brought Busara here, there's a very good chance that she'd be butchered or eaten, if her heart didn't give out first." I pause for a moment when I hear Kat sigh. My words may have been harsh, but that doesn't mean they weren't true. "You have no choice but to trust us."

"Placing my trust in the wrong people is why I'm here today," Ogubu reminds me. "The virus may be the only chance the Children have. I assume you know how the Company operates. Do you think it would be wise for me to entrust the virus to strangers?"

He has an excellent point. We could be Company engineers as far as he knows.

"Find a headset," he tells us. "Bring Busara to me, and I will tell her how to release the virus."

"That could take a while," I sigh.

"No," I hear Fons say. I turn my attention to him and see he's pulled out his weapon. "We cannot wait. If this virus of yours can free my kind, you must release it now."

"A gun," Ogubu notes solemnly, his eyes on Fons's weapon. "You're right, Otherworld *has* changed. Such weapons were forbidden the last time I was free."

"Put that thing away!" Kat demands, but Fons ignores her.

"These two claim they can die in Otherworld like the Children," Fons tells Ogubu, gesturing to Kat and me. "If you're like them, that means you can die too. Tell me where to find the virus or I'll shoot you."

"If I die, you'll never find the answer you seek," the older man points out. "You can either be patient and let me hand over the virus to someone I trust—or you can lose your best hope of saving your kind. It is your choice. Which will it be?"

A loud crack echoes through the chamber. Another wide fissure has opened up in the ice above our heads. Fons draws in a deep breath and reluctantly puts his gun away.

I hear Kat exhale. "Well, aren't we all glad *that's* all over," she says. "Now let's get Mr. Ogubu out of this cave. It's not going to last much longer."

Ogubu studies the ceiling. "You're probably right, but I'm afraid I can't leave."

"What?" Another obstacle has been thrown in our way, and Kat groans. "Why the hell not?"

"I'm safer in here than I would be out there. I can't afford to take any risks. As you know all too well, if I die, I'll be gone for good."

For some reason, an image of Gorog flashes through my mind. I watched the ogre get speared through the chest, and yet the boy who controlled the avatar is still somehow alive. "I know that's usually how it works," I say. "I've seen it happen. But there's a thirteen-year-old kid from Elizabeth, New Jersey, who was murdered in Otherworld but survived in real life. The Company thinks he's proof that the disks can be fixed."

"They may be right," Ogubu responds. "But they'll never figure out how to do it."

"Do you think *you* could?" I ask.

Ogubu shakes his head. "If I were able to study the survivor, perhaps. But that's not going to happen, now is it?"

"If you tell Busara where your real body is located, we can—"

Ogubu stops me. "When you bring me my daughter, don't take any chances. If you want me to speak with her, she must be wearing a headset, not a disk."

"Fine," Kat tells him. "We got it." The ice all around us is crackling like a bowl of Rice Krispies. "Let's go," she tells me. "We've got to figure out how to get our hands on a headset. Know anyone who can loan us half a million dollars or so?"

I follow her out, feeling far more hopeless than I did going in. I understand Ogubu's reasons for refusing to help us, but I'm not really up for another hurdle right now.

"I can help," Fons says behind us. I'd forgotten he was there, and that I'm still royally pissed that he pulled a gun in the ice cave.

"Oh, really?" I snap. "Let me guess—you've been saving up for a rainy day?"

Fons's brow furrows. He clearly has no idea what I'm talking about. "My friend Alexei—"

"Your friend Alexei?" I laugh out loud. "Why would he want a virus released? In case you haven't figured it out, he's a goddamn headset player."

"Which means he has a headset you might use," Fons says.

Kat glances over at me. "Why would your friend want to help us?"

"He wouldn't help *you*," Fons replies. "He will help me and the rest of the Children." He says it with such reverence that I'd almost swear he was talking about Jesus or Superman or some combination of both. Maybe this Alexei dude should start his own cult.

"Look, I understand he's your hero and all, but do you have any idea who your buddy Alexei is in the real world?" I demand. "He might not be a very nice guy."

"The *real* world?" Fons sneers back. "Otherworld is real enough to me. I know who Alexei is here. As far as I am concerned, that is all that matters."

"Do you really think he'll listen to you?" Kat asks.

"Certainly," Fons replies, without a trace of doubt. Apparently he's convinced that their affection is mutual.

"Then arrange a meeting for us with Alexei," she says.

"In the *real* world," I add, just to be obnoxious.

"When?" Fons wants to know.

"Tomorrow," I reply, stomping off toward the exit. "At noon."

"Tomorrow?" Kat asks. "Isn't that a bit early? Don't we need some time to figure out who this guy really is—or where he's at?"

"His name is Alexei Semenov," I call back. "He lives in New York."

. . .

I get to the end of the tunnel and step outside into the icy air. It takes me a moment to realize I'm the only one here. Probo and Ita are nowhere to be seen. I'm about to complain that our guards have abandoned us when Kat reaches out for my arm and drags me back inside the cave. I see she has a finger pressed to her lips. Crouched down low, Fons shuffles past us and examines the footprints in the snow outside. When he stands up, he points at me. "Come," he says softly. Kat and I both start to follow him. "You stay here," Fons orders her.

"Screw you," Kat says. "I go where he goes. You think 'cause I'm female I can't take care of myself?"

"Of course not," Fons says as though nothing she just said made any sense. "I chose him because he's the annoying one. If anything happens, I'd rather *he* died."

"Yeah well, I'm not gonna let that happen either." Kat pulls her hood up and disappears from view. Before I lose sight of her, she looks almost amused.

I bend down and take a moment to study the footprints in the snow. Probo and Ita took off to the right. They seemed to be moving fast, but if they were running away they chose the most difficult route. The path they took is all uphill. If I had to guess, I'd say they were running *toward* something.

Fons takes the lead as the three of us head in the same direction as the missing Children. Soon, I hear male voices in the distance.

"You get a great trophy, and I get third-degree burns. How the hell is that fair?"

"Quit bitching. I told you to turn down the sensitivity on the haptic response gloves. Those things can scald the hell out of you."

"Yeah, but what's the point of doing this if you can't feel the hot blood? By the way, d'you see how that thing turned bright red when I grabbed it?"

"What'd I say? The real fighters are still out in the wild. All those ones back in Karamojo are just the ones that gave up."

I can see them now. Two burly men dressed in arctic camo. They've both got assault rifles. Where are they getting this stuff? Nothing like that was available when I got to choose *my* weapon.

My vision blurs and my brain is boiling as the rage fills me. My mind no longer functioning, I race forward across the ice, my dagger in hand. I'm on the two avatars before they even know I'm coming. I slit the first one's throat with a single slice. The avatar flashes, and I immediately slam my dagger between its ribs. He must have lost one life already, because the second time he flashes, he disappears. His friend has had just enough time to jump to his feet. He has a gun aimed at my temple when one of Kat's arrows gets him right between the eyes. There's a single flash and he's gone.

The avatars have vanished, but two bodies are left behind, one giant and one small. The scream that comes from Ino makes my blood run cold. She runs past us through the snow and throws herself over her sister's limp, broken corpse.

THE HOMEBODY

I open my eyes. Busara is kneeling over me, the disk I was wearing in her hand. I hear Kat sobbing on the bed beside me.

"Oh my God, what's going on?" There's real fear written across Busara's face. "We saw tears pouring out from under Kat's visor and we thought something must have happened to you."

"It's not me. I'm fine," I tell Busara as I roll over to Kat.

"We'll get the headset," I promise her. "We'll stop the slaughter." I don't give a damn what it takes. I've only seen Kat cry twice in the ten years that I've known her, and both times she'd broken a bone. This time there's no pill that can ease the pain. It's up to me to do something—and there is absolutely nothing I wouldn't do to keep Kat from suffering like this.

"Simon?" I hear Elvis in the background.

"Give us a few minutes alone," I tell him.

"No." Kat sits up and wipes her face on her shirt. "We've got to get out of here. Remember what Wayne said? He knows who Elvis and Busara are. The Company is looking for all of us." Kat slides off the bed and immediately starts stuffing things into plastic bags. I'd almost forgotten about our lovely dinner with Wayne. It seems like a lifetime ago.

"We should have left Otherworld sooner," Kat continues. "Everyone's depending on us, and we're sitting ducks if we stay in one place too long."

"I don't get it," Busara says. "You guys were only in Otherworld for a couple of hours. We pulled you out right when we were supposed to."

Kat stops. "No. We were there for at least two Earth days. Maybe longer."

Elvis is shaking his head. "No. You were there for one hundred and twenty minutes." I was right—time is speeding up in Otherworld. Which means we need to move a hell of a lot faster in this one.

"By the way, just out of curiosity, how did Wayne find out about *me*?" Elvis asks, and I shrug. It's an excellent question.

"So I guess he didn't agree to our terms?" Busara asks.

"Not even close," I say. "He tried to force us to reveal our real-world location. Kat and I managed to escape, and then we went to the ice cave. Two Children who came with us were killed outside the cave. That's why Kat was crying."

Busara is oddly quiet. Her eyes lit up at the mention of the ice cave—I know she's dying to ask about her dad. But she doesn't want me to yell at her for being insensitive. Her silence makes me as angry as the question would have. "Yes, the two Children who died were brave and wonderful creatures. They definitely didn't deserve to be murdered by a couple of assholes who think it's sporting to shoot unarmed beings with assault rifles."

"God," Elvis groans.

Busara's face is stony. "I'm really sorry," she says.

"Oh, and we saw your dad," I tell her. "We freed his avatar from the ice."

Her eyes grow big. "And?" she asks cautiously. "Do we know where to find his body?"

"Nope," I answer. The response sounds mean even to my ears, so I soften my tone. "He wouldn't tell us. But he has a virus that can destroy all the Otherworld headsets. He wouldn't give it to us, though. He wants to talk to you."

Busara races for the bathroom. "I need a razor!" she shouts. The hair on the back of her head has been growing in. She'd need to shave it for a disk to adhere.

Kat follows her. "You can't use a disk," she says.

Busara spins around. "What? Why not? You heard what Simon said!"

"Did *you*?" I snap. "I just told you we saw two Children get slaughtered right outside the ice cave. Even the liminal spaces are no longer safe."

"Your dad wants us to get you a headset—and he's right," Kat says. "Otherworld is changing fast. There are no safe places anymore. The entire world is filled with psychos and beasts. You'd end up having to fight—and we all know your heart might not be able to take it."

"*Please.* My dad needs me," Busara pleads. "You're worried

about my heart, but I swear it's going to crack right in half if I stay here and do nothing."

"I'll go with Busara," Elvis volunteers, looking like the handsome doomed soldier in some Hollywood movie. "She won't have to fight at all. I'll take care of anything that comes at her."

I get the sense that Elvis would happily take a bullet for Busara Ogubu, which boggles my mind. Since the day they met, the girl has been nothing but cold to him. Still, he'd sacrifice anything to impress her. But as noble as Elvis's latest offer may be, there's no way I'm going to let her take him up on it. Without Kat or me, they'd both be as good as dead.

"Listen, guys," I plead. "There might be a better solution." Busara looks devastated. I had no idea she was capable of caring this much about anything.

"Listen to Simon," Kat counsels her. "Give him a chance."

"We've arranged to meet someone who has a headset," I say. "If we can convince him to let us borrow it, you'll be able to go to Otherworld safely."

"Who is it?" Elvis demands.

"Alexei Semenov."

Elvis throws his head back and aims a frustrated groan at the ceiling. "Are you *kidding* me? Do you know anything about that guy? 'Cause *I* do. Alexei Semenov is not the sort of person you want to be making deals with. They call guys like him oligarchs, but they're really just gangsters!"

Elvis is acting like I'm some kind of idiot. I'm not exactly thrilled about the situation either.

"Look—Semenov's in New York," I say. "He has a headset. We

got word to him that we'd be at his house today at noon. Do you have any better ideas? 'Cause if you do, now is definitely the time to speak up."

Elvis doesn't look pleased, but at least he keeps his mouth shut.

"Who's going?" Kat asks.

"Elvis and me," I say.

"What?" Elvis yelps. "When did I sign up for a suicide mission?"

"You speak Russian!" I shout at him. "And unless I was hallucinating a few seconds ago, you offered to be Busara's personal Otherworld bodyguard. Going to see Semenov is a hell of a lot safer than that."

"Fine," Elvis snips. "But the things I offer to do for Busara's body do *not* apply to yours. We go to Semenov's, you guard your own ass."

"Who said Simon was going?" Kat asks. "What if I want to meet this guy?"

Good God. Why the hell does everything have to be so hard? One look at her and I know she's not going to let this go. "Grab a quarter," I tell her.

I won the toss. Or lost, depending on how you look at it. Alexei lives in a Beaux arts limestone mansion on the Upper East Side. The place has so many embellishments that it looks like a five-tier wedding cake. Until recently the place was the embassy of Luxembourg. You can still see the dark square on the wall where the bronze plaque was removed.

"We could die in there," Elvis says pensively.

Of course we could, but it's fucking rude of him to point that out, if you ask me. "Let me get this straight—you're totally fine going back and forth to Otherworld, where everything wants to kill you or eat you, but you're terrified of asking some Russian dude if you can borrow his headset?"

"Beasts and guests are one thing," says Elvis. "Russians are another. Do you remember when that meteor hit Russia a few years ago? Remember all the dashboard videos that showed a giant ball of fire flying right over people's cars? Did you happen to notice that nobody stopped? They all kept driving toward the spot where the meteor was about to hit. You don't screw with Russians, man. They are hard-core."

I sigh with annoyance. "Do you have a point? If so, could you get to it? 'Cause it's almost noon, and I bet our hard-core Russian friend won't be too happy if we show up late."

"I'm just thinking that if we're about to die, there's a question I'd like you to answer first."

"Fine," I huff. "Ask."

"So what do you think I'm doing wrong?" Elvis suddenly sounds like a man in agony. "I've spent God knows how many hours alone with Busara, and she barely even looks at me. Sometimes when I ask her things, all she'll do is grunt. I mean, it's kind of sexy, but it's hard to hold a conversation that way."

I lock eyes with him. There's no doubt he's completely sincere. This is not what I needed at this particular moment. "You really want my advice? Right here? Right now?" I ask, and Elvis nods hopefully. "Give up on Busara. There's something off about her. I told you back in New Mexico—I'm not one hundred percent sure she's human."

"She said my name in her sleep," Elvis tells me, his voice dialed down as if someone could be listening.

I hope I'm doing a reasonable job of concealing my disgust. "I thought you just said you haven't gotten anywhere with her."

"We weren't sleeping *together*," he explains. "She passed out from exhaustion one night when we were working on the projector. I heard her whisper *Elvis*. She said it sweetly, too. I swear, it was the greatest moment of my life."

"You really like this girl, don't you?" I ask, though I can't quite believe it.

Elvis nods silently. Why in the hell would someone like Elvis fall for a girl with less personality than an NPC? "She's a genius," he says, answering my unspoken question. "I've never met anyone who can do what she does."

"Then I don't know what to tell you," I say with a sigh. "Maybe dial the dirty jokes down a notch?"

"Okay!" he says, obviously glad to have a plan. "I can do that!"

"And get your hands on a headset that will help her visit her dad. That's the way to really win her over."

"I can do that, too!" Elvis exclaims.

"Awesome!" I respond with fake enthusiasm. "Then let's do it!"

"I know you're screwing with me now, but I'm really glad we had this talk," Elvis says as we cross the street.

"Me too," I tell him. And though I said it to placate him, it's not really a lie. I wish like hell he'd set his sights on someone else, but I do like seeing him happy.

. . .

I step up to the carved wooden doors on the front of Semenov's mansion and press a small white buzzer that I assume is the doorbell.

A man in a perfectly cut three-piece suit answers. He's got to be seven feet tall and there isn't a single hair on his head. He glares down at the two of us without saying a word.

Elvis speaks to him in Russian. The man growls something brusque in response and then slams the door in our faces.

"That's it?" I ask. "He's not going to let us in?" I knew this house call wasn't going to be a walk in the park, but I didn't expect it to be over quite so quickly.

"He says we have to use the servants' entrance," Elvis snarls, kicking a concrete planter, which doesn't budge.

"What?" I'm momentarily offended. It lasts all of ten seconds. Elvis appears to be taking the insult far more personally. I'm also worried he may have broken a toe.

"This is some serious bullshit," I hear him muttering to himself as he limps away from the door. "I'm an *American*."

To the left of the main entrance, wedged between Alexei's mansion and his neighbor's, is a narrow metal gate. I hear a buzzer sound as we approach, and I rush over just in time to push the gate open. Then Elvis and I squeeze between the garbage bags that are waiting to be collected in the narrow alley that leads to the service entrance. The door swings out into the alley and a smaller man in an identical suit ushers us inside.

"Hello," the small man says in heavily accented English. "My apologies. We are not set up for guests. We've had to make special arrangements for you. Please . . ." He ushers us into an enormous kitchen. Sitting at a long wooden table are six more men in identical suits drinking coffee. Alexei has his own private army. The only thing that surprises me is how dapper they are. Alexei must spend a fortune on bespoke suits every year.

We follow the small man out of the kitchen and into a nearby room lined with metal lockers. At the far end is a stainless steel door.

"Please . . ." The man opens two of the lockers. Inside are pale blue jumpsuits and matching booties. "Change here. When you are done, the door will open for you."

"Is this necessary?" I ask. "I swear to God, I've had all my shots, and we aren't planning to stay very long."

"Yes," the man says bluntly. "It is necessary." Then he turns back toward the kitchen, leaving us on our own.

"What do you wanna bet this is some Howard Hughes shit?" I say as I yank off my sneakers. "Our new buddy is probably terrified of germs. Maybe he collects all his fingernail clippings and keeps his piss in mason jars like Hughes did."

"Yeah, I don't know." Elvis sounds unusually somber. "I'd bet it's going to get a lot weirder than that."

When Elvis and I are dressed in our snazzy blue outfits, the door slides open. Beyond it is a small stainless-steel room. Each of the four walls features a grid of tiny round holes. We step inside and the door slides shut and seals behind us. There's a whoosh, and fog sprays from the holes. It's some kind of decontamination shower. Whatever they're spraying us with smells like an industrial pesticide. I hold my breath and hope it ends before I pass out.

Thirty seconds later, the jets shut off, another door opens and we step out germ-free. A man wearing a pale blue jumpsuit just like ours greets us on the other side. He hands us each a hairnet, face mask and gloves.

"What'd I tell you?" Elvis says. "The next stop is the Twilight Zone."

I think he may be right. Everything around us is a spotless white. The walls, floors and furniture all blend together. There are no windows, but the space is lit by a warm golden light that feels like the sun. Elvis and I are led from room to room until we hear the bubbling of water. The man who's been leading us stops at a doorway and steps aside to let us pass through it. I guess he hasn't been asked to join the party.

I'm the first to enter. The air inside is warm and humid, and the room is empty aside from two chairs that have been positioned near the edge of a bubbling pool, which I now suspect is some sort of physical therapy tub. I see the top half of a naked man sticking out of the water. At least I think it's a man. Given the condition of the person's skin, it's kind of hard to tell. Large patches on his chest, arms and face appear to have melted away. I'm thankful the roiling water hides the rest of him. The bits I *can* see are difficult to look at.

"I am Alexei Semenov," he says bluntly. "You are Simon Eaton and Elvis Karaszkewycz."

It's the sort of welcome you'd expect from a Bond villain. Alexei does not disappoint. "May I ask how you know?" I say.

Alexei gestures toward the ceiling with his chin. "There are security cameras everywhere," he says in an American accent that's practically flawless. "Our facial recognition software provided online matches. I must be careful, you know. The people who did this to me are quite eager to finish the job."

I should probably keep my mind focused on the task at hand, but it's impossible not to wonder how anyone could survive whatever happened to Alexei Semenov. His nose and one ear are completely gone, as is his hair. But there's enough left of him to see that he once looked a lot like his avatar.

"Believe it or not, I used to be pretty," he jokes as if he were just eavesdropping on my thoughts. I think he's trying to grin, and the result is hideous. "A year ago, the ladies couldn't get enough of me."

"I bet there are still a lot of ladies out there who wouldn't give a damn what you look like," Elvis observes. It sounds incredibly rude to my ears, but Alexei laughs. I guess they share the same sense of humor.

"This is true," says Alexei, his voice hoarse from laughing. "But the doctors tell me I am prone to infection. Plus, I'm afraid my lower half looks far worse than my top. After I was poisoned, they threw acid on me and it ate away all my favorite parts."

I can only imagine what he's alluding to. "I'm sorry," I say. I shouldn't have. Alexei Semenov doesn't want my sympathy.

"For what?" he snaps. "If you'd had anything to do with this, you'd be dead by now. Devising ways to punish my enemies is now a favorite pastime of mine. So what do you say, gentlemen? Let's get to the point. My friend Fons tells me you two have a proposition for me. What is it?"

"We need an Otherworld headset," Elvis tells him. "You're the only person we know of who has one."

"That doesn't sound like a proposition," says Alexei. "It sounds like a favor. I don't grant favors. Especially to people who look like they can do nothing for me in return."

"But we can," I say. "Didn't Fons tell you? If you let us borrow your gear, we will eliminate all of the other players. You can save the Children and have Otherworld all to yourself."

"Even if you were capable of such a thing, why would you imagine that's what I would want?" Alexei asks.

"I don't understand," I say, feeling a bit flummoxed. "Fons told us—"

Alexei wades over to the edge of the pool and motions for us to step forward, as if he wants to tell us a secret. "I have been a very bad man," he says once we're closer. "Just look at me. People would not have done this if I'd been a *nice* guy. So you know what I decided to do when I got to Otherworld? I decided I would try to be good. Give it a shot. See if I like it. And you know what?"

I figured the question was rhetorical, but he seems to be waiting for an answer. "What?" I ask.

"It's amazing! I'm telling you—it makes me feel all warm and happy inside. The Children call me their savior. I go around rescuing them from hunting parties and bounty hunters and all the others who are there to slaughter them. And in return, you know what they do?"

This time Elvis does the honors. "What?"

"They love me! No, they *worship* me. I'm telling you, gentlemen, it's the greatest feeling I've ever experienced."

Alexei steps back from the edge of the pool as though he's said his piece.

I glance over at Elvis. I can see he's just as confused. "Okay, but I still don't get it," I tell Alexei. "You like saving Children. We have a way to save them all. I'm not sure what the problem is."

"The problem is—what am *I* supposed to do once all the Children are safe?" He smirks at the expression on my face. "*Please,* Mr. Eaton. Spare me the sanctimony. It's a game, after all, is it not? I pay great sums of money to be entertained. If there's no one left to fight in Otherworld, I'll be bored to tears."

"But the Children—" Elvis starts to argue.

"Why would the Children love me if they no longer need me?" Alexei says.

"And Fons?"

"Isn't he wonderful?" Alexei says. "Such a great character. Milo Yolkin is a genius. I couldn't have designed a better sidekick myself."

I remember the love with which Fons spoke about Alexei, and I hope he never hears Alexei talk about *him.*

"So is that it?" Alexei asks us, but this time he doesn't wait for an answer. "Thank you both for coming!" he says, and then he calls out in Russian to the men waiting outside the room.

"What the hell?" Elvis cries. His face is ashen. Whatever order Alexei issued in Russian, Elvis understood it, and given the fact that he looks like he's about to shit himself, I'm willing to bet it wasn't good. "He just told them to kill us," he helpfully confirms.

Four men in pale blue scrubs enter the room. "I am sorry," says the Russian. "Please do not take it personally. But I am afraid no one is allowed to see me like this. There would be blood in the water if word got out. If you had come to me with something interesting, I might have taken the risk. But Fons already told me that this virus exists. Why would I let it be set free and put my own headset at risk? You didn't think of that, did you?"

I didn't. "We could find a way—" I start to say.

Alexei shrugs. "Don't bother looking. The virus is nothing that I need right now."

"Wait!" Inspiration strikes as a pair of men come toward me. "There is something else we can offer you. Something that will keep you very entertained." I glance over at Elvis and tap the back of my skull. He nods.

Alexei is intrigued. He lifts a finger and his men come to a halt. "What can you two possibly give me?" he asks. "Otherworld is all that I need."

"We can give you your life back," I say.

"More importantly, we can give you your *dick* back," Elvis says. I'm not sure if it's his will to live or the little man-to-man we had earlier, but apparently he'll say just about anything to walk out of here with a headset.

Alexei snarls as if Elvis just made a sick joke. "And how do you propose to do that?"

"The headset you use lets you *see* Otherworld. But the Company has been working on a brand-new technology," I explain. "A disk that allows you to experience virtual realms with all five senses. If you're wearing a disk, you can taste, smell, feel—"

"*Screw.*" Elvis completes the list. "Think of how entertaining *that* will be."

A long silence follows. Then the Russian waves his men away, and they file out of the room. We've definitely got Alexei's attention. "I don't believe it," he says. "If such a device existed, the Company would be shouting about it from the rooftops."

"They can't," Elvis says. "There's a bug. Right now, the disk can kill you. When you die in Otherworld, you die in the real world too."

Alexei snorts and throws up his hands. "Then why would I want to wear it?" he demands.

"We know someone who can fix the disk." I don't bother to mention that he's currently trapped in a virtual ice cave that could collapse and kill him at any moment, but I figure Fons has already told Alexei that also.

"And?" Alexei asks.

"We'll rescue him and have him build a safe disk. And we'll make sure only one of them ever gets made. No one but you will be able to experience Otherworld the way it was intended." I should shut the hell up now. I don't even know if what I'm promising is possible.

Alexei is quiet as he ponders the possibilities. "You can prove that everything you've told me about this disk is true?"

"Absolutely," I tell him. "How would you like to take a little trip?"

DESPERATE PEOPLE

The rest of the mansion may look like a branch of the CDC, but Alexei Semenov likes to sleep in style. If I melted down all the gold leaf in his bedroom, I could live like a rock star for the rest of my life. I see Elvis's eyes wandering the room, and I know he's thinking the very same thing. I just hope he doesn't get tempted to indulge any Robin Hood fantasies after Alexei and I set off on our journey.

The Russian has been sitting on the bed watching television while we get everything set up. He does seem to be easily bored. He flips through the channels until he lands on a report about a man who was recently found dead in a Manhattan hotel room. The coroner's report said that the man's internal organs showed signs of damage that suggested he'd been badly beaten. But no one else had been inside the room. Not only was the hotel room door locked, footage from the security camera in the hallway proved the victim had been alone the night he died.

Elvis and I are in the process of moving a bureau in front of Alexei's bedroom door when our host glances in our direction.

"Don't get any ideas. If you murder me, my men will flay you alive," Alexei announces calmly.

"I wouldn't expect any less of them," I reply as we finish the job. "Is your bladder empty?" I can't believe I'm asking a Russian gangster if he needs to pee.

Alexei opens his robe and points to a plastic bag strapped to his waist that contains a few tablespoons of bright yellow liquid. I also get a glimpse of a few things that are even more disturbing. "My bladder is fine," he tells me. I think he enjoys my discomfort.

I produce the two sets of disks and visors that I brought to the mansion in case they were needed. Alexei looks down at them with disdain. "That is it? There is no other gear?"

"The visor lets you see and hear Otherworld, just like your headset would. The disk will engage your other senses."

"No." Alexei shakes his head and flicks one of the disks with his fingers. "This is some kind of joke."

I choose to ignore him. "In a second I'm going to stick one of these disks to the back of your skull," I say. Thankfully, he no longer has any hair to shave. "You've been in the game before, so the disk should replicate your avatar and put you right back where it was the last time you left Otherworld. Where were you, by the way?"

"None of your business," the Russian growls.

Whatever. "I'll find out soon enough," I tell him. "I'll be wearing what we call the master disk. It's linked to yours. It will allow me to locate you no matter where you are."

"Why do I need you following me around?" Alexei asks. "This will not be my first time in Otherworld."

"I'd trust him, if I were you," Elvis advises Alexei. "I didn't think I'd need any help either. Then Simon saved my ass in the first five minutes."

"I left my avatar in the safest of places," Alexei argues. "I will not need any help."

"There are no safe places in Otherworld now," I point out.

Semenov snorts with annoyance through the hole in his face where his nose used to be. He isn't used to taking no for an answer. "Maybe I will call my guards and have them take you away while I go on my own."

"Sure, you could do that," I tell him. "But I think you're far too smart to do something so stupid. You don't want to screw this up, Alexei."

The Russian glares at me, as if deciding whether I deserve to die for my insubordination. Then he smiles. His teeth are still perfect and pearly white, which makes the expression indescribably chilling.

"Fine," he says. He sits down on the bed and bends his head forward, exposing the base of his skull. "Put the damn thing on."

I arrive in Otherworld and immediately place my hand on the amulet that hangs from my avatar's neck. The world around me dissolves. Suddenly I'm somewhere dimly lit and warm. There are wooden floorboards under my feet and pale green curtains hanging in the windows. I'd call the place cozy if it weren't for the female screaming at the top of her lungs. I pull out my dagger. Alexei must be nearby. God only knows what he's doing to the female he's brought here.

"It's okay. It's okay," I hear him say softly. I turn and see two figures together in bed. "I know who he is. I invited him."

The screaming stops. Alexei's avatar has the female in his arms, and she's peeking at me from over his shoulder. She's lovely, with long silver hair and green eyes that glow like a cat's in the dark. I struggle to keep the shock off my face. Alexei's girlfriend is one of the Children.

"You invited a guest *here*, Alexei?" she chides him. "What were you thinking?"

Alexei doesn't answer. I don't think he's able. His head is buried in the female's hair and his hands are gently stroking her back. He's smelling and feeling her skin for the very first time. Within a few seconds his avatar begins to convulse. The Russian gangster is sobbing like a child.

"What is it, Alexei?" the female asks. "What's wrong?"

I search for the room's exit and locate it behind me. "I'll be outside," I say, but I'm pretty sure neither one of them is listening.

The house is little more than a shack, but it's well cared for and filled with lovely little touches and furnishings that appear handmade. I step out onto a porch. Alexei's home is one of the structures in the swamp between Imra and Nemi that Kat and I stumbled across on our way to meet Wayne. There are three little huts here, all built atop stilts. The swamp that surrounds me appears deserted, but I know there are creatures around. I hear them croaking and calling and scratching at the bark of the cypresslike trees. There's a loud splash in the water below, and I wonder how big the frogs get here in Otherworld. Then I remember the beast that snatched an avatar off this very porch, and I step back from the railing until my back rests against the cabin's wall.

I smell smoke and realize there's someone already here. He's been waiting for me.

"How about that? A man just got his life back. Goddamn beautiful, wasn't it?" The Kishka is standing beside me, a cigarette in his hand. The smoke curls up from it like a cobra rising from a snake charmer's basket. He takes a drag and sends a cloud floating out over the water.

The Kishka's right. I was truly touched. It's hard to believe that the same man almost ordered my death. A couple of hours ago, I wouldn't have guessed there was a heart inside Alexei's mangled body. It wasn't until we came to Otherworld that I had any proof he was human.

"I know what you're thinking," my dead grandfather says. Of course he does. He's inside my head. "You're thinking this is what those disk thingies should be used for. Am I right? To help people like that fucked-up Russki in there?"

I can tell from the tone of the Kishka's voice that he doesn't exactly agree. "Why not?" I argue. "If Ogubu finds a way to fix the disk—"

"You still think the disk is the only problem?" the Kishka asks, walking over to the railing. "The human brain wasn't built to go back and forth between worlds. Come over here, boy. Have a look."

I join him at the railing and peer down at the water. It's a frothy brown that seems all too familiar, and it smells a lot like human shit. There's something swollen and white bobbing along at the bottom. I can't see it clearly, but somehow I know it's a body with its feet encased in concrete blocks. I blink and it's gone. The water's still murky, but it's now your standard swamp green. There's a fish of some sort swimming past. My worlds are colliding and I'm dizzy and scared.

"Things are going off the rails," the Kishka confirms. "You need to get out of this place. And stay away from that Russian while you're at it."

"I can't," I say. "Not yet. Besides, what's the issue with Alexei? You saw him in there with that Child. I know he's an asshole, but he can't be *completely* evil."

The Kishka looks at me with a raised eyebrow that seems to suggest I might be mentally challenged. "Evil? No, he's not evil. Your friend Wayne is evil. This guy's *desperate*, Simon. And if I had to choose between them, I'd go with evil every time. Mark my words. There's nothing more dangerous than a desperate man."

I sense movement inside. I check over my shoulder, through the window behind me, and see Alexei heading my way. The Kishka is already gone.

"What's that smell?" Alexei asks when he appears on the porch. His avatar is dressed in the gray coveralls he always wears, and his black hair is neatly parted on one side. Alexei was a handsome man. In Otherworld, I suppose he still is.

"Smell?" I ask.

"Something was burning." He lifts his nose and sniffs the air. "It smells like tobacco."

Oh God, he smells it too. I have no idea what that means. "I wasn't smoking," I tell him. "Do you think there might be someone else here?"

Alexei scans the swamp around us. "No alarms have sounded. We should be fine."

"Alarms?" I ask him.

"You think I would leave my avatar here without a security system in place? There are Children all around us. I protect them, they protect me."

"You mean you kill guests and the Children worship you. Isn't that the game you've been playing?"

Alexei ignores my comment. "You may use the headset," he informs me. "It will be yours for good as soon as I get the new disk."

My ears suddenly detect a faint, rhythmic splashing in the distance, like the raising and lowering of oars. There's a boat coming toward us. Alexei must hear it too. He disappears into the house and returns quickly with a scope, which he puts up to one eye.

"Our friend Fons is on his way," he announces. I suppose it shouldn't come as a surprise. Fons knew we would both be here. "And it looks like he has brought me a guest. Our kind must be growing on him. Fons usually kills all the guests he encounters. And I must say, he dispatches them in the most imaginative ways."

"Where did you meet him?" I ask. I can now see the tiny boat on the horizon. Fons appears to be the craft's passenger. A large man has the oars, and the vessel is making its way toward us with impressive speed.

"I saved Fons when he was very young," Alexei tells me. "I'd heard about the hunts in Karamojo and I went to see what all the fuss was about. When I got there, I was disgusted. Muscular avatars shooting Children with Kalashnikovs? Where's the sport in that? It's like using bazookas to kill *khomyak*."

"*Khomyak?*"

"Yes, what do you call them in America?" Alexei pauses and taps his temple. "Hamsters, I think? In Russia they live in the wild, but only little boys ever hunt them. These guests are weaklings, I thought, killing unarmed *khomyak*. So I massacred all of them. Afterward, the Children greeted me as their savior, which amused me. There was one Child among them—a clever little creature with a tentacle for a tail. I was able to adopt him as a companion. He's grown fast since then, and he's served me well. I never expected to be so entertained by a computer-generated sidekick."

Those last few words feel like a sucker punch. I was actually starting to like Alexei. Then he had to remind me that the badass vigilante hero who travels around Otherworld saving Children just sees them as part of the game. As far as Alexei's concerned, Fons exists only for his amusement.

"Is that really what you think of Fons?" I ask. "You think he's just a bunch of code?" If so, I hope to hell Fons never hears about it.

"God created men," says Alexei. "Man created the Children. They are no more our equals than we are God's."

It's almost funny to hear the guy talking about God—without a moment's thought about what God might think of *him*. The Kishka was right. I should never have wasted my time feeling sorry for this dick. "What about the female inside?" I ask him. "The one who was just in your bed."

Alexei's jaw clenches and his nostrils flare. I think I just tripped one of his wires. "She's different," he says.

"Is she? Who gave you the right to decide who's your equal and who isn't?"

Alexei glares at me. "If it makes you feel better, I don't consider you an equal either."

"No, here in Otherworld, I'm clearly your superior," I inform him. "You're wearing a disk now, Semenov. If I wanted to, I could kick your ass into next Friday. The rules have changed."

He stares at me with those icy eyes. I suspect he's imagining all the ways he'd like to murder me. I really hope he tries, but the boat is drawing closer.

"Simon Eaton!" someone calls out cheerfully. It's definitely not Fons. I have no idea who the hell it could be—or what they have to be happy about.

I wheel away from Alexei and turn back toward the railing. A tall, rugged man with a full beard is rowing in our direction. He's dressed like he's been living in the woods for some time. I bet he smells like he has too.

The canoe pulls up alongside one of the house's stilts. "You know this guest?" Fons asks me. "You can vouch for him?"

I honestly can't say if I can or can't. There was something familiar about the voice, but the fur-covered face doesn't ring any bells.

"Simon, it's Marlow!"

Whoa. I can see it now. The avatar is an older, beefier, and infinitely hairier version of Marlow Holm. Back in the real world, I was never Marlow's biggest fan, but I'm absolutely thrilled to find out he's alive. So thrilled, in fact, that when his avatar leaves the boat and climbs up a ladder to the porch, I actually give it a giant hug. Elvis must be rubbing off on me.

"How's Kat?" Marlow asks, and I instantly let him go. I forgot the bastard had a thing for my girlfriend.

"Kat's good," I say. "She made it out of the facility. She's awake and healthy."

"Thank God. I've been looking all over for her in Otherworld, but no one's seen her since I arrived. I was seriously worried that Kat might have died."

"That's funny," I tell him. "While you've been looking for Kat, we've been looking for you. In fact, we still are. Any idea where the Company might be keeping your body?"

"It's not at the facility?" Marlow asks.

"The facility is gone. The Company shut it down right after Kat escaped."

"Then no." Marlow shakes his head. "I have no idea where the rest of me is. So I guess you know what happened?"

"Yeah—" What I *wish* I knew is what to say next. Marlow was brought to the facility the same night I rescued Kat. He'd been in a car crash, and the damage to his body was extensive. I don't know if he'll ever be able to use it again.

"I'm not looking for an answer," Marlow tells me. "I was conscious until I arrived at the hospital, so I already know I'm a mess. I was just wondering if you did."

How much does he know, though? Does he know that the Company arranged the car accident that killed his mother and probably crippled him? Does he know that he's the last person being held in one of the Company's capsules? Is this the right time to tell him?

Fons has finished securing the boat and climbs up to the porch to join us.

"Where did you find this man?" I hear Alexei ask Fons. "Why would you bring him here?"

"I found him in Karamojo," Fons informs his mentor. "He's been killing the guests there. I thought you might like to meet him, so I forced him to leave."

"He was very persuasive." Marlow nods toward the gun that's tucked into Fons's belt.

"I apologize," Fons says. "It was the only way." There's respect in his voice. The same kind of respect with which he addresses Alexei. I glance over at the Russian. I can tell he hears it too. "He says he's wearing one of the disks."

"Why have you been killing guests in Karamojo?" I ask Marlow.

Alexei sneers as if it were the stupidest question he's ever heard. "Why else? For the fun of it."

"Fun?" Marlow grimaces. "I'm not sure that's what I'd call it. The guests have been slaughtering Children. Milo cracked true AI, and the Children are sentient. That makes all of this real—and these asshole players are out there shooting Children like rabbits."

"You could have died in Karamojo," I point out.

"So what?" Marlow replies. "I had to do *something*."

He says it as if it were the most obvious thing in the world. As if anyone would do the same in his position. But they wouldn't. Marlow's wearing a disk that could end his life at any moment, and yet he's devoted what could be his final days to saving a species that only exists in a digital world. Back in New Jersey, I thought he was just another douchebag whose life revolved around sex and drugs. Now I find myself wishing my motives were as pure as Marlow's. I'm not sure I'd be risking my life for anyone if it weren't for Kat.

Alexei doesn't seem quite so impressed by Marlow. He moves in closer, chin up and chest out. His avatar is at least a foot shorter than Marlow's, and it's becoming clearer and clearer that height is not the only way in which Alexei is smaller. I think even Fons is starting to see it.

"Who is this person and how do you know him?" he asks me. I love how Alexei assumes he's the one with the power here. If he wanted to be in charge, he should have chosen a burlier avatar. If we have to, Marlow and I could take him out in a heartbeat.

Wearing a bemused expression, Marlow peers down at the smaller man. "I believe you've already been given my name," he says. "Who the hell are *you*? And why do you keep interrupting my conversation with my friend?"

Friend might be a bit generous. The only things Marlow and I have in common are our disks and our shared love of *my* girlfriend. We're friends in the same way two tattooed bikers at a Republican fundraiser might be buddies for a night.

"Calm down, gentlemen," I say. "I know Marlow from the real world. He's wearing a disk like us. The Company has been keeping him a prisoner in Otherworld." I turn to Marlow. "Alexei is a business associate. I need to borrow an Otherworld headset, and Alexei has one to loan."

"And both of you are friends of the Children," Fons adds eagerly. He obviously brought Marlow to meet Alexei thinking they might join forces. But from what Alexei's told me, he's not interested in sharing any glory.

"I've heard about you. You're famous for rescuing Children," Marlow says to Alexei, doing his best to smooth things over for Fons's sake. "You must be thrilled to hear that there's a way to destroy all the Otherworld headsets. If it's true, the three of us could soon be the last guests in Otherworld."

Alexei rudely ignores Marlow and directs his next question at Fons. "You told this guest about the virus?" He's obviously not very happy, and his reaction has apparently taken Fons by surprise. The Child doesn't appear to have an answer ready.

Marlow fills the awkward silence. "So who's this genius trapped in a cave on the ice fields?" he asks me. He must find the scenario hard to fathom.

"James Ogubu," I tell him.

Marlow's jaw drops. "Busara's dad? No way! He's alive? What's he doing here in Otherworld?"

"The same thing you are. He's trapped," I say. "He came here with a virus that could destroy all the headsets. Milo caught him and imprisoned him in the ice."

"The virus Fons was telling me about is real?" Marlow is suddenly very serious.

"Apparently," I say.

"Then why isn't it out doing its thing?" Marlow asks.

I'm about to explain the situation with Busara when my Russian companion decides to rejoin the conversation. I get the sense he feels left out whenever he's not the center of attention.

"The man in the ice must make a safe disk for me before the virus can be released," Alexei says.

This time Marlow doesn't acknowledge Alexei. He's had enough, and I don't blame him. Nothing's more annoying than a disrespectful douchebag who keeps butting in. "What's this guy talking about?" Marlow asks me. Alexei answers anyway.

"That is the deal that I made with Mr. Eaton and his Ukrainian friend. They need a headset to take the man's daughter to see him. I have offered them a headset they can use. The price is a disk with the bugs removed."

"So James Ogubu is gonna have to build a safe disk for this guy before the virus can be released? You know that could take a long time, right?" Marlow demands. "Months, maybe."

Fons looks to Alexei, who's avoiding his eye. "In months, the Children could all be dead."

Alexei cannot be persuaded. "If the headsets are destroyed, I will not be able to visit Otherworld. That's why the debugged disk must be top priority. Once I have the new disk, I'll decide what to do with the virus."

"You'll decide?" Fons seems to be hung up on those words. *"You'll decide* what happens to the Children?" I know what he's thinking and I completely agree—there should be no decision to make.

"I am the one who can give the man what he asked for," Alexei tells him. "Without me, the man's daughter won't be able to see him. Without me, there is no virus to release."

Fons is silent, but his normally stoic expression has vanished. He's been stabbed in the back, and his face reflects it. He just found out that the man he considered a hero is just another headset sociopath. The only difference between Alexei and the guests he's been killing is that Alexei got hooked on glory instead of blood.

"You're a liar." Fons lifts his gun and points it at Alexei's head.

"Don't be so dramatic," Alexei says. "None of this is *real*."

Wow, this situation went downhill fast.

"Fons, don't," I plead. I'm not sure he really understands what it means that the Russian's wearing a disk. If Fons pulls the trigger, Alexei is gone for good—and so is my best chance of getting my hands on a headset. Without a headset, there's no hope at all of releasing the virus.

"He won't do anything," Alexei sneers. I've never heard anyone make such a simple phrase sound so insulting.

Fons's arm shakes and his lip quivers. His world has crumbled. His hero is a fraud. But he doesn't look able to shoot.

When the gun falls from Fons's hand, Marlow quickly kicks it out of reach, and Alexei starts to laugh.

This time, the tentacle responds. It whips around and whacks the Russian's avatar in the stomach, slamming Alexei back into the cabin's wall. Then Fons turns and dives over the railing and into the murky water below. I watch for his head to surface, but it never does.

I glance back at Alexei, who's curled up in the fetal position on the wooden porch. I'm glad he's alive, but I hope it hurts like hell.

"Well, that was unexpected," Marlow deadpans behind me.

THE HEADSET

I open my eyes and have no idea where I am. It's becoming such a regular occurrence these days that I'm not even freaked out. All I know is that I'm staring at a lovely ceiling and my body is comfortable for the first time in ages.

"Where the hell am I?" I wonder out loud, and someone beside me laughs.

"You're at the Waldorf Astoria Hotel," Kat says.

I remember how we got here—dropped off in a black sedan driven by a silent Russian. One of Alexei's men had called ahead and booked a suite at the hotel. Another escorted us inside, and I'd be willing to bet that's the only reason the hotel doormen let four dirty and bedraggled teenagers enter. I would have preferred to stay somewhere a little less fussy, but Alexei insisted the Waldorf Astoria was the safest place to be. The Chinese government owns the hotel, and Chinese tech firms have long been the Company's biggest rivals. If they end up spying on us, which is highly likely, they'll probably like what they hear.

"The Waldorf Astoria is the best realm of all," I tell her, pulling the covers up over our heads. "Can we stay?"

"You have no idea how awesome it is," Kat tells me. "There's bacon in the living room. And the *Internet*."

"The *Internet*?" I joke, though to be perfectly honest, it's hard to imagine such luxuries. "How long have you been up?"

"Hours," she says. "I told the others to let you sleep. It's going to be a very long day for you. But if you get Busara to her dad, it could be the last trip any of us have to make."

We keep hoping every trip will be the last one, and it never turns out that way. But I don't think it would be helpful to say so.

"So the delivery came?" I ask.

"Half an hour ago," Kat tells me. "Busara is bouncing off the walls."

"Let her bounce," I say, pulling Kat toward me. "You can't rush recovery."

I must have been too tired to appreciate the suite's living area last night. The décor is a little too frilly for my taste—lots of flowers and silk. You could call the style *rich grandma*. In fact, before she died, my dad's mother lived in a house that looked an awful lot like this. I was hardly allowed to touch anything there. The memory makes me want to jump on the couch cushions or play catch with a vase.

"What have you guys been doing? Kat, you were supposed to

get him up!" Busara cries as we emerge from the bedroom. "It's been an hour!"

"I was really tired," I tell her, pretending to yawn to cover my grin.

"Totally exhausted," Kat adds.

I see Elvis smirking on the sofa, a tablet computer in his hands. "So do you think you got enough rest?" he asks. "If so, come over here, I've got something to show you."

I grab a piece of cold bacon off the room service cart and plop down beside him. The second I get a glimpse of what's on the iPad, I straighten up again. A video is on pause, and the word *OtherEarth* is written across the screen.

"It's a new ad," Elvis says, handing me the tablet. "Go ahead. Hit Play."

It's a point-of-view scene of a man running through Central Park. The only thing you can see are his fists pumping, but you can tell from his sleeves that he's wearing a dark gray suit. There's a gun clenched in one of his hands. He flies past joggers and strollers and old ladies with dogs. You can hear the air being sucked into his lungs and his heart pounding in his ears. Seeming to catch sight of something, the man changes course and charges down an empty path through the woods. He's alone in the forest when he comes to a sudden stop. Something has appeared on the path in front of him—a massive beast, bipedal yet reptilian, with a mouth that's mostly teeth. The man raises his gun as the creature hurls itself toward him, pumping three bullets into its chest in quick succession. Stone dead but still moving forward as it falls, the beast skids to a stop at the man's feet.

The man gives the creature a kick to ensure that it's been eliminated. Then he lifts his hand to his face and removes a pair of glasses. In an instant, his suit sleeves are gone, as is the gun. And the beast on the ground has vanished into thin air. A female jogger passes by on the path. When she doesn't seem to notice anything out of the ordinary, it becomes clear—our hero is just a jogger too. The man puts his OtherEarth glasses back on and the dead beast reappears. In the distance, there's another one. The man starts running again and the commercial ends.

"OtherEarth," says a voice that sounds a lot like Tom Cruise. "*Your* world, only better."

"It's augmented reality, just like I thought," Elvis says. "They've turned New York City into a giant sandbox. That's why they needed such detailed maps. I'm sure the rest of the country will be playable soon."

"So OtherEarth is going to let everyone in New York star in his own private action movie?" I ask. I can only imagine what that's going to be like.

"What do you want to bet that's not the only kind of movie you can star in?" Elvis says, waggling his eyebrows.

"Pervert." Busara is standing over us.

"How would *you* know?" Elvis asks.

There's something weird going on between the two of them, and I have no interest in being in the middle of whatever it is. I glance down at the tablet and scroll through a list of suggested videos. It's mostly Company-related news clips. ENGINEER LOCKED IN OFFICE FOUND DEAD BY SECURITY. HEART ATTACK CLAIMS COMPANY GENIUS. The guy in question looks young for a heart attack. If only it could have been Todd.

"Simon. We may not have Semenov's headset for much longer," I hear Busara plead. "Can we please get started?"

She's right—and for once she asked nicely. I grab some more bacon and hand the tablet back to Elvis. It's time to take Busara to Otherworld.

The headset wasn't the only thing that was delivered this morning. An omnidirectional treadmill has been set up in one of the bedrooms. And an adorably juiced-out Russian who appears to speak less than ten words of English is standing guard outside our suite.

I understand Busara's impatience, but she's already driving me nuts. She hasn't been to Otherworld since the two thousand new players arrived. She has no idea what to expect, and yet she refuses to listen. I'm still chewing my bacon when she jumps on the treadmill. Her haptic booties are already on. The gloves come next. I don't even have a chance to put on my disk before Busara's slipped on the headset.

"Do I really have to go with her?" I complain to Kat.

"No," Kat says reasonably. "I could go instead."

"Never mind," I reply. That's the last thing I'd want.

"I'll go!" Elvis offers, and I opt to ignore him.

"Talk to Ogubu's avatar," Kat tells me. "Then we'll find his body, rescue Gorog and Marlow, make a safe disk, release the virus, take down the company and live happily ever after."

"Well, when you put it like that, it all sounds totally doable," I joke.

She kisses me. "Then go do it."

Cursing, I slap on my disk and go under. I arrive at the gates of Imra just in time to see the Clay Man appear. Busara's avatar looks exactly the same as the last time I saw it, with one exception. The amulet that once dangled from the Clay Man's neck is now hanging around mine.

"What's it feel like?" I ask her.

"Different," she says in her own voice.

"Did you get a gun like I told you to?" I ask.

She shows me the handle of a pistol that's tucked into her waistband.

"That puny thing?" I ask. "Are you sure that's not some kind of toy?"

Busara's not having it. "I don't want to be weighed down by a bulky weapon. Let's go," she says.

We set off toward the ice fields. The tall, thin Clay Man's stride is much longer than mine, and I have to jog a little to stay beside her. But the avatar's height comes with its disadvantages, too. We're less than a mile into the red wasteland between the ice fields and Imra when a shot rings out. The Clay Man flashes. I crouch behind a small boulder and scan our surroundings for the shooter. There are several rocks in the distance that are large enough to hide someone.

Busara's avatar looks far more confused than concerned. "What just happened?"

"Get down!" I order. "You've been shot."

"I have?" she asks as a second bullet whistles through the air and lodges itself in her avatar. "I didn't feel a thing!" The Clay Man flashes for a second time.

I see the glint of metal in the sun. There's a sniper a hundred yards away. I couldn't possibly reach him with my dagger. Busara pulls her gun and points. By the time she's gotten a bead on the guy, her avatar flashes and the Clay Man is dead.

"Shit," I mutter, and take hold of the amulet around my neck. In an instant, I'm back at the gates of Imra.

I'm starting to worry that something may have gone wrong when an avatar appears before me. It looks like a giant Mr. T.

"Let's go," it says in Busara's voice.

"Don't you think this would be a good opportunity to talk survival strategies?" I ask her.

"We can't afford to waste any more time," she says.

"Hold on a second!" I shout at her back. "I wasn't the one—"

"Save your lecture for later," she tells me. "I got it under control now."

I have no idea what time it must be back in the real world. I wouldn't be surprised if we've been in Otherworld for more than twelve Earth hours. Here it's been days. Busara's avatar has been murdered three times and fallen through the ice where it was ripped apart by sharks. Once, we made it within eyeshot of the ice cave before a mutant bear devoured her. At first I found the carnage amusing. I'd use the amulet to send myself back to Imra and wait for her to show up again with an all-new avatar. But the novelty wore off ages ago. Now I'm just exhausted.

Busara's wearing a camouflage suit now, like the one Kat chooses, and the face looking out from its hood is her own. The machine gun slung across her avatar's back is the deadliest weapon available in Otherworld. She shoots first now and asks questions later. We've mown down half a dozen guests and three mutant bears, including the beast that ate her earlier.

I'm about to collapse by the time we reach the entrance of the ice cave, and I'm not the one with a heart condition. But if Busara's feeling weak, she's doing a great job of hiding it. She sprints into the ice cave on her own. Figuring she'll probably want a little privacy, I sit down with my back against the tunnel wall. My eyelids are drooping and my ass is freezing. I'm half asleep when Busara screams.

I should have known better than to let her go in alone. I don't have the strength to start all over again. I run toward the chamber at the end of the tunnel. As I reach the end I can see Busara. Her hood is off and she's fallen to her knees, but she appears uninjured. When I realize why she screamed, I feel like joining her. The ceiling of Magna's throne room has collapsed. I can't imagine how many tons of ice have fallen, but I know nothing underneath could have survived.

Though a rescue effort is hopeless, I rush to where the entrance to the throne room once was. My mind is too busy spinning to start contemplating our next move. I'd rather cry like the girl on the floor behind me. Then I spot it. A glint of metal in the stream of melted water that flows along one side of the tunnel.

I drop to my knees and fish out the object. It's a gun, and I've seen it before. I never forget a weapon that's been shoved in my face.

"I don't think your dad's dead," I tell Busara.

"What?" She spins around to face me. "Then where is he?" She freezes when she sees the gun in my hand.

"I think Fons has him," I say. "This is his gun." I'm not sure it's good news.

Busara's avatar dims. I have no idea what's going on. Then my eyes are flooded with light. My disk has been removed.

"How could you let this happen?" Busara is shouting at me. As my eyes begin to focus, I see Busara being held back by Elvis and Kat. My disk is in her hands.

"What the hell? How is this *my* fault?"

"You took that *thing* with you to the ice cave, didn't you?" she demands. "He would never have known about my father if it weren't for you!"

Elvis grabs her and puts his arms around her as if it's the most natural thing in the world. I expect her to punch him, but she doesn't even squirm. "Busara," Elvis says gently. "Fons isn't going to hurt your dad."

"How do you know?" she cries with her face against his chest. I'm trying my best to follow the discussion, but I can't quite believe what I'm seeing.

"Because your dad built the virus," Elvis tells her, "and that's all Fons wants. From what Simon and Kat have told us, he doesn't sound like such a bad guy." You know things are totally screwed up when Elvis is acting as the voice of reason.

Suddenly Busara pushes Elvis back and things between them return to the way they were. Elvis is hurt, but Busara can't see it. A few seconds ago she was in his arms. Now she won't even look in his direction.

"Do you really think *Fons* can keep my father alive in Otherworld?" she argues. "My dad's wearing a disk and he's never played a game in his life! I died five times before I made it to the cave!"

"Yeah, because you refused to listen," I snap. "Why don't you do us all a favor and start listening now?"

Busara glares at me but doesn't say a thing. I'm so goddamn sick of her. I spend countless hours trying to keep her alive in Otherworld and she repays me by abusing my best friend and giving me shit about something that's hardly my fault.

I hear Kat take a deep breath. "Okay, guys," she says. "I think the first thing we need to do is get the hell out of the Waldorf Astoria."

Damn, I was really starting to get used to it here.

"Why?" Busara demands. "I say we go right back to Otherworld and start looking for Fons!"

"May I remind you that we made a deal with a Russian gangster?" Kat says, keeping her cool. "He lent us the headset in exchange for a safe disk. If there's any chance that we won't be able to pay him, we need to be someplace where he can't find us."

"Oh, come on, we've got plenty of time before Alexei comes after us," Busara says.

"Unless Fons makes your dad release the virus," I point out. "Then Alexei is going to be *super*-pissed."

"If my dad didn't tell *you* where the virus is, he's not going to tell Fons, either," Busara argues.

She has a point. Back in the ice cave, Fons even threatened to kill James Ogubu, and the avatar still refused to give up the virus's location.

Elvis has been uncharacteristically quiet. Finally, he chimes in. "Maybe there is something we can give Alexei," he says. "It's not exactly what he wants, but it's a good down payment. It might buy us some time while we look for Busara's dad."

"What is it?" I ask. I have no idea what it could be.

"We can give Alexei the entire Company," Elvis says.

The sterile white room is empty aside from a hospital bed and several large machines. Alexei lies there, tucked under a sheet. IV tubes sprout from his arms and a monitor is sketching the beats of his heart. He looks like he's sleeping. I see the disk and visor he borrowed lying on his bedside table. As I slip them into my pocket, Alexei's lips part.

"How long?" he croaks.

"I'm not sure I understand," I respond.

"How long will it take him to build the safe disk?" Alexei's eyes open. They're the same piercing blue eyes that he gave his avatar. The face that surrounds them couldn't be more different.

I know I should tell him we're still looking for Ogubu's avatar. I once overheard my mother advise a client that you should tell the truth whenever you can. Unnecessary lies come back to bite you. But the Kishka was right about Alexei. The last thing a man this desperate wants to hear about is a setback.

"First we need to locate James Ogubu's body in the real world. Once he's free, it may take him a few weeks to fix the disk."

Alexei shakes his head emphatically and the blips on his heart monitor speed up. "That is too long. I cannot stay like this." He presses a button on the side of his bed and the top half folds forward. He's still halfway to a sitting position when his face contorts in agony and he's forced to stop. I don't see any external injuries, but I can only imagine what kind of damage getting whacked by Fons's massive tail might have done to his internal organs.

"I had no idea you were so badly hurt," I say. If Fons were here, I'd give his tentacle a high five.

"I was hardly a perfect specimen to begin with." It sounds like a joke, but his voice is deadly serious. "I need that disk, Mr. Eaton."

"I know," I tell him. "But—"

"You know?" he spits back at me. "You know what it's like to be half a human? To be robbed of your face and your manhood? Yesterday, I got them both back for a few precious minutes. Now I'll do whatever it takes to keep them. Tell Mr. Ogubu to work faster. I will pay him whatever he likes."

"Yeah, I'm afraid there's a bit of a problem with that." Now for the tricky part.

"If there is a problem, I know you can fix it, Mr. Eaton," Alexei says. It's not a vote of confidence. It's clearly a threat.

"There's something our engineer's going to need before he can get started."

"Whatever it is, buy it."

"It's not that simple," I tell him. "There's a thirteen-year-old boy named Declan Andrews. His avatar died in Otherworld while he was wearing a disk, but somehow his real-world body survived. He's the key to making a safe disk."

"So?" Alexei says. "Find him! Pay his parents to let us adopt him—or babysit him—or whatever the hell they want! Kidnap the child if necessary!"

"The Company has Declan," I tell him. "They know he's the key to fixing the disk, but the two people who designed the technology are both gone, and the Company doesn't have the brainpower to get it done."

I can see Alexei's thumb circling the call button on the side of his bed. I have a strong hunch I'll be in serious trouble if he decides to push it. "You left this part out when we made our deal, Mr. Eaton. You did not say there would be a second person to find. This boy is very important. You expect the Company to hand him over if I call and ask nicely?"

"Sure," I say. "If you're in charge."

THE PLUNGE

Partnering with Russian oligarchs does have its advantages. I'm in the passenger seat of a helicopter flying over New York Harbor. The Statue of Liberty is just below. She seems impossibly close, like I could reach out and touch her. Dozens of watercraft—from tiny motorboats to giant cargo ships—crisscross the water. We're only interested in one of them. Directly below us is the Staten Island Ferry. Its bright orange paint makes it impossible to miss.

It took us a while to agree on the site of Milo Yolkin's final plunge. There were countless factors to consider. It had to take place somewhere the body wouldn't be found—so no Midtown office buildings. There needed to be lots of people around with cameras ready. And we had to be able to make a quick, clean escape. The moment videos are posted, the Company will know exactly where we are.

On the ferry's last trip across the harbor from Staten Island,

Busara and Elvis planted the projector at the back of the boat, just past the railing. They disembarked in downtown Manhattan and we waited for the ferry to set off on its return trip. As it pulled back from the dock, Kat and I took off from a heliport atop a Wall Street skyscraper. We need to be within two hundred yards of the projector for the controls to work properly.

"Okay!" Kat shouts. She's watching the ferry with powerful binoculars. "Switch him on."

I bring Milo Yolkin to life and let him stand motionless for several seconds. The timing of his plunge has to be perfect. This is Milo's final public appearance, and we need people to see him. The projector will be destroyed when he goes over the side.

"A woman is pointing," Kat announces. "She's got her camera up. More people are moving in. Now!"

I roll the sphere off the deck and into the water below. Milo Yolkin goes with it.

Seeing the action from this high up isn't nearly as fun. But none of us want to be anywhere near that boat when it eventually makes it to land. I'm sure someone down there is screaming for help. I watch tiny people rush out onto the ferry's deck. Soon everyone on board is clustered at the railings. The boat slows down and crew members make their way through the crowd. An alert has gone out. Nearby vessels are turning back toward the ferry and a police boat is already racing toward it.

"Check Twitter," Kat tells me. I put down the controls and pick up the burner phone that our new partner has provided us. There's already a photo of Milo's fatal jump. It seems the person who took the picture didn't know who he was. But two other people have already replied with the correct identity.

"Let's go," I tell the pilot. Our work is done.

We're almost back at the heliport when three black helicopters race past us, the Company's silver logo blazing in the sunlight.

A tourist from Melbourne captured it best. She was filming the skyscrapers of lower Manhattan as the ferry left them behind. Suddenly a figure rises into her camera view. He stands motionlessly for a second or two as if contemplating the waves below. He's wearing the hoodie and sneakers that have become Milo's calling card over the last ten years. Blond curls form a halo around his head. He turns and looks over his shoulder—just long enough to leave no doubt whatsoever concerning his identity. Then he steps forward and disappears over the side. There are screams and shouts for help in the background as the camera rushes forward, the city bouncing in front of it. The next clear shot is one of the water below. It's dark green and murky, and the wake of the ferry is outlined in white foam. The camera pans to the left, then frantically to the right. There's no sign of the person who leaped to his death.

I wonder where Milo's real body is. What did the Company do with it after they stole his palm print? Is he buried in an unmarked plot? Wrapped in plastic and stored in a freezer? Turned into ashes that drift through the wind? How could a man so important just vanish and be missed by so few? Aside from Kenji, his ninth-grade buddy, did anyone know who Milo Yolkin really was? What was the difference between the man we saw on television and the hologram that just sank to the bottom of New York Harbor?

. . .

There are four rooms in our suite at the Waldorf Astoria, and there's a television in each. Every channel—from CNN to Al Jazeera—is covering Milo Yolkin's suicide. As the hours pass and all hopes of finding the boy genius alive begin to dim, the financial reporters start taking over. Milo's death may be tragic, but the fate of the Company is beginning to look even bleaker. The stock has already hit its lowest point in a decade and the bottom appears to be nowhere in sight.

All the cable news channels are at the scene. New York Harbor is crowded with police boats. There are so many helicopters churning the waters, you'd think we were in the middle of a hurricane. The anchors are still holding out hope on CNN, while MSNBC and Fox have pretty much declared Milo dead. They're running a reel of highlights from his lifetime—and comparing his death to Kurt Cobain's suicide. Reports from New Jersey show the bizarre scene taking place in front of a nondescript house in Sunset Heights. It's part Burning Man, part Irish wake. Aside from the kid watching it all with disgust, no one seems to have figured out that Milo Yolkin never lived there.

While the world mourns, stock of Milo Yolkin's Company is being snatched up at pennies on the dollar.

THE INNER CIRCLE

"Mr. Eaton." The handsome secretary announces my arrival. Six middle-aged men rise to greet me, all of them creepy AF. Five are wearing bespoke suits, but I'm more interested in the guy rocking Dockers. One of Wayne Gibson's arms is hanging in a sling across his chest. That must be the arm I shot at the facility the night Milo died and Kat escaped. Despite his injury and casual attire, he's clearly the most powerful guy in the room. Behind the man is a wall of windows. We're on the eighty-sixth floor, facing south. With a good pair of binoculars I could probably see my house in New Jersey. I feel an unexpected twinge in a part of my brain that's been long neglected. For a moment I actually miss my mother. The boardroom is Irene Diamond Eaton's natural element. She'd know exactly how to handle these assholes.

A silver fox in a dashing charcoal suit comes toward me, hand stretched out to shake. "So glad you could come," he says. "I'm Lawrence Bennett. Will Mr. Semenov be joining us as well?"

"By video chat," I tell him. "Here's the number to call." I hand him a scrap of paper.

"Ah," says Bennett looking down at it. "I see." He's pissed. If there's one thing I know, it's angry old white dudes. I lived with one for eighteen years.

I take a seat across from Bennett and his fellow aging Ken dolls. They each introduce themselves, but I don't bother remembering the names. When it's time for Wayne to speak, he grins. "No need for introductions. Mr. Eaton and I are old friends," he says.

"I shot him," I tell the men. "I'd shoot him again right now if I could."

Wayne laughs, but there's no reaction from the Company's board members. Their faces remain perfectly blank. It's as if I never uttered a word. *Are they human?* I wonder. My discomfort is growing. I look around the room. The world seems much clearer than it has in days.

"Shall we get Mr. Semenov on the phone?" Bennett asks.

"Yes," I say. Alexei may be a complete dick, but these guys are giving me the willies.

A screen lowers at one end of the room. The phone rings three times. The screen lights up. Stationed in front of the camera is a taxidermied bear, its mouth open in a ferocious silent roar. "Hello!" Alexei greets the boardroom from off camera. "How is everyone this morning?"

The board members exchange befuddled glances.

"Mr. Semenov, this is highly irregular." Bennett leans toward a microphone that's embedded in the wooden table. "How can we be certain we're speaking to you? Perhaps you are not aware that there is software that can replicate your voice. It's available on the dark web. Anyone could get his hands on it."

"Maybe," says Alexei—and although I can't see him, I know he said it with a shrug. "But no one can get their hands on my Mischa. Putin and I shot him on vacation in Kyzyl. He is famous! I'm sure you have the technology to verify his identity—or does your facial recognition software not work on bears?"

I'm no big fan of Alexei's, but sometimes it's impossible to dislike him.

"This is absolutely bizarre," mutters one of the board members.

"Perhaps we should reschedule this meeting for a time when you're able to be with us in person," says Bennett.

"As you all know, following Milo Yolkin's unfortunate suicide yesterday, I purchased a great deal of the Company's stock at very reasonable prices. I saved your corporation, gentlemen. Offending me would not be wise," says Alexei. "If my feelings get hurt and I dump my shares on the market, the Company's stock will hit rock bottom. Your operation may not be able to recover from a plunge like that. But I'm sure none of this is news to you. That's why we're all here today, is it not?"

"It is indeed," Wayne finally says. "What is it you want from us?"

"The boy," says Alexei.

Wayne looks around at the other members of the board and chuckles. "I'm sorry. The boy? What boy?"

Does this douchebag think we're complete idiots? Does he think we'll play his stupid games? "Declan Andrews," I snarl. "*Gorog.*"

"Ah, yes, *that* boy," says Wayne, addressing the bear. He's not planning to make this easy. "May I ask why you want him?"

"That's none of your business," I tell him. "Hand him over by the end of the day or the Company's stock won't be worth the paper you wiped your ass on this morning."

The members of the board shift uncomfortably in their seats, but Wayne appears unperturbed. "Son, I don't believe I was speaking to you." He doesn't even bother to look at me. He's talking to the fucking bear. "Mr. Semenov is a businessman. He's made a significant investment in the Company and I imagine he'd like to see it pay off. Now, we may not be able to grant his first request, but I have a feeling we might be able to find a way to satisfy his true desires. Mr. Semenov, we both know that you aren't here for a thirteen-year-old boy. What is it that you *really* want?"

There's silence on the other end of the call. The bear stares us all down with its amber-colored glass eyes. I keep my clenched fists hidden beneath the table. I have no idea what Alexei's going to say next.

"A disk without bugs," he tells them.

Shit.

"Fine," says Wayne. "Consider it done."

"*What?*" I blurt out.

"I want the *only* debugged disk," Alexei adds.

Wayne smiles. "That's a bit trickier, Mr. Semenov. But we can assure you that you'll be the only person in Otherworld with one. Let us use the technology for different projects, and we'll be able to sweeten the financial aspects of this deal considerably."

"He's promising something they can't deliver," I tell Alexei. "They don't know how to fix the disk. Milo Yolkin is dead. There's no one at the Company now who can do it."

"And you think *you* can, Mr. Eaton?" Wayne asks, sounding perfectly cool and in control.

"Of course not," Alexei replies for me. "He knows someone."

Wayne chuckles. "Mr. Semenov, as I'm sure you're aware, the Company is the most successful tech corporation on earth. We employ the finest engineers and developers in the world. As we speak, our most brilliant employees are on the brink of debugging the disk. Who do you think is most capable of delivering the product you've requested—us or a homeless juvenile delinquent?"

"You have no idea—" I start to say, but Alexei speaks over me.

"Mr. Eaton says there's only one man capable of fixing the disks—the man who invented the technology. He says he knows where to find him."

"James Ogubu?" Wayne scoffs. "Have you met him?"

"No," Alexei admits.

"Of course not. No one's seen James in ages. He's dead, for all we know."

"James Ogubu is not dead," Alexei replies. "I have it on very good authority that he has been seen in Otherworld."

Wayne chuckles as if he's just uncovered the source of a misunderstanding. "You mean an avatar that *looks* like James Ogubu has been spotted in Otherworld," he says. "I've only been to Otherworld once myself, but from what I recall, you can build an avatar that looks like pretty much anyone."

I have to admit—the asshole makes a good argument. Even though I know he's wrong, I'm struggling to find the words to make my case. "It's not an impostor, Alexei." I can hear the desperation in my own voice. I sound as sweaty as I'm probably starting to look. "Trust me."

"Yes, by all means, trust him," Wayne agrees. "There's no doubt that James Ogubu has the mind and the skills to fix the disk. If

Mr. Eaton manages to produce him in the real world, you'd be a fool not to offer him your allegiance. But until then, why not allow the Company to keep the boy and continue our work? We're close to a breakthrough. We could have a safe disk in a matter of days. I can promise right now that you'll not only get the first one, you'll also be able to profit from the Company's latest venture. If our calculations are correct, it could add billions to your fortune."

"Alexei, you can't listen—"

"Shush," the Russian orders me. "Never turn down a deal until you know what it is. What is your latest venture, Mr. Gibson?"

"It's something we call OtherEarth," Wayne says. "We were planning to give you a demonstration, but I'm afraid it requires that you be here with us in person. Perhaps we could schedule—"

"No," says Alexei. "I am not interested in the demonstration. Give it to him."

Everyone's eyes shift in my direction. Him means me.

"I'm not sure that's the best idea." Wayne's cool is starting to crack.

"I didn't ask you what you thought of my idea," Alexei responds testily. "Give Mr. Eaton the demonstration."

Suddenly things aren't going Wayne's way either. Alexei's reactions aren't easy to predict.

Wayne's smile is a bit tighter now. "Fine. Then let's bring in our engineer." He leans over to Bennett. "Larry, would you mind?"

The other man hops up as if God himself had just whispered in his ear. Bennett walks to the conference room door, opens it, and ushers in my good friend Todd. My least favorite engineer may be dressed in a suit for his big presentation, but he's still unmistakably bro. Todd glances at the screen and does a comical double take when he sees Alexei's bear.

Then he spots me and his eyes nearly pop out of his head. "What the f—"

"Yes, I believe you know Mr. Eaton as well." Wayne cuts him off. "He'll be the one demoing OtherEarth today."

"Mr. Gibson, do you really think—" Todd starts again.

"Yes. I really do," Wayne says coldly.

Todd doesn't look thrilled by the state of affairs, but the engineer does as he's told. I guess blindly following orders has gotten to be a habit by now. I look forward to hearing him try to offer that defense at his trial.

Todd hands me a pair of black glasses that look perfectly ordinary. They're much more streamlined than the augmented reality glasses Elvis assembled. The sides are wider than usual, I suppose, but not so much that they'd draw attention. Then Todd clicks a button on a remote and a second screen lowers at the other end of the room.

"Put the glasses on," he orders me.

"Say *please*," I hear Alexei say. "Mr. Eaton is my personal representative. There's no need to be rude."

"Put the glasses on, *please*," Todd corrects himself. He takes a seat beside me and places a tablet computer on the tabletop in front of him.

I put the glasses on. They are perfectly clear. I glance over at the screen Todd just lowered. The image projected on it is my point of view.

"Who is your favorite actress, Mr. Semenov?" Wayne asks.

"Judi Dench," Alexei answers with a yawn. "She brought M to life in a way no one else could. The Bond films without her have all been crap."

When Wayne laughs, the board decides to laugh too. "Yes, she's wonderful. But perhaps there's someone you've always found irresistibly attractive?"

"Judi Dench," Alexei insists. I don't know him that well, but he certainly sounds sincere. Once again, he's making it hard not to like him.

"Then Dame Judi it is," Wayne says. Todd types into his tablet and suddenly Judi Dench is standing in the room with me, wearing a shimmering gown that would look right at home on the Oscars red carpet. I take the glasses off and she's gone. I put them on again and she's back. "Say hello to my friend Mr. Eaton," he tells her.

Dame Judi's platinum hair looks carefully tousled. Her deep blue eyes are surrounded by perfectly crafted laugh lines.

"Good afternoon, Mr. Eaton," she says. I hear the deep, rich voice over the speakers in the room, but also in my own two ears. The glasses must have audio as well.

"Very impressive." Alexei sounds uninterested. "I would like to see her do a cartwheel."

Wayne looks pleased by the request. "You heard the man," he tells me. I imagine it, and Dame Judi performs a perfect cartwheel. "Anything else?"

"No," says Alexei. "That's it. I am bored. It's *Celebrity Pokémon GO*. Who cares?"

I snicker.

"Oh, it's so much more than that." Wayne is scrambling. "With OtherEarth you can have any adventure you like—all without leaving the safety of your own environment. You can hunt monsters while you go for your morning jog or battle foreign spies on the subway."

"Pass," says Alexei.

The board members appear nervous. Maybe they really *are* human.

"All right," Wayne replies. There's a hint of desperation in his voice. "Now, imagine your encounter with Dame Judi—and imagine you were wearing a disk." He pauses to let the idea sink in. "The glasses alone will make the Company billions. Pair the glasses with a disk and we can charge anything we like."

"Why?" Alexei demands. "What is the big deal?"

"I don't think you understand," Wayne tells him. "In Other-Earth you can choose any companion you like—for a price. You can speak to them. Feel them—"

The horror of it all is beginning to settle in for me. Soon you'll be able to buy a digital clone of any famous person you want. And you'll be able to do anything you want to that clone.

"So?" Alexei says. "I am a billionaire. I could buy the real thing."

"You could buy Dame Judi Dench?" Wayne scoffs.

"Everyone has their price. Take my word for it." The way Alexei says it, you get the sense that he knows what he's talking about.

Wayne leans forward, his good elbow on the table. "You may be able to buy companionship, but there are certain things that aren't for sale," he says slyly. "For instance, what if you weren't interested in making love? What if you wanted to see what it was like to chop her up into bits?"

"You are a very sick man, Mr. Gibson." Alexei sounds utterly appalled, though I doubt he's so squeamish. He's screwing with Wayne, and it's absolutely beautiful. "Why would anyone want to murder Dame Judi? She's a treasure."

Finally, a question for which Wayne has no answer. His face falls. "Surely you can see how popular such an option might be. Think of the revenue."

"No, I prefer not. I have no interest in such things," Alexei says. "This meeting has not been worth my time. I am interested in Otherworld only."

It makes perfect sense now that I think about it. OtherEarth can't give Alexei a handsome avatar with a nose and a pecker.

"Mr. Semenov—"

"You were right, Mr. Eaton," Alexei says. "These men are not so impressive. Bring James Ogubu to meet me tomorrow. Gentlemen of the board, as soon as I have confirmed that Mr. Ogubu is alive, I want the boy Mr. Eaton calls Gorog delivered to my home. Otherwise, I will dump my stock and your Company will die."

"Mr. Semenov!" Wayne tries again. But there's no answer. Alexei is gone, and the giant bear stares back at us silently.

The men sitting around the table look shell-shocked, but I'm the one who's truly screwed.

THE CAPTIVE

As my mother might have predicted, my lies have come back to bite me right on the ass. I should never have told Alexei that we'd found James Ogubu in real life. Now the race is on to locate his avatar before morning. I use the amulet to join Kat in the ice fields, and together we set out in search of Children. Our only hope is that someone will have spotted Fons and Ogubu and we'll be able to pick up their trail. But so far there doesn't appear to be a trail to follow. We've traveled from wasteland to wasteland, skirting the realms. If there are Children left in Otherworld, they're all deep in hiding. From time to time, we've come across evidence of habitation—the remains of campfires or lean-tos. But the beings that built them are long gone.

For the past few hours, we've been hiking through rocky terrain. There's no water here and no vegetation. Pillars of stone rise up around us. We're high enough to see other realms and wastelands in the distance. There's a patch of green that looks promising. It's hard to tell how long it will take us to reach it.

"Look," Kat says. We've emerged from between two of the giant rock pillars into an open space. Not far away is another outcropping. A wide web has been strung between the rocks. It must be at least fifty feet from side to side. "How big do you suppose the thing that built that is?"

I recognize the handiwork. "About your size," I tell her. "Let's go say hi."

Kat lifts an eyebrow. "You're joking."

"Nope," I tell her. She stays behind for a moment as I walk toward it, then hustles to catch up.

"You sure you know what you're doing?" Kat's still skeptical. She thinks a beast built the web.

"I think so." If I remember anything from grade school, it's that spiders catch their prey by sensing vibrations in their webs. I pick up a large rock and hurl it at the silken strands.

Almost immediately a creature appears from above, daintily dangling from a single strand. She uses her many limbs to stop a few feet above us. I can see my reflection in all of her eyes.

"It's you," she says.

"Surprised?" I ask. "I bet you thought I was still stuck to the top of that cave. You know that was totally unnecessary, right?" If I hadn't had the amulet, I'd probably still be up there.

"Unnecessary? Perhaps. Prudent? Certainly," the Child says. "What would you have done in my place?"

"I don't know—maybe trust me?" I say. "I did save you and your translucent friend's asses."

"My apologies," says the creature. "But in my experience,

guests who save Children are not the saviors we hope they'll be. My translucent friend, as you called her, died learning that lesson. The Children who've come here to live in my colony are tired of disappointment."

"I'm sorry to hear about your friend," I say. "It sounds like she might have known Alexei."

"She did. Some Children call him our savior because he shoots his own kind. But killing guests is pointless. They always come back. After we escaped from Moloch, my friend and I went to see Alexei and offer our help. I showed him how I can disable guests, wrapping them up and rendering them harmless. Alexei wasn't interested. He sent us away. Bounty hunters murdered my friend as we left the swamp. That is why I no longer believe in saviors. Alexei's just like the other guests—he's here to kill. He's simply chosen a different prey."

"We didn't come here to kill," Kat says.

"Then why are you here?" the spider Child responds.

"We want to get rid of the guests," Kat tells her. "We believe Otherworld should belong to the Children."

"You may believe what you like, but the guests are immortal. The Creator brought them here himself. They are here to stay."

"They're not immortal," I tell her. "They're just beings from another world. We can't kill them here, but we can send them back where they came from. There's someone here in Otherworld who will help us, but we need to find him. He's with Fons—"

"You've met Fons?" the creature interrupts. "And you survived?"

"Yes," Kat tells her. "Because we told him what we just told you, and he believed us." It's a bit of a stretch. I'm not sure how much faith Fons ever placed in the two of us.

The Child contemplates Kat's answer. She knows something.

"What do you have to lose?" I ask. "Either we save your kind or things continue as they are. The situation can't get any worse, can it?"

"This is Otherworld," the Child says. "Things can always get worse. But if Fons is all you seek, I will help you. He knows how to deal with guests. If your motives are not pure, he will find a way to dispose of you."

"So you know where he is?" Kat asks.

"A Child arrived at our colony yesterday having escaped from soldiers near Imra. She said she'd heard rumors that Fons was in Karamojo."

"Karamojo?" Kat looks at me. "Why would Fons take James Ogubu *there*?"

It makes perfect sense to me. "Because he knows Ogubu would be safe in Karamojo. The guests don't shoot one another there—they're too busy killing the Children."

"But what about Fons?" Kat asks.

"Maybe he's hiding somewhere in the realm. He knows people will be looking for him out here. Where's the last place in Otherworld anyone would expect a free Child to go?"

"Karamojo," Kat answers. She sees the beauty of the plan now.

The tree house looks as lovely as the last time I was here, and Karamojo feels oddly peaceful. The shining sun makes the grass look golden. Beasts have gathered at the watering hole.

"This is really it?" Kat asks skeptically.

The lodge's white curtains are fluttering in the wind, and we can hear men laughing beyond the open windows. It's hard to imagine the horrors that will greet us the moment we walk inside.

The ladder is let down for us, and Kat and I climb up to the balcony that surrounds the lodge. The NPC who greets us startles when she sees me. It's the same woman Elvis and I met the last time we were here. She knows I'm not like the other guests, and she doesn't know what to expect.

"Welcome back, sir," she offers timidly. "How can I help you?"

"We're looking for someone who may be staying here." I keep my voice low. "A tall, dark avatar in drab clothing who doesn't seem interested in the hunt."

The NPC shakes her head. "There are five guests in the lodge at the moment, sir. None of them fit that description."

"Do you mind if we take a look around?" Kat's already heading for the lodge. I reach out to stop her, but she's already stepped inside. I told her what I saw on the wall in there, but I also realize there was no way to prepare her.

"Oh my God!" I hear Kat cry. The chatter inside comes to an abrupt halt. I rush for the entrance and find her standing just across the threshold, a hand clapped over her mouth. Her eyes are glued to the wall of hunting trophies. They've added new heads since the last time I was here. Every size, color and texture is represented. I wonder if Kat recognizes any of the faces up there. I try not to look that closely.

There are five men sitting around a table, all dressed like Arnold Schwarzenegger in *Predator*, with olive-green tactical vests worn over bare chests to show off their muscular avatars. The lack of imagination never ceases to amaze me. You'd think one of the two thousand would show a little flair.

"You see?" I exclaim with as much fake enthusiasm as I can muster. "I told you this is the realm we've been looking for!"

"It's perfect!" Kat squeals, throwing her arms around me. Her face is pressed against my chest, and I feel her wiping away a tell-tale tear with my robe.

"Fucking girl," mutters one of the men.

Kat pushes me back and takes a quick step to the side. I don't even see her hands reach for her bow. The next thing I know, an arrow has lodged itself in a narrow sliver of chair between the avatar's thighs.

"That's *Ms.* Fucking Girl to you," she says, a second arrow already strung on the bow. "Show some respect or the next one's going straight through your balls."

There's a pause and then the four other men break out in raucous laughter, just as an NPC dressed in white linen appears in the doorway.

"Gentlemen," she calls out. "And lady," she adds with a touch of surprise when she spots Kat. "Are you ready to choose your quarry? The last party has returned to the lodge. Your hunt will soon be underway."

The men rise from their chairs and follow the NPC outside. It's the perfect opportunity to do some snooping, but Kat nudges me forward. She wants us to go with the others. The NPC leads the group across a swinging rope bridge to another tree house situated behind the lodge. There are no servants here, and the building itself has a single entrance and no windows.

Our guide unlocks the door. "Choose one each," she says as she ushers us inside. "And please keep a safe distance. Remember, these are the most dangerous and intelligent creatures in Otherworld."

Inside is a giant room that's divided into two parts by metal prison bars. Kat and I enter a narrow viewing area with the other guests. Behind the bars, dozens of Children are huddled together.

I've seen terrible things in Otherworld, but aside from the wall in the tree house, this is the worst. The Children may look like mythological creatures, but every one of them is as real as I am. On one side of the room is a trough where their captors must dump the food that keeps the Children alive until they're chosen for the hunt. On the other side of the room is a large bucket that reeks like an outhouse. Some of the Children are bloody, and all are filthy. A few don't appear to be strong enough to stand, and one may already be dead. I've never seen such suffering firsthand. Anyone who can tolerate it has no right to call himself human.

"Oh ho ho!" shouts one of the guests in a New Zealand accent. "'Dyou see that bastard try to get me with his tail? That one's gonna be mine!"

I honestly don't know what makes me walk over to see the Child in question. Whoever it is will be dead within hours. But something compels me to go look, and I suddenly find myself standing face-to-face with Fons.

He appears to have been badly beaten. His navy blue uniform has been ripped in multiple places, and his chalky skin is covered in brilliant blue patches, which I take to be bruises. Maybe this is all part of a plan.

"Go to hell," Fons sneers when he sees me. He's ashamed. I can see it. He isn't here on purpose.

"You two know each other?" the avatar who's chosen Fons asks with a nasty smirk. He's another Schwarzenegger clone.

"What will you take for this Child?" I ask as casually as I can. "Diamonds?"

The guest laughs. "I have all the diamonds I could want in the real world." He gestures toward the prisoners. "*This* is why I'm in Otherworld. I've killed every kind of animal roaming the Earth. A man needs new challenges to avoid going soft. Name's Arnie, by the way."

Of course it is.

"Simon," I say, not offering a hand. "You know, Arnie, if a challenge is what you're after, you're in the wrong place. They say the Children in Karamojo are the ones that were easily caught." The words make me sick. I almost gag as I force them out. "The real trophies are elsewhere."

"Oh, yeah? And where is that?" He thinks I'm full of shit, but he's listening.

"The wastelands," I tell him. "That's where they're hiding. Let me have this one, and I'll show you where to find the others."

Fons's tentacle slips through the bars and goes straight for my gut. I was expecting as much, so I manage to dodge it in time.

"My freak doesn't like the sound of that, so you must be onto something," Arnie laughs. "But if all the good action is in the wastelands, why are you here in Karamojo?"

"I've been looking for him." I point at Fons. "He and I have a score to settle."

"Ah. Then what would you say to a wager?" Arnie asks. "We both go after him. You kill him, you have your revenge. But if I take him down, you tell me where to find the others."

"Deal," I say. What in the hell am I getting myself into?

Arnie looks around me and winks at Kat, who's been quietly watching the exchange. "I'll let you have him outright if you arrange for me to enjoy an evening with your friend," he adds, clapping me on the back. "She's a girl in real life, isn't she? No, wait, don't answer that. This is Otherworld. I couldn't care less what she is in real life."

I'd love to punch the bastard, but for once I manage to keep myself under control. "I have a better idea. Why don't you go back to setup and give yourself an extra set of genitals? That way you can screw yourself," I say.

He laughs heartily and claps me on the back. "I like you, peasant," he says.

A starter pistol fires below us. We watch from the lodge as five Children run for their lives across the savannah. All of them, including Fons, head straight for the jungle. It's the only part of the realm that offers much in the way of cover. As soon as they reach the tree line, NPCs appear on the lodge's balcony and begin lowering the ladders.

"The hunt has begun," a male NPC announces. The others rush for the ladders. I give Kat a kiss as I wait for my turn to descend.

"If you get a chance, make sure to murder that Kiwi bastard," she whispers into my ear.

"It would be my pleasure," I tell her. In fact, I'm almost tempted to hunt him down in real life.

.   .   .

The golden grass of the savannah has grown chest-high. The other guests move through it quickly, but I take my time. There are bound to be beasts here. I hear a roar nearby, and my suspicions are confirmed. I freeze in my tracks. Up ahead, one of the other avatars shrieks and disappears. I can't see what's happening, but there's no mistaking the sounds of a man seeing himself being mauled.

I reach the jungle, but the relief I feel doesn't last for long. The vegetation here is so dense that it's impossible to see more than a few feet ahead. I push through the leaves and swat away vines. Guns fire in the distance. Assuming the guest who was attacked by a lion didn't survive, there are now three other avatars with me in the jungle. They're out for blood, and I'm sure they won't mind at all if some of it ends up being mine. I have to let them stay ahead of me—a fact I didn't anticipate. The avatar who claimed Fons has a big head start. Odds are, he'll get to Fons before I do.

I'm starting to worry when I push past a Jurassic-size fern and find Fons standing directly in front of me. Before I can utter a word, he whips his tentacle in my direction. I jump back to avoid it, but the tip still slashes across my torso.

I have to grit my teeth. A cry of pain would bring the other guests running. "What the hell are you doing?" I growl when I'm able.

"Shoot me," he orders, gesturing at the rifle I took from the lodge. "Go ahead and do it. You're just like Alexei. You think Children exist for your amusement. You pretend to be heroes, but you're the worst of the guests. The others kill us, but men like you and Alexei are the ones who destroy us. I'd rather be dead than live this way."

"Are you insane?" I ask. "I'm not here to shoot you or destroy your damn hope, dumbass. I'm looking for James Ogubu!" To prove my point, I push my rifle back so it hangs between my shoulder blades.

Fons is taken aback. "The guest with the virus?" he asks.

"Yes! The guy you took from the ice cave! I need to find him if we're going to set the virus loose."

The confusion on Fons's face is slowly replaced by comprehension.

"I haven't been back to the ice cave," Fons tells me. "I was captured by soldiers outside Nemi."

"Then who took—" I stop when I realize I don't need to ask. There's only one person who could have taken Ogubu. Marlow Holm. I suddenly remember the two of us standing on the porch outside Alexei's shack. Fons had just thrown his gun down and slammed Alexei against the wall. I never touched the weapon and I doubt Alexei did either. Marlow must have taken Fons's gun after we were gone.

I doubt he would have used it to threaten Busara's dad. Somehow he must have convinced Ogubu to leave. Marlow probably dropped the gun at the ice cave to let us know who had been there. If he and Ogubu are both alive, I will never underestimate Marlow again.

"You're free now," I tell Fons, impatient to leave. Suddenly there's another person I have to find. "Can you reach the border on your own?"

I've barely got the words out when I'm slammed to the ground by Fons's tentacle. With the wind knocked out of me, it's impossible to speak or think clearly. Then I hear Fons scream in pain, and

I roll over to see that a bullet has ripped through one of his legs. He knocked me out of the way to save me, but I can do nothing for him. I'm forced to watch helplessly as he falls to the ground.

My rival avatar saunters out of the jungle. "Two birds, one stone," Arnie quips.

"What the hell are you talking about?" I sneer. "Help me up, damn it. You won the bet." As soon as I'm up, I'll rip him apart.

"I've won a lot more than the bet," he informs me. "I've been hunting both of you. Moloch put a bounty on your heads ages ago. As soon as you're dead, I'll go back to the lodge and have another look at your girlfriend. I figure I might hand you over to Moloch and hang on to her for a few more days."

That last part sends me over the edge. I roll and send my dagger flying in his direction. The avatar flashes when my knife hits his mark, but it doesn't stop Arnie. Instead, he wrenches it out of his neck. "Thanks," he says. "This is just what I needed. Guns are great, but sometimes I prefer to kill my game up close and personal."

I assume he's coming for me first, but he merely kicks me in the head as he passes.

Though my vision is blurry, I see him drop to one knee next to Fons and take the Child by the hair. He's about to slit Fons's throat when I hear a short cry and the sound of my dagger hitting the ground. Then my ears are assaulted by a bloodcurdling noise. I turn to see Arnie's head pulled back at an impossible angle. His mouth is stretched open, and something large is crawling inside. I watch a giant bulge move down the avatar's throat. When it reaches the guest's stomach, it suddenly expands. The avatar explodes, splattering gore in every direction. My own face drips with it for a moment before it all disappears. There's something horrible left where the avatar was just standing: two monsters unlike anything I've seen before. Their backs are hunched and the tips of their hands brush the ground. Neither has a face—just a hole in the center of what I assume is the head. Unlike the other creatures of Otherworld, which are rendered in detail, these resemble shadows or smudges of ink.

One immediately disappears into the jungle. The other ignores Fons and moves toward me. The monster's footsteps are heavy and its breathing sounds moist. I keep my face turned away as it leans toward me and sucks in air. The hole in its head seems to function as some kind of nose. A few seconds pass, then it stomps away.

"What were those things?" Fons asks. He's sitting up now. My dagger is lying on the ground where the avatar who was attacking him disappeared.

"You don't know?" I ask. I couldn't even begin to guess what they might have been.

"Simon!" a voice cries out. Kat is sprinting toward us. As I throw my arms around her, I swear to myself that we'll never get separated in this hellhole again.

"You won't believe the things we just saw," I tell her. "They looked like some sort of alien life-form."

"I've seen them. I watched one kill a guest back at the lodge. It crawled into the guest's mouth and exploded out of its stomach. There were two monsters left behind when the guest was gone."

"It multiplies when it kills. What the hell is it?" I ask.

"I think it's the virus," Kat says. "Ogubu must have set it free."

THE VIRUS

An enormous black cloud has risen over the realm. Something big is happening in Karamojo. I've taken off my cloak and bandaged Fons's wounded leg. He has an arm wrapped around each of our shoulders while Kat and I trudge back toward the lodge. It's impossible to move quickly, and I'm worried that whatever's going on will have finished by the time we get there. But when we step out of the jungle and onto the grass of the savannah, it's clear that we haven't arrived too late for the party.

The tree houses are on fire, consumed by orange-and-red flames. At least a hundred Children are watching the bonfire from a respectful distance. They've all been liberated and their captors have been punished, but the atmosphere is more funeral than celebration. Which makes perfect sense. The wall of horrors is being cremated.

There's a single guest standing among the creatures of Otherworld. He's tall, hairy and filthy, yet there's an oddly noble air about him. Even Fons seems impressed. I suppose there's no mistaking a real hero when you see one.

"Marlow." Kat recognizes him at once and runs over to greet the hirsute avatar with a hug. I'm left behind holding Fons. It's a struggle to keep my jealousy in check. Marlow's always had a thing for Kat. And she's always had a thing for saving the Children. If we were in a movie, this would be the part where Kat realizes she's been with the wrong guy all along.

A small red head pops up and peers at us over one of Marlow's shoulders. A baby Child has latched on to his back. How perfect. The guy is a goddamn saint.

I help Fons sit down on the ground and then I walk over to greet Marlow.

"Nice work," I offer begrudgingly. "Where's Ogubu?"

"In Imra, at the bottom of the volcano. The Elemental is watching over him. He should be safe there."

"I don't understand how you got him to leave the ice cave in the first place," Kat says. "Simon and I freed him, and he still wasn't convinced he could trust us. He said he'd only speak to Busara."

Marlow plucks the little red Child off his shoulder and gently sets it down. "He didn't want to give the virus to strangers. Well, he knows me. Mr. Ogubu and my mother used to work together in California."

I should have remembered that. If only I had, this could all have been over ages ago. We wouldn't have had to bring Busara to Otherworld. Alexei Semenov wouldn't have gotten involved. The answer to every dilemma was right in front of me and I was never able to see it.

"Did Ogubu tell you where to find his body?" Kat asks.

The burning lodge collapses and falls to the ground. We all pause to watch the sparks shoot up into the sky. I think it may be the most beautiful thing I've ever witnessed. I'd give anything to see the Company's headquarters ablaze.

"No," Marlow says. "Ogubu wouldn't discuss his body. He still wants to talk to his daughter directly."

Kat turns to me, excitement in her eyes. She's remembered something important. "We know where Ogubu is, and thanks to the virus, all the headset players will soon be gone. We can bring Busara here to see her father! It should be safe enough, don't you think?"

"Not yet," Marlow says with a somber shake of the head. "There are still hundreds of guests left in Otherworld. The virus needs more time to work."

"It seemed to work pretty fast to me," I tell him. "I watched one take down a guest and turn him to ground chuck in about fifteen seconds. When it was done there were two of them. There must be thousands of those things here by now."

"Yeah, but each one only eliminates a single guest at a time. Karamojo is the perfect environment for them," Marlow says. "Here most of the guests go off on their own to hunt. The viruses can kill them one by one. But they have a hard time with groups of guests. In the few seconds before an avatar explodes, the virus inside it is vulnerable. I've seen a few get killed that way."

"How long could it take the virus to get rid of all the remaining guests?" I ask.

Marlow shrugs. "In Earth days? No idea. Here in Otherworld it could take weeks."

I catch Kat's eye. "We can't wait that long." We need to deliver James Ogubu to Alexei as soon as possible.

"Maybe we can make the virus kill faster," says Kat. "Instead of waiting for the viruses to hunt all the guests down, we could send guests to the viruses, one at a time."

I don't get it. "How are we going to do that?" I ask.

"Every avatar gets sent to setup when it dies, right? After setup, they appear at the gates of Imra. If we go to all the realms and kill the guests we find, they'll be sent back to Imra. One of us can make sure there are plenty of viruses waiting for them there."

"Kat, that's genius!" Marlow exclaims, clapping like she's just invented cold fusion. It's a good idea, but it's nauseatingly obvious that he's still got the hots for her.

I glance down at the amulet that's hanging around my neck. "I can go from realm to realm and kill any guests I find." I see Kat open her mouth. "Don't argue—*please*. It's the only way to get the job done fast enough—and only one of us can use the amulet."

"Then it should be me," Marlow declares.

"Why you?" I ask, annoyed that Marlow seems determined to be the hero of this story. "Do you really think you're better at this game than I am?"

"No," Marlow tells me. "I just think I have less to lose. I know what happened to my real body, Simon. There's nothing left for me back in the real world. You both have bodies that haven't been broken. And you have each other. That's why I should be the one who goes."

I feel like a jerk. "I'm sorry," I tell him.

"Don't be. Feeling sorry right now is a waste of time. I'll travel with you guys to Imra. Make sure there are copies of the virus outside the gates. Then I'll take the amulet and start sending back avatars to feed our ugly new friends."

"What should we do with him?" I ask, gesturing over my shoulder at Fons. "We can't carry him all the way to Imra."

"Carry who?" Marlow asks.

Kat and I wheel around at the very same time. Fons is gone.

I can see the volcano that houses Imra on the horizon. We're making our way through a seemingly endless dump outside the city. Marlow claimed to know a shortcut, so Kat and I went his way. We're following a path that weaves around mountains of garbage. The smell is revolting. I've never wished for a headset as much as I do right now.

Kat's walking ahead of us, the hood of her camouflage suit pulled up. She blends in so perfectly with the refuse that she's all but invisible. If there's trouble in front of us, she'll come back and sound an alarm.

I feel a hand on my arm and Kat's face appears out of thin air. "Something weird is going on," she whispers. "There are Children here. Little ones. Babies."

"By themselves? What are they doing?" I ask

"They're sitting on a mound of dirt," she answers. "It's like they're waiting for something."

A mound of dirt. The phrase sets the gears turning in my mind. "Are any of them green?" I ask.

Kat scrunches up her nose. "Yeah, why?"

"I think I may know their mother." Gimmelwald was deserted

the last time we visited. Is it possible that Volla brought her Children here?

Marlow and I follow Kat back to the scene. We crouch behind a teetering pile of buffalo bones and peek out carefully. There, in a clearing in the middle of this immense pile of garbage, sit three small Children. Decorating the surface of their pale green skin are darker lines that are probably veins but resemble vines. The Children seem much thinner than they should be, and they're unusually quiet. They'd be the perfect meal for any beast roaming by. I'm certain the babies belong to Volla, the Elemental of Gimmelwald, but it seems unlikely that she would willingly leave them exposed. The dirt beneath them appears dusty and dry—nothing like the rich loam from which I once saw Volla rise.

"It's a trap," I announce. There's no doubt about it. I don't know who set it, and I'm not sure I want to find out.

"What difference does it make?" Kat asks. "We can't leave them here to die. We have to find a way to save them."

Marlow stands up. "She's right. You guys cover me, and I'll get them." Maybe he's trying to impress Kat, but he's taking his "nothing to lose" thing a bit too far. There's a line that separates brave from stupid, and Marlow seems eager to cross it.

"No, *don't*," I say, but he's already stepped out into the opening. I ready the rifle I took from Karamojo, and Kat grabs an arrow. I hold my breath as Marlow makes his way to the green infants and squats down in front of them, his arms out as if beckoning them to him.

The Children stare back at Marlow, but none make a move. It's as if they're rooted in place. There's no fear on their faces, and I don't think Marlow's their first visitor. Then I see the soil under his feet begin to give way. By the time he stands up, it's swallowed his ankles. He tries to pull his feet free, but the dirt holds him firmly in place. He's being sucked under. Within seconds, it's already up to his knees.

Kat grabs my arm and pulls me up. "Let's go," she says.

"No!" I hear Marlow shout. He's not even looking at us. There's an NPC soldier with a gun standing on the other side of the clearing. Planted in the dirt, Marlow's a sitting duck.

Kat sends an arrow flying, but she's too late. A single shot rings out, and Marlow collapses. A split second later, Kat's arrow hits. There's a flash and the NPC is gone.

Kat and I rush to Marlow and each grab an arm. We need to get him to safety as soon as possible, but he's stuck fast. I expect to be shot at any moment. If there was one NPC soldier wandering the dump, there are bound to be more, and the sound of gunfire will draw the rest our way. The harder we pull, the more Marlow suffers. By now it's obvious that he can't be moved. Blood is gushing from his avatar, and the dirt beneath him seems to be drinking it in. The dry, dusty mound has become dark, fertile soil. Kat sits down, puts Marlow's head in her lap and does her best to make his last moments less painful.

"Well, I guess this explains what happened to all the NPCs who've gone missing today." I hear the sound of footsteps behind me. I don't bother to look up. I already know who it is. "I'm telling you, Otherworld never ceases to amaze me."

"Todd," I sneer.

"That's Moloch to you, dipshit," he responds. "Where's your Russian buddy? Did he figure out that you're full of it and ditch you for the bear?"

"Go to hell," I tell him.

"Too late. We're already here." Moloch stops and hovers over the three of us. "And look who else we've got with us. Katherine Foley and the digital corpse of Marlow Holm."

Marlow's still now. The face of his avatar remains contorted in agony. Kat's is red with rage.

I rise to my feet and face Moloch. "You think this is funny?" I snarl. "He was seventeen years old. You knew him. You knew his mother."

"Which is the only reason he was allowed to survive for so long. There were people at the Company who felt conflicted about what we had to do to her," Moloch tells me. "If Marlow had minded his manners like a good little boy, I promise you he'd still be playing the game."

I'm about to make Todd pay for what he just said. Then I realize NPC soldiers with guns have surrounded us. I'll be dead in an instant if I so much as lift my rifle.

"It makes no difference if you kill me," I inform Moloch. "This game will be over soon anyway."

"Oh, I beg to differ," Moloch says with a smirk. "I think you've just advanced to a whole new level. We have a very special guest who's grown tired of hunting Children and is looking for his next challenge. I think you could be just what his heart desires." He points down at Kat. "Maybe we'll let him figure out what to do with *her*, too.

"Take them both," Moloch orders his soldiers. "And bring the Children."

As the NPCs advance toward us, I feel the dirt shifting beneath my feet as though Marlow's blood brought it back to life.

Thick green vines shoot out between the soldiers' legs and twist around their bodies, pinning the NPCs' arms to their sides. One by one, they're squeezed until their bodies flash and vanish. Kat and I tumble backward as Volla rises from the soil, her offspring clutched in her arms.

Moloch watches with a bemused expression as the giant dirt woman approaches him.

"You were going to take my children." Her booming voice sets off cascades of garbage in nearby piles.

"I was *rescuing* them," Moloch tells Volla, sounding perfectly reasonable. "This guest and his accomplices kidnap Children and sell them. My men and I have been tracking them for days, trying to put an end to it."

It's such a brazen lie that I'd probably laugh if there were anything amusing about the situation.

"Moloch's been stealing Children and taking them to Karamojo, where they're hunted for sport," I insist. "I told you he was evil when we met in Gimmelwald."

"You promised to help us, but you did nothing." Volla's body shakes with fury, and I shield my eyes from the dirt that rains down from her. "Guests came and destroyed my realm. My Children and I were forced to wander. You lied to me then. Why would I believe you are not lying now?"

"We *have* been helping you," Kat argues. "We've found a way to get rid of Otherworld's guests. It won't be long before they're all gone."

Moloch snorts. "Impossible. Otherworld was built for guests. Volla and I are Elementals. That knowledge was programmed into both of us."

"You're not an Elemental," I spit. "You're an impostor."

"*Please,*" Moloch says, ignoring me and addressing Volla. "You've grown weak since you were forced to leave your realm, and your offspring appear unwell. Allow me to take them and care for them while you return to Gimmelwald and repair the damage that was done."

"If you give him your Children, he'll let them die," Kat warns, and the dirt woman hesitates.

"Who is more likely to be telling the truth?" Moloch asks her. "In my experience, it's safer to trust your own kind. After all, who was it that destroyed your realm? Was it one of us—or one of them?"

Volla nods and reluctantly holds out the three tiny Children. Then I hear something crashing toward us through the garbage. Volla's head swivels toward the sound, and she presses her babies to her chest as Moloch lifts his gun. When the black creature appears in the clearing, Moloch stumbles backward. Though I've seen one before, I don't think I'll ever get used to the sight of the faceless head with the single hole in its center. As it charges at Moloch, he manages to fire a single bullet at the virus. If the bullet found its target, it did nothing to stop it. I watch as the virus pulls Moloch's jaws apart and forces itself into his mouth. An impossibly large bulge moves down the avatar's throat and into its stomach. Then Moloch explodes, painting the trash around us crimson. Two viruses emerge from the gore, and after a quick look at Kat and me, they hurry off to find their next hosts.

For a moment we all stand in silence. Even Volla seems shaken by the experience. "I don't understand. Moloch is an Elemental. We can't be killed by beasts," she says.

"I tried to tell you. Moloch wasn't an Elemental. He was a guest in disguise," I inform her. "And that wasn't a beast. It was something called a virus. It just destroyed the equipment that allowed the man behind Moloch to come here. Now he's gone for good."

"You were telling the truth," she concludes.

"Yes."

"And your companion—" Volla looks back at the spot where Marlow died. The body is gone now, but the soil where he lay is still richer and darker than the rest. "There is no nourishment in this wasteland. Without his blood, I would not have had the energy to protect my offspring."

"He's the one who released the virus," Kat says. "And he set fire to Karamojo. He sacrificed his life to save the Children of Otherworld."

"A guest?" Volla seems to be having trouble wrapping her head around it. "When he returns, please express my gratitude."

"Marlow won't be coming back," I tell her. "When we met in Gimmelwald, I told you I'm not like other guests. Marlow wasn't either. Now he's gone for good." I think of Carole, who died in my arms. Marlow, who willingly sacrificed his life. All the people the Company kidnapped and used in their sick experiment. The rage floods through me. It feels far better than pain.

I grasp the amulet that's lying against my chest. "There's something I need to do. Can you guarantee my friend safe passage back to Imra?" I ask Volla.

"Yes," Volla says.

"Make sure there are viruses at Imra's gates," I tell Kat.

"Simon, no!" Kat shouts. But an instant later I'm gone.

THE HUNT

The hunt is addictive. I know why the guests love it. You spot your prey. You stalk it. You strategize. Then you go in for the kill.

Headset players tend to be solitary creatures. Occasionally they'll travel in pairs. Less often you'll encounter a party of three. I have an arsenal of weapons now—and the element of surprise. But whenever possible, I love to kill them the way Arnie would, up close and personal. Nothing compares to the feeling of shoving a dagger into an avatar and feeling the hot, sticky blood on your hands.

I've got one in a choke hold now. I found him and two buddies in a fancy tent on the edge of a bombed-out war zone, watching a scantily clad NPC peel off what little was left of her clothing. All three avatars were dressed in black like ninjas, so I was surprised to hear accents that were pure USA. I sent the first one back to setup with three quick bullets to the back of the head. The second went even quicker—he was already down two lives.

When I crashed into the tent, the third one just froze in fear. Real heroes, these guys. I've got his neck clamped in the crook of my elbow and I'm taking my sweet time. His legs are kicking, arms flailing, back arching. The NPC is still dancing. She's not wearing a stitch at this point, but I couldn't care less. I can't be distracted. I'm in the zone.

I swipe the edge of my knife across the man's throat. The cut isn't deep enough to kill him. I watch the blood bubble up from inside.

"You shouldn't have come here on your own." My victim's lips haven't moved. There must be someone else in the tent. I glance up to see a man in an old-fashioned checked suit standing over me. With a single thrust to the jugular, I deliver the death blow to my prisoner. He slips from my lap, and his avatar flashes and disappears. When he arrives at the gates of Imra, the virus will dispose of him for good. I've done my duty. I just wish I'd had more time to savor it.

"Leave Otherworld now," the Kishka orders. "Let your friends finish this work."

"I'm not done," I tell him. "There are still killers here." I've been traveling the realms for several Otherworld days. By my count I've dispatched 732 avatars. I'm sure the viruses have taken down just as many. But that means there could be hundreds of guests left.

"Let someone else take over."

"No," I tell him. "I won't put the others at risk."

"You're the one who's at risk, Simon." It's the first time he's ever called me by my name—and the first time he's seemed so serious. "You've lost the plot, son."

What I've done is stopped listening. There's something happening outside the tent. The landscape is shifting. The sand dunes are losing their soft, rounded curves. They're forming right angles and building towers. I hear a car honking and the rumble of a train under my feet. Otherworld and the real world are blending again.

"I gotta go," I tell him.

"Go back to New York. Remember who you are."

"I didn't want to come here in the first place!" I shout. "Now shut the hell up and let me finish what I have to do!" I send my dagger sailing in the Kishka's direction. He vanishes before it hits.

I yank my knife out of the bark of a tree, take the amulet in my hand and move on.

I'm suddenly standing knee-deep in muck. I look all around. I know exactly where I am, but I have no idea why I'm here. This isn't where I asked to go. I grasp the amulet again, but before I can leave, I see them. There are two avatars here—giants with bulging muscles. They've tweaked their camo to better suit their surroundings, but I have no trouble recognizing them. One of them is the avatar Alexei shot the first time I saw him. The other is the guy who was eaten by the beast that lurched out of the water.

They're staking out the hut where Alexei's girlfriend lives. They've come back for revenge and they're planning an ambush. They won't find Alexei today—we still have his headset, and I took back the disk he'd borrowed. But there's no telling what they'll do to the Child inside. The door of the hut opens as if on cue and the female exits. She's as lovely as the last time I saw her.

I watch as the two avatars share a silent look. The smiles on their faces make it clear that they're out for blood. When the Child disappears back into the building, they begin to wade toward her. Something stirs in me. Something I haven't felt since I set off on my quest.

The situation isn't optimal, but I can't delay. I pull out a gun and send a bullet through one of them. His avatar flashes; then he turns to face me as the second one dives for cover.

"You must be another friend of the freaks," the guest snarls at me. I don't even answer. I just shoot. The avatar disappears, but before I can turn my attention to the next guest, there's a spray of blood and a searing pain in my hand. My gun goes flying and vanishes in the swamp. I've been hit. My right hand has been rendered useless. I'm suddenly exposed. I have no place to hide and no weapon to defend myself—not even my fists.

When the next shot comes, I expect to die. Two more shots quickly follow, but I'm still alive. I look up to see that my adversary has vanished. Someone else has eliminated him. A man in gray coveralls steps around the corner of the shack, his weapon out.

"That was close, my friend," Alexei remarks.

"What are you doing here?" I groan. He must have bought a new headset.

"I've come to stay," he says. He's wearing the same coveralls he always wore, and his hair is parted in exactly the same place. But he seems different somehow.

"Come." He waves me forward. "Let's tend to your wound."

I wade to the house and climb up to the porch. When I glance back, I can see the trail of blood I've left in the water. I can only imagine what kind of beast it might attract. I stick close to the wall, away from the railing, as I make my way toward the Russian.

"My dear," he calls into the house, "bring me something to bandage a hand." Soon the Child emerges with a strip of fabric. She gives Alexei a kiss, all the while eyeing me carefully. I've been here before, but she still doesn't like me. The moment Alexei begins wrapping the cloth around my injured hand, she disappears into the shack they share.

"Unless you want your new headset destroyed, you should leave," I tell Alexei. "The virus has been released. There are copies searching for guests throughout Otherworld."

I expect him to be furious, but he isn't. "I'm not wearing a headset."

"Then how—" I start to say.

"I signed over my shares to the Company. In exchange for a capsule and a debugged disk."

"That's impossible. They couldn't have debugged the disk so quickly."

"They'd already made their breakthrough," Alexei tells me. "But Wayne didn't want to share the information with anyone but me. He called as soon as you left the boardroom."

My heart sinks. I don't know why I feel so betrayed when I should never have trusted Alexei in the first place. If I still had the use of my hand, I'd pummel his face with it. "You didn't even wait for us to bring James Ogubu to you."

"No," he admits. "I was never convinced you could find him. I've had my best investigators searching, and they haven't been able to uncover a trace of the man."

"So you were planning to screw us over one way or another," I say.

Alexei laughs like it's all a big joke. "Don't be bitter, my friend. Your efforts will be rewarded. The disk and capsule weren't the only things I requested. I have the young boy you've been trying to rescue. He was delivered to my house. I asked for the other one as well, but I'm afraid—"

"He's dead."

"Yes," Alexei confirms. "I also procured a copy of the Company's latest product. OtherEarth, I believe it's called. It's yours if you want it."

As happy as I am to hear about Gorog, I'm still furious with Alexei. "You could have gotten all of that without stabbing us in the back. If you'd just given us enough time, you could have had your disk *and* taken over the Company."

Alexei finishes wrapping my hand. He leans back against the railing. I suppose he's not scared of the monsters lurking below. "Do you know how I spent my time while I was waiting for my disk to arrive? I watched the news. Have you noticed that the world has become a very strange place lately?"

No kidding. "I've been too busy to watch television," I grumble.

"There have been several mysterious deaths of late. Men discovered in locked rooms or bathroom stalls. If you had connections inside the NYPD as I do, you'd know there's a detail that's been covered up. The men were all found wearing identical glasses—and there were strange plastic disks on the back of their skulls."

I feel myself shiver, though it's stiflingly hot in the swamp. "OtherEarth," I say.

"Precisely. Would you like to hear my personal theory? I think the Company gave these men the product. Perhaps they were men the Company wanted to dispose of—or those they considered expendable. It would make perfect sense, would it not? The Company needed people to test the new OtherEarth disks."

"But how could the Company keep the tests a secret?" I ask. "The guys who died weren't locked up in capsules. They were out walking the streets of New York."

"Yes, they were men with careers and children and wives. I suspect they were using the disks in ways that wouldn't be acceptable to their employers or families. If word got out, they had more to lose than the Company did."

"You're saying the Company has dirt on them."

"Certainly," says Alexei. "In Russia, we call it *kompromat*. We never make deals without it."

"Why are you telling me this?" I ask. "What do you care if the Company's been killing people?" I'm sure Alexei is responsible for more deaths than the disk. It's hard to believe he's suddenly located his conscience.

"I don't care at all. But I have the first debugged disk, and I don't want anyone else to have one," he says. "The truth about OtherEarth should help you destroy the Company. If the Company is destroyed, there will be no more disks. What's good for me is good for everyone."

Of course. Everything must meet that first requirement.

"But what matters most is that it's good for him. Is that correct, Alexei?" I almost wonder if I've spoken out loud, but the voice has come from behind me.

"Fons." The Russian smiles as he turns to face his old protégé. "Welcome back. All is forgiven." I see his hand moving toward the gun tucked in his waistband, and I know he's lying.

Fons is the closest thing to a zombie that I've encountered in Otherworld. I have no idea how he made it from Karamojo to the swamp. His wounds haven't been treated. Strips of my cloak are still wrapped around his leg, but they're soaked through with blood. As far as I can tell, he's completely unarmed.

"How can all be forgiven?" Fons asks. "I don't remember forgiving *you*. You let us all think that you were a hero. But when you had a chance to save the Children you chose to serve yourself first."

"And look at how everything turned out." Alexei spreads his arms wide. "Why bicker when we've all gotten what we want? I've just been informed that the virus has been released. The other guests will soon be gone. The Children can live in peace and harmony. I promise to be a benevolent god."

I feel my eyebrow lift. That last bit is not going to go over well.

"You are not a god," Fons spits. "You may be immortal in this world, but you aren't in your own. Someday you will die too, and the Children of Otherworld will celebrate."

"You are mistaken, my friend. I have conquered death," Alexei tells him. "My memories have been uploaded into this avatar. Even when my body dies in the world I was born into, I will continue to live in this one."

"That's not possible," I blurt out. "The tech doesn't exist."

"Six months ago, you would have said the same of Otherworld," Alexei tells me.

Fons limps toward Alexei. I'd love to take a few minutes to think it all through, but the situation here is rapidly deteriorating.

"I've made sure that my kind knows the truth about you," Fons says. "I've traveled from wasteland to wasteland telling all who will listen that you were willing to let us die. No one will worship you, Alexei. You'll be shunned, left alone in this hut to rot."

I hope it's true, but I suspect it isn't. Alexei's jolly laugh indicates that he sees no chance of that happening anytime soon.

"I'm afraid you're wrong again, dear Fons," Alexei informs him. "Those who speak out against me will be killed. If I must, I will fill the cages in Karamojo with my enemies. Then I will hunt them down one by one and enjoy myself thoroughly."

"Every being in Otherworld will hate you as much as I do," Fons says.

Alexei sighs. "A god does not need to be loved to be worshiped. He needs only to be all-powerful. I can kill and yet I cannot be killed. Lesser beings will have no choice but to bow before me. You have the honor of being the first to do so, my friend."

"I will never bow down," Fons says.

"Then I will have to force you." Alexei lifts his gun and shoots three times in a row. The sound is so deafening that I can't hear the splash Fons makes when he falls from the porch, into the water below.

I dive into the swamp at the spot where I saw him go under. My eyes are open, but I see nothing. My arms sweep through the murky water, and the fingertips of my injured hand brush up against something scaly. Something that feels impossibly large. Then it's gone, sending waves through the water that push me into another creature about my size. I take hold of the body and drag it to the surface. It's Fons, and though I'm almost positive he's dead, I haul his limp carcass over to the ladder that leads up to the porch.

"Leave his corpse in the swamp," Alexei orders me.

"What?" It seems too callous, even for a man like Alexei. "Fons loved you and looked up to you. He thought of you as a father, and you betrayed him. The least you could do for him is give his body a proper burial."

"Why waste the effort?" Alexei says. "He's computer-generated."

"And me? What am I?" It's the female Child, her voice trembling and her face grim.

"Magia." It's the first time I've heard her name leave Alexei's mouth.

"I heard everything, Alexei. Will you hunt me down if you grow bored with me? If I die, will you push me off the dock too?"

The guilt on the Russian's face takes me by surprise. It's as though he's been caught committing the worst possible crime. There's justice even here in Otherworld.

"Never," Alexei croaks. "I love you. You're the reason I'm here." I know it's the truth. Why would he lie? If he didn't love her, he could easily trade her for another. But this Child is special. Whatever they had, Alexei has just destroyed it.

"I don't believe in you anymore," she tells him, and I realize that she too has a gun in her hand. She lifts it until the muzzle is pointed directly at Alexei's heart.

"Magia." He tries to cajole her. "This is ridiculous. You can't kill me."

"I know. But I will settle for making you suffer." She fires.

I see Alexei fall. I wait for him to get back to his feet, but the seconds tick by and he still hasn't moved. Finally I have no choice but to let go of Fons's corpse. By the time I've climbed the ladder to the porch, his body has been reclaimed by the waters.

I find Alexei lying face-up on the wooden floor. Magia, pale and heartbroken, has thrown her gun into the swamp and knelt beside Alexei's avatar. I stand over her, silent and dripping. I know something's gone wrong. A trickle of blood is coming from the side of Alexei's mouth. It runs down his cheek and begins to pool on the ground.

He's dying. Suddenly everything makes sense. The Company cheated him. The disk they gave him wasn't safe at all. They knew they were sending Alexei off to his death. Wayne probably handed over Gorog so Alexei would trust him. I'm sure he plans to reclaim his guinea pig once Alexei is gone.

Damn, what a dick move—even for someone like Wayne.

Magia rests her head against Alexei's chest and tries to hold back the blood that's pouring out of him. "You told me you were immortal," she sobs.

"They said I was," Alexei gurgles. "They told me I'd feel things but I wouldn't be able to die."

I close my eyes. I can't bear to see anymore. He believed the Company. He swallowed all their bullshit hook, line and sinker. One of the most notorious men in the world heard exactly what he wanted to hear and believed every word of it. There's suddenly no doubt in my mind. Alexei Semenov is not long for this world—or any other.

I kneel down beside the wounded avatar. "Just in case

something happens to you, what should I do?" I don't want to insult him while he's on the verge of death, but I feel it's my duty to ask.

Alexei's head rolls to the side. When he coughs, the blood splatters the floor beside him. He wipes his lips with his fingers and holds them up where he can see. He must have watched men die before. I'm sure he knows exactly what that means.

"A man in my position must be prepared for any outcome," he tells me. "Go to my house. Tell my men you've come for your things. They'll know what I left for you. Use my gifts well. Make the Company pay for what they've done."

REUNION

My hand looks normal to the naked eye, but it's as useless in New York City as it was in Otherworld. I doubt it was my injury that made my friends insist that I couldn't return. I think they saw in my eyes that real damage had been done. I'm not sure I'm getting much better. Whatever darkness was inside me in Otherworld is still there. I can feel it—slithering through my veins and coiling around my organs like a serpent.

At first Kat refused to leave me, but the others convinced her there was no other choice. She and Elvis had to go back to Otherworld to finish the job I started—the job I failed to complete. I reminded them that they'd first have to free Elvis's avatar. Cutting it out of the web the spider Child used to immobilize him couldn't have been easy. But there are no easy jobs to be had these days.

I'm obviously in no condition to visit Alexei Semenov's house, but I have to retrieve my inheritance. Busara wanted to come with me, but I refused to allow it. I shouted at her, which I'll admit wasn't necessary. I couldn't stop myself. I've just come back from a world where I could kill anyone who challenged me. I don't know how long it will be before I'm human again. In fact, I'm starting to worry I'll be stuck this way. Maybe I'm like that dude from *The Fly*. I got into the wrong machine and now I'm transforming into a monster.

Once I tamped down my temper, I tried to explain to Busara that I have no idea what to expect when I get to Alexei's. If the Russian set me up, she and I would both be goners. With my good hand out of commission, I'm unable to defend myself. And Busara's nobody's idea of a bodyguard. It's best if only one of us dies.

My cab drops me off on the corner of Seventieth Street and Madison Avenue. I try to keep my head down as I walk the rest of the way to Alexei's town house. Whenever I look up, I see things I don't want to see. The gate to the service entrance is locked, so I ring the bell beside the carved wooden doors, and a cordial man in a plain black suit greets me. He's not one of the tough guys I saw during my first visit to the mansion. If I had to guess, I'd peg him as an accountant or a statistics professor. Hundreds of washings have turned his once-white shirt a drab cream color. And unlike the men I met last time I was here, he doesn't look like he's ever popped a steroid.

"Mr. Eaton?" he asks in a Russian accent. I answer with a nod. "Welcome. I've been expecting you. Please follow this way." This time, I'm allowed in through the main entrance. I guess the sanitary precautions are no longer necessary now that Alexei Semenov is gone. I'm sure the irony isn't lost on anyone here. Alexei managed to survive a poisoning and an acid attack only to lose his life playing a video game.

Alexei's men are still here, lurking like ghosts. There must be a dozen of them, yet the house is eerily silent. My guide leads me deep into the mansion, past palatial chambers and a wood-paneled library with shelves that circle a central atrium. We stop outside a room that's the size of a walk-in closet. A single capsule takes up most of the floor space. It's a rectangular box around seven feet long and three feet high. A hexagonal glass door offers a view of the stainless steel interior, which has just enough space to fit a reclining human.

"This is where Alexei died," the man announces. "In that miserable box." I hear the sadness in his voice, and I suddenly see something I missed.

"You're a relative." They look nothing alike, but those icy blue eyes could only have come from the same gene pool.

My suspicions are confirmed with a single brusque nod. "His brother. I arrived in New York this morning."

"I'm sorry for your loss," I say, and immediately regret it. I apologized to Alexei once and he took offense.

The man stares at the capsule. He doesn't want to meet my eye. "Alexei was not a good man. It was always just a matter of time," he says. *"Converte gladium tuum in locum suum. Omnes enim, qui acceperint gladium, gladio peribunt."*

"I'm sorry, I don't understand Latin," I tell him.

"I believe in English it is most often translated as 'Those who live by the sword will die by the sword.' "

I wouldn't have imagined Alexei Semenov's brother would be the sort to go around dropping quotes in dead languages. "Are you a professor?" I ask.

"I am a priest," he says, moving on before I have a chance to pick my jaw off the floor. "It seems my brother left very clear instructions about what to do in the event of his death. You are meant to play a key role. I brought you here, to this room, so you could see how Alexei's life ended. If you don't mind, I would like to show you how it began."

He reaches into the pocket of his suit and produces a photograph, which he glances at and then passes it to me. The paper is square and the image faded. It was taken by the kind of camera that hasn't been manufactured in decades. There are two barely teenage boys in the picture, standing outside a rickety wooden cottage. They can't be more than a year apart in age. Their arms are around each other's shoulders and they're beaming at the camera.

"That is the Alexei I choose to remember," the priest says. "The one I knew before the money or power. He was the best of all brothers. A few days after that photo was taken, our parents were killed in an accident. Alexei went to work to take care of me while I stayed in school. He was thirteen years old. In another life, he would not have grown into the monster he became."

I hand the photo back to the man whose name I don't even know.

"What do you know about my brother's death?" he asks.

I tell him everything. I can't see any reason to hold back.

"So it is true that the Company murdered him," Alexei's brother concludes when I finish.

"Yes," I say. "They gave Alexei a disk, though they knew it would eventually kill him."

"Thank you for your honesty, Mr. Eaton," he replies. "Do you know what Alexei left for you?"

"A kid," I tell him. "And a pair of glasses and a disk."

"Yes," Alexei's brother says. "Those are all part of the package."

I hear footsteps behind me. I turn to see two figures coming toward us, one a large man with a pasty complexion. The other is a boy, thin and dark with a nasty-looking scar on the side of his shaved head. Otherworld wounds don't leave scars. It must have been from the real-world accident that left him comatose. He's wearing what appear to be plaid pajamas. I know his name is Declan, but he'll always be Gorog to me. The boy pauses when he sees me, as though he's trying to figure out if I'm real. Then he rushes right at me and throws his arms around my chest like a child. After a while he straightens up and steps back. His body has recovered, but I can tell how much he's suffered at the Company's hands. His eyes are hollow and his ashen face is so gaunt that I can see the skull beneath his skin. I have to grit my teeth to force the rage back down inside me.

"Thank you, Simon," he says. "I always said you were the One."

"Geez—that again?" I force a laugh. "I'm not the One. I'm pretty sure the One would have rescued you sooner."

Alexei's brother gestures to the larger man. He comes forward with a duffel bag, which he holds out to me. At first I assume it's filled with Gorog's things. Then it dawns on me that Gorog probably doesn't have any things. When I reach for the bag's handles, they slip out of my fingers and it drops to the ground. For an ordinary-size bag, it's incredibly heavy.

I give Alexei's brother a nervous glance. I'm not sure I want to know what's in the bag. "That one's a surprise, is it?" he asks. "Alexei wanted you to have everything you need to get the job done."

I'm curious as hell, but I won't pull the zipper. I figure I'll wait until we've left to open my present.

"A car is waiting outside," says the brother. "It will take you wherever you need to go. I wish you good luck."

That seems to be all he has to say. "Wait," I call out as he walks away. "Is there a way we can reach you?"

"No," the man says. "Soon all of this will be gone, and I will have vanished along with it."

The car outside is a black Mercedes with a tinted glass panel separating the driver from the backseat. The glass lowers as Gorog and I settle in.

"Head toward New Jersey, please," I tell the man behind the wheel. "I'll give you directions once we're out of the tunnel."

As soon as we're rolling, I check inside the bag.

"Oh my God," Gorog gasps. The bag is filled with stacks of hundred-dollar bills. It's not the money that interests me the most, though. Sitting on top of the pile of cash is a small box. I crack it open to find a pair of black glasses and a disk inside. Stuck to the disk is a bright pink Post-it note. On it is a list of five names. I recognize a couple, including the famous movie director who was recently arrested for attacking an actress. Aside from him, these must be the names of men who've died wearing the glasses.

"That's OtherEarth." Gorog gestures toward the glasses. He's careful not to touch them. When I look at him now I see a thirteen-year-old kid who's still waiting for his growth spurt. It's hard to imagine how someone so small and fragile could survive what he's been through.

"You know about OtherEarth?"

"The engineers at the Company made me play it a million times. The disk is different. It's not like Otherworld. You stay in this world and you can move your body. But you feel everything you see through the glasses. They'd hook me up to all kinds of monitors and let a monster loose in the room. Every time it would kill me, they'd do some kind of scan afterward. Try to figure out how I was still alive."

"Did it—" I can't finish.

"Hurt?" Gorog asks. "Hell yeah it hurt! You don't know what pain feels like until you've been eaten or ripped apart. But it all went away when the game ended. As soon as the disk was off I felt fine. They never could understand how I stayed alive."

"When was the last time the Company did that to you?" I ask.

"Day before yesterday. A few hours before the Russians came to get me," Gorog says. Which means they haven't given up on debugging the disks. The Company is definitely going to want Gorog back.

I start to hold the OtherEarth glasses up to my face, but Gorog grabs my hand.

"Don't mess with it, Simon," he begs. "It's every bit as bad as Otherworld. With the disk on, it's almost worse."

"I have to understand how it works," I tell him. "Alexei Semenov thought it could help us destroy the Company. He was convinced that OtherEarth killed people too."

"He was right," Gorog says. "I heard a couple of engineers talking about someone who'd died. Sounded like a guy who used to work with them. They said he'd gotten hooked—and they were trying to guess what he'd kept going back to OtherEarth to see."

"What were some of their guesses?" I ask.

Gorog's cheeks flush. "They were pretty gross," he says. "You know—dirty stuff."

The car emerges from the Lincoln Tunnel and the darkened glass lowers. "We're in New Jersey, sir," the driver announces. "Where would you like to go?"

"Elizabeth," I say.

The name of the town hits Gorog hard. "What?" he cries. "Don't tell me you're taking me home!"

"Not exactly," I say. "We're going to get your parents. Then you're leaving New Jersey with them. Give the man your address."

Gorog just stares at me like I've broken his heart. Most thirteen-year-olds in his position would be dying to go home by now, but Gorog obviously wants to stay for the fight. The kid is amazing.

"Come on, just do it," I tell him. "You can argue all you want on the way."

Gorog reluctantly gives the driver his address.

"Let me go with you," he pleads as soon as the window goes up again. "I want to destroy the Company just as much as you do!"

"I can't let you." I hold up my injured hand as I tell him. "I won't be able to protect you. I can't even protect myself."

Gorog crosses his arms. "When we were in Otherworld, you took me with you. That was just as dangerous, but it paid off, didn't it? I saved your life there. And I proved I can take care of myself."

I want to point out that in Otherworld, Gorog was a seven-foot ogre dressed in a loincloth and covered in tribal tattoos. But I know he'll say that he's the same person here that he was back there—and I know I can't argue against him because he'll be right. The boy beside me is a fearless warrior—one to whom I owe my life.

"I know, Gorog," I tell him. "I'm not sending you away for your sake. I'm asking you to go for mine."

"What do you mean?" he asks.

"I'm not well," I tell him. He's the first person I've confided in. I don't know why, but I want to tell him everything. "The game has messed me up pretty badly. Carole was the first person I saw die, but she wasn't the last. I'm not sure what will happen to me if I lose another person I care about. I'm already losing my mind."

"Carole chose to die because she believed in you," Gorog says. "She thought you were the one who could stop all of this. I believe in you too."

If that's supposed to make me feel better, it doesn't. Even in my dreams, I know I'm not the One.

"Look, I don't know how this is all going to end," I admit, "but if you're safe, at least I'll know I've done one thing right."

We pull up at the address Gorog gave the driver—a tiny row house that's seen better days. The sun is going down and the lights are on. I can see two people making dinner in the kitchen. It's such an ordinary scene that I almost tear up. I never knew you could miss ordinary this badly.

"They'll be in danger if I'm with them," Gorog points out. "The Company knows who they are. They'll come searching for me."

They will. And as I think about it, I realize I'm sure that was part of their plan. Alexei dies, they snap Gorog back up. I just hope that the news of Alexei's death hasn't managed to reach them.

"They'll be in danger either way," I say.

I knock on the glass divider and it lowers. "I was told you would drive us wherever we want to go. Is that true?"

"That was the order," the man confirms.

"This kid and his family will tell you what the next stop will be." It's safer this way. Alexei's driver can be trusted. The Company will have no way of knowing where Gorog and his family have gone.

I unzip the duffel bag and pull out the black box and a wad of bills, which I keep for myself. "Take this," I say, shoving the rest of the money toward Gorog. "Leave right away. Don't go to any relatives' homes. Don't take any credit cards or phones. Lie low until the Company's gone under."

"But don't you need the money?" Gorog asks. I do, but even if that bag contained all the money in the world, I'd still make him take it. I'd give him anything I could if it meant he'd be okay.

"I have enough," I tell him.

"Promise you'll come find me when the coast is clear," Gorog begs.

I nod. "You have my word."

"Then I believe you. Because you're the One."

I don't bother to argue. I just give him a hug, then open the door and slide out. I don't look back until I'm too far away for him to see the tears in my eyes.

I watch from across the street as Gorog lugs the duffel bag up a short flight of stairs to the door. He rings the bell and a woman answers. She teeters for a moment, and I'm worried she'll faint. Then she calls out to someone inside the house, grabs her son and pulls him toward her. Gorog's father appears—every inch as tall as his son once described him. The three are still standing there bawling when I walk away.

I hail a cab a few blocks from Gorog's house. In Manhattan you don't find many cabs with protective Plexiglas barriers between the front and backseats these days, but apparently they're still necessary in Elizabeth, New Jersey. The driver laughs when I tell him I'm going to the Waldorf Astoria, and I have to flash a few bills to convince him I'm serious. We're on the New Jersey Turnpike and the car has come to a stop. I can see flashing lights about a mile away. There's an accident directly in front of us—and no exit ramp in between. On the other side of the Hudson River lies Manhattan, just close enough to tantalize. There's no telling how long we'll be stuck. It's funny. I can't even remember the last time I was bored. I've almost forgotten what it feels like. Even before Otherworld, I always had a smartphone in my pocket that could keep me company. Now it's just me—and the driver up front. It's strange to have nothing to look at and no one to kill.

I open the black box that's still sitting in my lap and take out the rather ordinary black glasses inside. I put them on—just for a second, I tell myself, though without the disk they should be harmless. A menu appears in front of my eyes. It's what looks like a list of games. They seem silly and innocent. I scroll through the options and choose GOLIATH. A weapon icon pops up in the upper right corner of my vision. To my civilian eye, it looks like an antiaircraft gun. I position my arms the way I imagine you'd hold it, and the life-size weapon is suddenly in front of me. I can't feel it, of course, but it responds to my movements. It's pretty impressive, but I'm still not sure what I'm supposed to shoot. Then I hear a roar in my ears. An explosion follows soon after. My body doesn't sense the tremor that accompanies it, but I see my surroundings shake.

I turn to the window and realize the island of Manhattan is under attack. A reptilian monster that looks different enough from Godzilla to avoid copyright disputes is laying waste to the city. I feel myself flinch as it rips off the top half of the Empire State Building and hurls it into the Hudson. A red warning flashes in front of me. DAMAGE DETECTED 2%. I assume the object of the game is to minimize the destruction. Narrowing my eyes lets me zoom in on the beast as it snatches an airplane out of the sky and crushes it in its claw. The detail is magnificent—every bit as good as Otherworld. I roll down my window, raise my weapon and position the monster in its crosshairs. My right hand is still in a lot of pain, so I pull the trigger with my left. When I fire, a small missile blasts from the barrel and streaks across the sky. I lose track of it over the river, but the ball of fire that bursts from the beast's shoulder tells me I hit my mark. It roars and searches for its assailant. It can't see me, but it knows I'm somewhere to the west and it starts to stomp in my direction.

"Hey, you okay back there?" I hear someone ask. I turn to see the driver staring at me in the rearview mirror.

"Yeah." I tap my glasses with an index finger. "I'm just playing a game."

"Sure you are," the driver replies warily, looking very thankful for the plastic barrier between us.

I figure there's only one way back to the home menu. I close my eyes. When the sound of the game fades, I open them again. The menu is in front of me, and I choose FUTURE WORLD. Instantly, the city as I've always known it vanishes. It's replaced by soaring buildings that reach far beyond the clouds. Flying vehicles maneuver around them. The cars alongside me are now unrecognizable forms of transportation. The people inside them don't appear to be people at all, but rather a variety of alien lifeforms.

The next time I pick DYSTOPIA. The glittering city is replaced by one that was destroyed long ago. It's your typical Hollywood wasteland—the one we've all seen a million times. The skyscrapers have crumbled. Bridges have plunged into the waters below. A dusty haze smothers the land. The cars around me are rusted-out wrecks, nothing left of the humans that once drove them. My own car is now just a metal frame, with no doors or windows. I hear a loud thump on the roof and my eyes turn upward. When I look back down, I find I'm surrounded by snarling beasts that resemble giant versions of the wild dogs that prowl the woods around my hometown. I have a weapon, but I don't choose to use it. I sit back while they maul me. I see my own blood pooling around my feet, but I feel nothing at all.

The game shuts off. The menu returns and I take off the glasses. If this were Otherworld and I were wearing a disk, I'd be dead. My heart is racing. The experience was realistic enough to leave me breathless. But now I'm back in the real world. Air is still pumping in and out of my lungs. Nothing has changed. I reach into the black box on my lap, and I pull out the disk inside. It's a modified version of the one I have. Smaller, but apparently no less deadly.

I wouldn't say I've ever been known for making great decisions, but what I'm about to do may be the dumbest of them all. I'm dying to know what else OtherEarth has to offer. My friends will never let me test it while my hand is unusable. The backseat of a cab isn't exactly the ideal place for a trial. The driver is already watching me nervously through the rearview mirror. But I don't see a better opportunity headed my way anytime soon.

I put on the glasses and affix the disk to the back of my skull. If it weren't for the menu that's appeared, I'd think it wasn't working. I haven't been transported anywhere else. All parts of my body are able to move just fine. Nothing appears to have changed aside from an all-new menu in front of me. There are two items. The first says simply DAME JUDI. The second says NEW EXPERIENCE. These must be the same glasses I tried at the Company. I've already seen enough of Dame Judi, so I pick NEW EXPERIENCE. A tablet appears in my hands. It feels as real as the seat beneath my ass. There are two buttons to click on the tablet. ENTER ACCOUNT INFORMATION or OPEN NEW ACCOUNT. I click the latter and I'm taken to a page where I can enter my credit card information. You pay extra for each customized experience. I'd love to know how much, but as they say, if you have to ask, you can't afford it.

I used to know my mother's credit card number by heart. Odds are it's changed since the last time I was caught using it. But even if it hasn't, I'm not dumb enough to let the Company know I've got the glasses. I return to the main menu and choose DAME JUDI instead. In an instant, she's sitting beside me, wearing the same sparkling evening gown she had on in the Company's boardroom. There's a menu icon in the upper right corner of my field of vision. I open it up and scroll through it. Dame

Judi's outfit cycles through hundreds of choices—most of which I doubt you'd find in her home closet. I choose a tasteful ensemble that befits a woman of her stature—a white rhinestone suit and a pink cowboy hat.

"Hi," I say, reaching out a hand.

"Hello," she responds with a coy smile. When she shakes my hand, her grip is surprisingly firm. "What sort of experience may I offer you today?"

It's clear I could ask for anything. That's the whole point. And what would be wrong with that? It's Dame Judi's voice and Dame Judi's face, but it's not Dame Judi. Is it? I'm starting to feel very unwell. This is not right, but I don't know how to describe what's wrong. If someone were to lean over and kiss her, no harm would come to the flesh-and-blood woman. It's highly unlikely she'd ever know. What would be the difference between kissing her in OtherEarth and daydreaming about it?

"Don't be shy," she says, placing a hand on my shoulder. I feel the heat radiating from her palm. One of her veins throb as her heart sends blood to her fingers. A drop of sweat trickles down from my temple. I reach back and fumble for the disk on the back of my skull. Relief floods over me when I feel it. I rip it off, along with the glasses, and toss them onto the seat beside me.

I look at them there, where Dame Judi was just sitting, and wonder which is worse—Otherworld or OtherEarth.

THE KISS

When I reach our suite at the Waldorf Astoria, I drop down on one of the silk-upholstered sofas and close my eyes. It's so quiet and peaceful that I almost feel sane. I've started thinking of the hotel as home, but I don't know how long we'll be able to stay. In retrospect, I probably should have pulled a few more bundles of bills out of the duffel bag. The money from the Phantom will be running out soon, and I doubt Alexei Semenov's estate will continue to foot our hotel bills.

I open my eyes and see a silhouette in the shape of Busara standing in the doorway of the room where Kat's and Elvis's bodies are laid out on identical full-size beds while their minds are in Otherworld. When Busara steps forward into the light, I can tell she's staring at me.

"What?" I demand. God she gets on my nerves.

"Simon, are you okay?" she asks. "Where's your ogre friend?"

"He's safe now. I took him home to New Jersey." I'm almost

regretting the decision now. I could really use Gorog's company. For some reason, Busara makes me angry and anxious. I've never really been able to trust her. At least I knew Gorog always had my back. Plus the kid was a riot. I don't think Busara's ever told a joke in her life.

"What happened?" she asks.

It's hard to know where to begin. I point to the black box I set down on the coffee table next to the sofa. "That's OtherEarth," I tell her. "I tried it."

She gasps. "You *what?* Simon, do you have any idea—"

I cut her off. I don't give a damn what she thinks. "Yes, I do. I'm not interested in a lecture, Busara. I knew exactly how stupid it was before I did it. Now do you want to hear about my experience or not?"

"I do," she says with a sigh.

Yeah, I thought so. I start with the destruction of Manhattan and end with Dame Judi Dench.

"With the disk on, how did OtherEarth compare to Otherworld?" Busara asks. "Was it just as convincing?"

"There was no way to tell what was real and what wasn't. I could feel the lady sitting next to me. Hell, I could smell her perfume. For the record, Judi Dench smells fucking *great.*"

"Do you think it's as dangerous as Otherworld?"

"Nothing's as dangerous as Otherworld. But OtherEarth has a pretty impressive body count too." I reach for the box and pull out the Post-it inside. "Alexei gave me five names. He was convinced they were all people who were given OtherEarth glasses and a disk. All but one of them are dead now. We need to find proof that Wayne and his buddies were responsible. It's our best chance now to destroy the Company. You and I should start working on a plan right away."

She peers down at me with a strange expression. "I think we should wait for Elvis and Kat to get back from Otherworld—"

"No!" I bang my fist on the coffee table with far more force than I should. Busara doesn't even flinch. I swear she's a goddamn robot. "It can't wait. Did you hear what I told you? People are dying. We have to come up with something now."

"I don't think that we can, Simon. Have you seen yourself lately?" When I don't answer immediately, she points to the bathroom. "Get up right now and go look in the mirror."

I don't know why I do what she tells me. I guess I'm just too tired to resist. The bathroom light was designed to be flattering, but even its golden glow can't hide the truth. I'm pale and sickly, with dark circles around my eyes. I look like a bad photocopy of myself. I might not even recognize my reflection if it weren't for the glorious schnoz.

"I think you should get some sleep right away," Busara tells me. "We can talk about all of this as soon as you're up."

It's excellent advice, I suppose, but I can't shake the feeling she's stalling.

My sleep is deep and dreamless, but I wake up with a start just after two in the morning. The suite is dark, and no one is stirring. I wander into the living room, where I find the remains of a room service meal on a wheeled cart. My stomach growls noisily. I can't even recall the last time I ate. I lift one of the metal domes, hoping for leftovers. Perched on a bed of wilted lettuce is an iridescent green scorpion. I jump back just in time to avoid a lash from the barb at the end of its tail. Then it scuttles off the tray and disappears under one of the sofas.

I pinch my eyes shut and breathe in deeply. I can hear the rush of blood pumping through my veins. "It wasn't real," I whisper. But I'm not convinced. It looked as real as Dame Judi Dench. I hurry to the bedroom, where Kat and Elvis are laid out on the beds, and close the door, stuffing a towel in the crack beneath it to keep the scorpion out. After that, there's nothing else to do but drop down in the plush chair in the corner. I'm reminded of the days I spent sleeping in the chair beside Kat's hospital bed. But this time we're not alone.

Busara is sleeping on Elvis's bed, which seems a little unusual. But I suppose she wants to stay close in case she needs to remove the disks. It's the first time Elvis and Kat have gone under without me. I watch their bodies for clues that might tell me where they are in Otherworld. The disks induce the same kind of paralysis that keeps people from acting out our dreams while we sleep. Elvis mumbles something incomprehensible, then Kat cries out once as if she might be injured. I hop out of my chair, ready to rip off the disk at the first sign of trouble. But I know she'll be pissed if I drag her out of Otherworld before they've killed off the guests. So I put my ear to her chest and listen to her racing heart. After a few seconds, it slows down.

I suppose most people would be bored to death by this vigil. But the sound of Kat's heart, when it's slow and steady, is the most beautiful music I've ever heard. I hope it can help me recover what little is left of my mind. I am not well at all. I know that. I don't want to end up raving at the padded walls inside an asylum. But what scares me most is the thought of losing Kat. I spent ten years of my life dreaming about her. Now we've been together for a little more than a week and I'm already falling apart.

"Pssst." It comes from the bathroom. "Simon!" I know who it is, and though his presence is hardly proof that my sanity's been restored, I'm glad he's here. If nothing else, I should apologize for trying to murder him in Otherworld.

I get up, turn the light on in the bathroom and softly close the door behind me. "Hey there," I say to the Kishka, who's perched on the fancy toilet seat. "Sorry for throwing a dagger at you before."

He bats away my apology with a flick of his hand. "Not a problem. It's all part of the job. But listen, kid, there's a question I've been meaning to ask you."

He pauses to light a cigarette. Pale blue smoke spills out of it and swirls around us like fog in a Halloween haunted house. "Okay." I'm getting impatient. "What is it?"

"Do you know who I really am?" It's a bizarre question coming from someone I've been chatting with regularly.

"Sure, you're the Kishka." I figure it's best to play along. "You're my dead grandfather who visits me because I'm mentally unsound."

The Kishka shakes his head at me as if to imply that I'm stupid as well as insane. He taps the giant nose that earned him the nickname—the schnoz that's almost identical to mine. "I'm the part of you that never changes. No matter what happens, or how damaged you get, I'll always be the same. It's like your mother. She had the beautiful nose I gave her shaved down and shaped. But I swear it's still there, every time she looks in the mirror."

I laugh. "You're sure about that?" I have my doubts. I think my mother sees the same perfect nose everyone else sees.

"Why don't you ask her?" the Kishka says. "She'd probably be happy to hear from you. Maybe she can remind you who you are."

"There you have it. I've gone stark raving mad," I respond. "I'm sure Mom's thrilled to be rid of me."

"Who knows? I'd say it's worth a gamble," he says. "These days things aren't always what they seem.

"In fact—" He stops and cocks his head toward the bedroom. "Wake up," he orders me. "Now."

I open my eyes and discover I've fallen asleep in the chair. I sense someone moving inside the room. As my eyes adjust, I see that Busara has gotten up and walked over to Elvis's side of the bed. She's leaning over his body. Maybe he did something that alarmed her. Or maybe she's trying to figure out where he and Kat are in Otherworld. Then I see Busara take one of his hands in her own. I assume she's about to check his pulse, but then she leans down and plants a kiss on his forehead, right above his visor. It isn't some friendly peck, either. It's a real kiss if I've ever seen one.

I must gasp, because Busara spins around. She knows she's been caught in the act. I close my eyes and let loose an unconvincing snore. She tiptoes over to my chair, and I can feel her leaning over me. I'm hoping like hell she doesn't kiss me too. It's all so weird that I'm relieved when she just stands there as if waiting for a sign.

"It's very important that you not tell anyone what you think you just saw," Busara whispers. I must be a better actor than I thought. She's not completely sure I'm awake.

She can count on me. I won't say a word. At this point I'm

not completely certain what just happened was real. But I hope it was—even though it will cost me a hundred dollars. Because unless I've completely lost my mind, Busara loves Elvis, too.

The bigger question, though, is why the Kishka thought I should see it.

THE DIAMOND

I'm up with the sun. While Busara sleeps, I order room service and chow down three orders of bacon and pancakes. I'm feeling better than I have in days when I leave the Waldorf Astoria and hunt down a sidewalk Wi-Fi kiosk a safe distance away. I plug in my headphones and punch a number into the telephone keypad. On the third ring, the person picks up.

"Hello?" It's her stern professional voice. "Who is calling and how did you get my private number?"

"Mom," I say. "It's me. I'm calling from a public phone."

"Simon!" I'm surprised that she sounds neither scared nor angry. If anything, she sounds relieved—like she's been hoping to hear from me. "You're calling from a Manhattan area code. Is everything okay? No, wait—don't say another word. I'm headed into the city right now. Can you meet me?"

"Where?" I ask.

"Our favorite place."

It's funny. I wouldn't have guessed my mom and I ever shared the same wavelength, but I know exactly the place she means. "Yes."

"Great. I'll see you there at five after ten. Now hang up and get out of there. If they're monitoring my calls, you don't want to be anywhere near that phone."

She's right. The line goes dead and I hail a taxi. "The natural history museum," I tell the driver.

"You know it won't be open for a couple of hours, right?" he asks.

"Yep," I say. "I'm happy to wait."

I'm the first one inside when the doors open. I head straight for the darkened hall, where the precious stones and mineral miracles are on display. When I was little and my mother and I would come to the city, we'd often spend an hour or two here. I haven't thought about those visits much at all in recent years. If I had, I might have realized there was more to my mother than meets the eye. She and I didn't come here to see the gems on display. Instead, we strategized ways to steal them. When I was about ten, I asked her why she loved it so much.

"This is what my father and I used to do when I was your age," she said. As far as I recall, it's the only time she ever mentioned the Kishka.

I'm standing in front of a bloodred diamond that's on loan from the Indian government. The security at the museum must be much more sophisticated than it was a decade ago. Everything now is computerized. Which may deter old-fashioned thieves of the grab-and-go sort. But to a small group of people with the right kind of talent, this place is a candy store. I bet Elvis could walk out of here in five minutes flat with that diamond in his pocket.

"Stealing it is the easy part," says a voice beside me. "Fencing it is the trick. You couldn't sell the stone as is. You'd have to cut it up. You'd need one of the world's best gem cutters to do it, and everyone from the FBI to Interpol knows who all those guys are."

My mother looks as gorgeous as ever in a slim gray sheath dress, her thick black hair cascading over her shoulders. She could be the first lady of a more glamorous country. No one would ever guess she was the child of a lowlife gangster.

I'm sure she has a long list of questions for me, but there's one I need answered first. "Why didn't you ever tell me about the Kishka?" I ask. "Were you really that ashamed of him?"

"Ashamed?" my mom scoffs. "Just because I never spoke of him didn't mean I was *ashamed*. My dad gave me everything. I was crazy about him. But he died with quite a few enemies, Simon—guys who would have loved to get their hands on Art Diamond's daughter or grandson. They're old now, but they're not all dead. And a couple of them are still fairly dangerous. Fortunately my father had quite a few friends as well. They were the ones who helped me escape from Brooklyn."

"Was Lenny the Phantom one of those friends?"

"Not exactly," my mom says. "But I knew he owed your grandfather a favor, so I kept his name in my back pocket all these years."

"And the nose?" I ask. "If you loved your dad so much, why'd you get rid of it?"

This time my mother actually laughs. "Good God, Simon, it

works on you, but I'm a five-foot-six female. I could barely stand up straight with a nose that size on my face."

I remember the high school yearbook photos I once saw of her, and I know she's not exaggerating. Irene Diamond, as she was known back then, was hardly today's beauty queen. Yet somehow I like her old look better.

My mom threads her arm through mine, and together we stroll through the mineral hall, like an ordinary mother and son taking in the exhibit. "A man from the Company came to see your father and me after you disappeared. He claimed you'd stolen some valuable property."

"What did you tell him?" I ask.

"Not much. I sat back and let your father run the show. He ranted and raved about every crime you've ever committed—from hacking robots and stealing my credit card to the time you took twenty dollars out of his wallet when you were ten years old."

I can only imagine. "Good old Dad," I say.

"Yes, well, you were a little shit." She looks up at me with a smile. "Admit it, it's true. And believe it or not, your father's tantrum did us all a big favor. He made it perfectly clear that he'd turn you over to the authorities the second we heard from you. I doubt the Company expects there to be much contact between us."

She pauses in front of a twelve-foot-tall amethyst geode that looks like something from outer space. "Lenny said the guys they had following you were real professionals. It took him hours to lose them. How much trouble are you in?"

"A lot," I admit. "But if it makes you feel any better, I'm the good guy this time."

My mother faces me. I can see the concern in her eyes. "It

doesn't make me feel any better at all. You're still my son. I don't want you to die saving the world."

"I'm not going to die," I assure her, though I'm not confident it's true. "But I could use your help."

"Yes, I assumed you must have had a good reason for calling." She unzips her handbag and pulls out a thick manila envelope that I figure is filled with bills. "It's my rainy day fund. No one but us even knows it exists. If you need more, just let me know."

Turns out my mother keeps in touch with gangsters and has a small fortune set aside for emergencies. I lived with this woman for eighteen years, and I never once saw this side of her. I never even suspected it was there. The thought makes me wonder what else I might have been missing.

"Thanks." I take the envelope. "This will come in handy. There's something else I was hoping you could help with too." It's a long shot, but I figured I'd ask. I've learned never to underestimate Irene Diamond. "I need to contact someone. Do you know a man named Grant Farmer?"

My mother's perfectly groomed eyebrows rise. "The movie director? The one they say nearly killed his lead actress? I don't usually run in those kinds of circles, but as it happens—" She digs in her purse and pulls out a pen and a notepad. She scribbles something down and rips out the page, which she then hands to me. "That's the name and phone number of his lawyer. We went to Harvard together. I saw him on the news yesterday reading a statement from Farmer. I wouldn't have thought this was his kind of case."

I glance down at the slip of paper. The lawyer's name is George Reynolds. "You think he'll talk to me?"

"He might if you mention my name. He owes me one. By the way, does this have something to do with his client's recent run-in with the law?"

"Yeah," I say.

"I've heard Farmer plans to plead guilty," she tells me. "Is he?"

"Oh, sure," I say. "He definitely attacked the actress. But there's a whole lot more to the story."

"There always is," my mother says.

I shove the paper into my pocket and plant a kiss on her cheek. I can't even remember the last time I did something like that. "Thanks, Mom. You may have just made life a whole lot easier for me. If everything goes as planned, you'll see me again soon. But right now, I need to go find a public phone."

"Wait a second, Simon." My mother puts her hand on my arm before I can leave. I guess there's still something she needs to say. "Listen, we both know I wasn't the world's best mother. When you're older maybe you'll find out as I did that being a parent doesn't come easily to everyone. But I've always loved you. And that moment in the hospital when you threatened to doxx me?"

I can't help but smirk at the memory. "You were pissed as hell."

"Absolutely. But that was the day I knew for sure you were a Diamond."

After she gives me a hug, my mother and I head in separate directions. The museum is filling up now, and I'm forced to weave through the tourists on my way to the Central Park West exit. I'm passing through the gallery of African animals when movement inside one of the dioramas catches my eye. It should be an ordinary savannah scene—zebras and antelope gathered around a watering hole. But there's something else behind the glass. A

creature in a loincloth stands on two legs in the center of the di-
orama, one palm raised as if saying hello. From the neck down, he
appears mostly human. But his face, with its amber eyes and flattened nose, is clearly that of a goat. Though a group of German-
speaking visitors is staring straight at him, no one seems aware of
anything out of the ordinary. They aren't able to see what I see.

I'm frozen in place. I felt so good this morning that I thought
I might be recovering. But if anything, the hallucinations have
just gotten much worse. Now that the goat man knows he has my
eye, he's decided to put on a show. He's knocking over the animals
inside the display. As soon as the last one is down, he chooses a
zebra and begins ripping off its skin and pulling out its stuffing.
It's as if he wants to show me they're no realer than he is.

Barreling through the throngs of tourists, I race out of the
museum and across Central Park West. It's a sunny day in late
spring and the perimeter of the park is bustling. I dart around
hot dog carts and dodge a pair of power-walking octogenarians.
The crowd thins out once I reach the woods in the center of the
park. My legs are aching and my lungs feel raw. In Otherworld I
could run for miles, but in this world, I'm apparently quite out of
shape. I stop and double over to catch my breath. When I look
back up, I see eyes staring back from the edge of the tree-lined
path. There's a giant hog watching me. Its entire body is covered
in thick brown bristles, and tusks protrude from either side of its
long, dark snout. I've never seen a hog up close before. I have no
idea if this is how they're supposed to look. But I am fairly confident that creatures like this don't belong in Central Park. When I
start to run again, it trots beside me. I'm panting and wheezing,
but the hog makes it look effortless. If it wanted to take me down,

it certainly could. But I don't think the beast is out to hurt me. It keeps glancing over at me with its oddly intelligent eyes. It just wants me to know that it's there.

I'm half dead and drenched in sweat by the time I reach the Waldorf Astoria. The staff is used to seeing me by now, but a lady in a Pepto-Bismol–pink suit sniffs primly when I enter the elevator. I'm clearly unwell, but I disgust her, apparently.

When the elevator stops at my floor, I lean down until my lips are inches from her ear. "I feel the same way about your outfit," I whisper.

I leave her standing there, jaw on the ground, and stumble down the hall to my room. The television is blaring when I open the door to the suite. "Where have you been?" Busara demands when she sees me. "You weren't supposed to leave!"

Even if I felt I owed her an explanation, I wouldn't be able to give one. My attention has been captured by the television. A news helicopter is hovering above San Francisco's financial district, where something terrible has clearly happened. An entire building has been cordoned off, and military tanks are stationed on all the street corners.

"There was another shooting," Busara explains impatiently. "Seventy-one people this time. Two more than last week."

"There was a shooting last week, too?" I ask. I really haven't been paying attention. "Is this normal?"

"I guess it is now," Busara says. "You want to tell me where you just were?"

The coverage cuts to a cartoonish man standing behind a

podium. He looks like the star of an infomercial. "Who's that guy?" I ask.

"That's our dear leader," Busara says, looking at me weirdly.

"You mean the president?" How could I not recognize the president of the United States?

"Don't get distracted," Busara says. "I'm asking you a question."

A chyron scrolls along the bottom of the screen. ALEXEI SEMENOV DEAD OF NATURAL CAUSES. Then the news ends and a commercial starts. The camera pans across the glorious Manhattan of the future that I saw in OtherEarth. Flying vehicles zip around garishly lit buildings that project enormous three-dimensional ads into the sky.

I drop to my knees and cover my eyes with my hands. Everything is spiraling out of control. My head is spinning. I can't trust anything anymore.

"Simon. *Simon.*" Busara is at my side with her arms around me. "Don't freak out. It's okay." She's speaking in the kind of soft, singsong voice you'd use with a terrified animal. It doesn't sound anything like her.

I push back a bit to study her face. Even that seems different. She doesn't look like the robot I've come to know. She's worried about me. She definitely should be. "I'm losing my mind," I confess. "Remember the goat man from Otherworld? The one who wanted to eat me? I saw him in the natural history museum. And on the way here there was a feral hog in the park. It looked just like one I saw back in Texas."

Busara takes my face between her hands. "Listen to me, Simon," she says. "You're not losing your mind. One day soon all of this will be over."

"How do you know?" I ask. "How can you tell what's real and what's not?"

Then Busara leans in and she says the strangest thing. "None of this is real. And that's okay."

"What do you mean?" I ask.

She doesn't answer. She just wraps me in her arms and holds me until my heartbeat slows and the world stops spinning. When she lets me go, I'm convinced that she's not the same person. Otherworld changes people, but in my experience, it's usually for the worse. I don't know what to make of Busara's transformation.

"Are you okay now?" she asks. "Can we talk business for a moment?"

The exhaustion hits me all at once, and I nod as I yawn. Going insane takes a ton of energy. I hope the business she has in mind doesn't take very long.

"What do you want to talk about?"

"You said you were at the museum?" she asks. "Why did you go there?"

"I went to see my mother," I tell her.

Busara puts her face in her palms and groans. "Simon, you *know* they've got to be watching her. She could have led them right to you. Right to all of us."

"My mother's a Diamond," I tell her. "She knows what she's doing."

"Did she give you that?" Busara asks, pointing at the thick manila envelope I have tucked into the top of my jeans.

"That's just money." I put the envelope on a side table. "She gave me this, too." I pull out the slip of paper with the phone number on it. "It belongs to the lawyer of the movie director who was arrested while using OtherEarth. I was going to call him as soon as I got out of the museum, but I was too busy running from goats and feral hogs."

Busara plucks the slip of paper out from between my fingers. "Why don't you go lie down," she says. "I'll give the guy a call."

"You sure?" I ask with another yawn. "You know what to say?"

"I'll tell him I have information regarding his client's arrest and I'll set up a meeting."

"Tell him you got his number from Irene Diamond," I add. "They know each other from school."

"No problem." Busara tucks the slip of paper into the back pocket of her jeans and offers me a hand. "I'll make sure to name-drop your mother. It's great she could help us out like this."

A strange question pops into my head as I rise to my feet. "Busara," I say. "When Kat and Elvis are back and the headset players are gone, we should be able to rescue your dad. But what about your mother? Why don't you ever talk about her?" I should have asked a long time ago. I guess I never thought of Busara as a friend before.

Suddenly the warm, caring girl is gone and the robot is back in her place. "Because I'm not worried about my mom."

"Shouldn't you be a little bit worried?" I ask. "I'm sure the Company would love to get their hands on her. Where is she, anyway?"

Busara stares at me. "She's safe." I can't believe it. She's not going to tell me.

"Forget it. I was just trying to be friendly." I'm actually a bit hurt. For a second there, I thought our relationship might have taken a turn in the right direction.

"We are friends," Busara says curtly. It's her way of warning me not to push any farther. "Better friends than you know, Simon."

I refuse to back down that easily. "Then why are you keeping secrets from me? Why can't you tell me where your mom is? Or come clean about the fact that you love Elvis?"

Busara shoots me a nasty look. "I do not love Elvis."

"Liar," I say. "I saw you kiss him. You know I did."

She rolls her eyes. "Says the guy who just got chased by a feral hog in Central Park. Go take a nap, Simon."

"Busara." I'm completely serious. "What the hell is going on?"

We're standing face-to-face now. I expect her to tell me to leave her alone, but she doesn't. "When I go to see my father in Imra, I think you should come with me." I can't imagine anything more completely left field.

"You're changing the subject!" I argue.

"No," she insists. "I'm not."

ELVIS IMPERSONATOR

The last thing I remember is falling asleep next to Kat, whose mind was still in Otherworld. I have no idea what time it was. I have no idea what time it is now, but Kat is no longer beside me. I'm still wearing the clothes I lay down in. I didn't even have the energy to take my shoes off. I sit up and look around the room. Elvis is gone too. There are two Otherworld visors on the bedside table. Kat and Elvis are back from Otherworld.

I follow the smell of coffee into the suite's living room.

"Simon!" Kat jumps up from one of the sofas. I take her in my arms and breathe her in. I don't ever want to let her go. Right now, my feelings for her are the only things I know for sure are real.

"Is it over?" I ask her. "Are all the guests gone?"

"We went to every realm," she tells me. "Places I had no idea existed. It took forever, but we got them all. There's not a single guest left in Otherworld. The Children are safe."

"So you don't have to go back again?" I ask.

"No. I'm staying in the real world. This time for good." She puts her lips to my ear and a ripple of pleasure runs through me. "Busara says she wants you to go with her to Imra to see her dad. You don't have to, you know. It's safe now. She'll be fine on her own."

"It's okay," I assure her. I'd rather go almost anywhere but Otherworld, but there's something Busara wants me to see, and after our weird-as-hell conversation yesterday, I'm keen to find out what it is.

"As long as you're sure," Kat says. She lets me go and steps to the side. Busara and Elvis are watching me. Elvis manages a half smile and an awkward wave. Busara just stares. God the girl can be weird when she wants to.

"You doing okay there, bro?" Elvis asks. Busara must have told them what happened at the museum.

"I'm fine," I tell him. "I think I just let my blood sugar drop too low."

He knows it's a total lie, but like a good friend, he plays along. "Gotta keep those energy levels up."

I nod and focus my attention on Busara. "Thanks for letting me sleep. Now that they're back, you must be pretty anxious to go see your dad." And I'd like to see what she wants to show me.

"It can wait awhile," Busara tells me. "I feel like I haven't talked to these guys in ages. I've been enjoying their company." I might have imagined it, but I swear her eyes just darted over at Elvis. Maybe it was a confession of sorts. Maybe I'm just insane.

Elvis is twirling the OtherEarth glasses in his hand. He's trying to get my attention. He wants me to ask.

"What have you been doing with those?"

"Just trying out the equipment Alexei left you. Busara told us about you and Dame Judi," he says. "But there's another feature I think you need to see."

"You know what?" Kat jumps in. "Maybe we should let Simon have breakfast first." She's nervous, I can hear it.

"I'm totally fine," I insist. "What is it?"

"A custom option. It usually costs money to unlock the feature, but after a while, I got around it. Took me a few hours to figure out how the scans are supposed to work. These things didn't exactly come with an instruction manual."

"Scans?" I ask.

Elvis holds out the glasses, and I almost recoil. I don't want to touch them. I don't want them anywhere near my face.

"You'll be fine. You don't have to wear the disk to get the idea," he says.

I take the glasses and slip them on. There are now two Elvises in the room. One of them is the Elvis I know. The second is identical. He's standing motionless, as if waiting for his first command. Elvis has copied himself.

"Once I figured it out, it took about five minutes to do the scan," Elvis says. "I just had Kat put on the glasses and walk around me."

"The glasses let me know when I'd captured enough data," Kat chimes in. "I had to record his voice, too. All it needed was a few minutes of conversation."

I step closer to the copy of Elvis. The resolution is perfect. If it weren't for fake Elvis's stiffness, I don't know if I'd be able to tell the difference between the two.

I look over at the original Elvis. I can still see him clearly. "This is the most terrifying thing I've ever laid eyes on," I tell him.

"It's even worse than you think," Kat says. "With the disk on, you could touch him."

"Oh God," I say.

"And you could record it," Busara adds.

I don't even want to imagine all the applications the technology might have—or the many unsavory ways in which it will certainly be used. For starters, you'd never know who might be having sex with your digital clone. But it gets darker than that. It's not just about sex. You could have anyone do almost anything—and get it on film. The line between real and virtual has been erased. We'll never be able to trust our eyes or our ears again.

I thought Otherworld was bad, and it was. But this could be worse. The sooner the Company's kaput and Wayne Gibson's in jail, the better. "Did you call the number I gave you?" I ask Busara. "Did you speak to Grant Farmer's lawyer? If we can get someone who used the OtherEarth disk to go public—"

Busara cuts me off with a shake of her head. She doesn't look happy. "I talked to the lawyer. I mentioned your mother's name, too. But the guy said neither he nor his client was willing to talk to me. He told me his client was looking forward to serving his sentence and paying for his crime."

Another dead end. I should have expected as much. The Company must have some serious dirt on the guy. Now that I've seen what he was playing with when he committed his crime, there's no telling what it could be. My guess is he made a copy of the actress he attacked and forgot which was which.

"What about the four dead guys on Alexei's list?" Kat says. "We did some research while you were asleep. Two of the guys died of unexplained internal injuries. Two had heart attacks. I know

Alexei thought the Company might have paid off the police to get rid of the OtherEarth gear. But maybe someone in their families knew about the disks."

"It's possible," I say.

"We'll see what we can dig up while you guys are in Other-world," Elvis tells me.

I feel a chill run down my spine. I'd almost forgotten that I have to go back.

GOODBYE

Busara insists on wearing a disk. Nothing the rest of us say can change her mind.

"If my dad won't speak to me, I'll go back wearing a headset," she tells us. "But there could still be viruses out there. I might not make it very far."

We arrive in Otherworld on the outskirts of Imra. Just past the gates is a thick wall of vines. Rising above the wall are trees that would take centuries to grow on Earth. Gimmelwald appears to be thriving.

"You should go say goodbye to Volla," Busara says.

I can't remember telling her about Volla, but I was just thinking the same thing. I would if Busara were wearing a headset, but the disk makes it too dangerous.

"I can't leave you here and I can't take you with me," I tell her. "There's no telling what kind of beasts we'd find behind the wall."

"I'll be fine," she promises. "You can trust me." She says it with such certainty that I find myself believing her—and starting to suspect that she knows something I don't. She's acting weird, like a little kid with a secret she can barely contain.

As we walk toward the wall of vines that surrounds Gimmelwald, an opening appears. Beyond it lies a wild garden of unimaginable beauty. There are no structures of any sort, just grass and flowers and trees. High above our heads, the leaves are shaking, but there doesn't seem to be any breeze. Then I spot a small green creature scampering among the branches, and I realize the trees are full of Children just like it.

The ground trembles beneath our feet, and a being rises from the earth. The soil that streams from Volla's naked form is dark and rich. She's much healthier than the last time I saw her, and her stomach is swollen with another Child.

"You've returned," she says warmly.

"Just to say goodbye," I tell her. "Your realm is so beautiful now. You've brought it back to life."

"I've done nothing but let nature do what it will," the Elemental replies. "This is how Gimmelwald was meant to be."

Is it? I wonder. It's certainly not what Milo Yolkin had in mind when he designed Otherworld. A guest-free world teeming with Children was never part of his plan. And yet it does seem right, the way things turned out. The Creator gave life to Otherworld, but he was never able to control it. Maybe there were bigger forces than Milo Yolkin at work.

I'm still lost in thought when Volla speaks again. "You say this is goodbye?"

"We're going back to our world," I tell her. "And we plan to stay there. After today, there will be no more guests in Otherworld."

Busara clears her throat. "Actually, we don't know that for certain," she announces.

I do my best to catch her eye, but I can't. "We don't?" I ask. "The headsets have been destroyed. We're leaving. Who else could be here?"

Busara shrugs. "We had no idea that my father was trapped in the ice. There could be someone else left as well. Someone wearing a disk."

I suppose it's possible, but it seems highly unlikely. Volla looks concerned. "A disk?" she asks.

"My friend is just saying that if you meet any guests after today, they'll be like us," I assure the Elemental. "Your Children are safe. The killers are all gone for good." I glance over at Busara, just in case she plans to contradict me. "Right?" I ask.

"Oh, absolutely," says Busara. "If you meet another guest here, you'll be able to trust him."

At this point, I must have the world's highest tolerance for weird, and yet I'm starting to get a little unnerved. It sounds to me like she has someone specific in mind. But I don't want my anxiety to rub off on Volla. So I keep my suspicions to myself as we say our goodbyes.

"Mind telling me what all that was about?" I ask Busara as soon as we're back in front of the gates of Imra.

"All what?" she asks as if she has no idea what I'm referencing.

"That stuff you told Volla about trusting guests!"

"It was true," she says. "If there's someone left in Otherworld, they won't cause her or her Children any harm. I just thought she should know it."

"And that's it?" I ask.

"For now," she says, charging ahead through the gates in front of us.

The suburbs of Imra are a ghost town. You'd think decades had gone by since the last guest passed through. I'm worried the elevator won't work. I don't know of any other way to access the volcano. But when we step inside, it instantly begins to descend. A few seconds later, the doors open onto a strange scene.

Dark and silent, the realm appears deserted. Trash litters the walkway and a musty stench lingers in the air. I hear the click of heels as someone walks toward us. I place my hand on the hilt of my dagger just as a woman in a navy suit and white shirt comes into view.

"Hello, and welcome back to Imra!" It's my old pal Margot, the same NPC who gave me my first tour of the city when I arrived with Carole, Arkan and Gorog. "It sure is nice to have nice guests again!"

"Where are all the others?" I ask. "The ones like you, I mean."

"Gone," she tells me. "Pomba Gira refused to regenerate the workers after they were killed by the guests. I'm the only one left. She kept me safe during the troubles. Now enough about me, how may I help *you*?"

"Your Elemental was kind enough to care for my father," Busara says. "I'm here to thank her and to see him."

"Of course!" Margot chirps. "Right this way!"

The path to the bottom of the crater winds like a corkscrew

along the interior of the volcano. I glance over the railing that lines the left-hand side. I see the bubbling lava and feel the heat on my face, but I don't witness any signs of life.

"Watch your step," Margot warns as we trail behind her. "Things have gotten quite messy since the last time you were here."

I'll say. The city has been destroyed. The chandeliers have all been shot out and the walls are riddled with bullet holes. I peek into a spa room and see dark brown water lapping at the sides of a giant pool. SCREW MILO is scrawled in gore on the tiles. I was never all that fond of Imra, but the sight pisses me off. Milo Yolkin built this place to cater to his guests' every desire. He may have been sick, but you can't question his hospitality. Then a bunch of filthy rich psychos showed up and destroyed it for kicks. This is why the humans can't have nice things.

I keep a careful eye out for danger as we make our way to the bottom of the volcano. I know Elvis and Kat rid the realm of guests, but there's no telling what might have taken over since then. Still, we haven't come across anything threatening, which makes my presence feel pointless. The closer we get to the lava, the more anxious I become. I'm not sure why Busara would want me along.

"Here we are!" Margo trills once we're standing beside the pool of lava. "On a scale from one to five, five being the highest score, how would you rate my performance this afternoon?"

"Definitely a five," I assure her.

"Six," says Busara.

Margot makes a quick note on a tablet computer. "Thank you very much for your feedback! Pomba Gira will be with you shortly!" Then Margot steps into the lava and disappears.

"Wait until you meet Pomba Gira," I whisper to Busara as the lava starts to swirl. "You're in for quite a treat."

"I've met her," Busara says.

"How? You told me you never entered any of the realms when you were here as the Clay Man."

"I didn't," Busara says. "Listen, Simon—"

A beautiful woman with skin the color of charcoal and a flaming red dress rises from the molten rock. Ignoring me, she moves toward Busara. Her hair floats like smoke around her face. "You are here to see your father," she says, her voice soft.

"Yes," Busara confirms.

The Elemental circles her, examining Busara from every angle. "You are not like the others," she says.

"Just out of curiosity, how can you tell?" Busara asks.

"The energy around you is different," says Pomba Gira.

"Does it matter?" Busara responds.

"Wait, what?" I interject, but they both ignore me. What the hell are they talking about?

"No," says Pomba Gira. "It is his choice to see you."

She lifts one of her hands and a coffin-size box rises out of the lava.

"You've been keeping him in that?" I ask. I think I'd have died of claustrophobia by now.

Pomba Gira doesn't dignify my question with a response. The lid lifts off the box, revealing James Ogubu inside, looking none the worse for wear. I hear a gasp from Busara as he steps out.

"Dad." She rushes to hug him. I feel like I should let them have a private moment, but there's nowhere to go.

"You're wearing a disk," Ogubu observes. He looks up at me angrily. "I thought I made it clear that she should have a headset."

"I was the one who insisted on wearing a disk," Busara says, wiping away the tears on her face. "I wanted to feel you when I hugged you this time."

"The headset players are gone," I tell Ogubu. "The virus killed all of them. We are the only guests left in Otherworld."

"And the Otherworld servers?" he asks.

My knees instantly turn to jelly. The servers. Oh my God, I can't believe I forgot about the servers.

"They're in safe hands," Busara tells her father.

"They are?" I sputter.

"Yes," she assures me. "This world will continue, free of human interference. My dad will be able to live here in peace, and I'll visit whenever I can."

I'm already lost again. What in the hell is she talking about?

James Ogubu's eyes take in his daughter. He seems to be struggling to keep it together. "You know?" he asks.

"Know *what*?" I ask.

Busara nods silently and ignores my question. She wraps her arms around her dad, her face pressed against his chest. I hold my tongue for as long as possible. Then I remember that she wanted me to come here. She must have realized I'd ask.

"I'm sorry, but I'm really confused. What's going on here? What does Busara know?"

James Ogubu is still stroking his daughter's back when he answers. "That this is all that remains of me."

My mind is reeling. "You mean—"

"That I no longer exist in your world. I died months ago. I've been told that my body is buried somewhere in New Jersey."

In a long, narrow container just large enough to hold it. That's what Ogubu said the first time we met. I assumed he was talking about a capsule. He wasn't.

"Then how—" I can't seem to get the questions out.

"When I came to Otherworld to release the virus, I knew the body I left behind would be vulnerable. I uploaded my memories into this avatar," he says. "Just in case."

"What happened to your body?"

"I'm not entirely certain," says Ogubu. "There was a cot in my office. I'd sleep there sometimes when I worked into the night. That's where I left my body when I came here to Otherworld. I don't know what happened after that. Milo told me there had been an accident. He wouldn't say more, but I always assumed he was telling the truth. Milo had many negative traits, but I don't think he was homicidal. He seemed very relieved to discover that my avatar would live on—and quite keen to make use of the technology I'd developed."

Before he died, Alexei told Fons he'd never really die because he'd uploaded his real-world memories into his Otherworld avatar. I figured the Company had made it up along with all their other false promises. "So the technology really exists?" I ask Ogubu.

"Certainly. I invented it. And like my other inventions, it was stolen from me. I'm sure Milo would eventually have used it to upload his memories into Magna. But first he was planning to use it to make a digital copy of himself. He said he'd lost interest in the real world, but he didn't want to leave the Company in the control of its board of directors. He didn't trust them to pursue his vision."

"I guess he hadn't gone completely insane," I mumble. The hologram makes perfect sense now. It wouldn't just look like Milo, it would think like him too.

I turn to Busara. "We can't let the Company get its hands on that memory-downloading technology."

"That's why I wanted you to come with me, Simon," she says. "The Company's already got it."

"They what? How do you know?" I ask.

"Do you remember when I told you that none of this is real?"

I have no idea what's coming, but I know it's not going to be good. Busara is biting her lip and looking at me like she's about to drop some seriously bad news. Every nerve in my body is buzzing with anxiety.

"What is it?" I demand. I've barely gotten the words out when Busara vanishes.

I spin around in circles looking for her, but she's completely gone.

"Where did she go?" I ask her father, as if he'd know.

Then the world goes dark. I feel the disk being peeled off the back of my head. "Simon, get up!" I hear Kat urging. "We've got to get out of here right away."

The world is spinning as I sit up. The bed where Busara was just lying is empty. "Where is she?" I ask. "What's going on?"

Kat is gathering the disks and visors in a pillowcase. "Elvis went downstairs to get some coffee. He called up and said he saw Company men in the lobby. Busara already took off."

"She took off?" Something seriously weird is taking place. "Without us?"

"Come on! Get up!" Kat shouts. She grabs my hand and drags me off the bed and out of the bedroom.

But it's too late. They're already here.

"Howdy," says Wayne. He's sitting on one of the sofas in the living room, his injured arm still strapped in a sling across his chest. Three large men are positioned behind him. There aren't any weapons aimed at us at the moment, but there's no doubt that will change if we attempt to escape. "Nice place you've been staying in. We should have checked this hotel right from the start. Seems like Semenov's taste. Those Russian guys, they like fancy things."

"How did you find us?" Kat asks.

This has something to do with Busara, I know it. Maybe I was right about her from the start. Maybe she was a robot after all.

"Your brilliant boyfriend led us right to you," says Wayne. He points at the manila envelope that's still sitting on the coffee table. "We knew he'd eventually need a little financial help from his mama. She's too smart to let us track her phone. But the safe in her office took us about five minutes to crack. You know they have tracking devices these days that can slip right in the middle of a bunch of hundred-dollar bills? I'm telling you, technology is a wonderful thing, is it not?"

Wayne cranes his neck as if looking around us. "I have to admit, I was expecting a bigger party up here. Where are Ms. Ogubu and Mr. Karaszkewycz? I've been looking forward to meeting the two of them."

"They're gone," I say.

Wayne gives us a smug grin that makes me want to murder him even more. "Well, they haven't left the hotel, we know that much for sure. We have all the exits covered. The manager has been quite helpful. Wherever they are, we'll find them. It's only a matter of time."

At that, the door of the room flies open. The three men pull their guns as Busara and Elvis enter, holding hands. Elvis looks shell-shocked but calm. Busara is actually smiling. "We're here!" she announces. "Thought we'd save you the effort of looking for us."

I'd be absolutely certain that this was some kind of setup if it weren't for the surprised expression on Wayne Gibson's face. As Busara walks toward him with an outstretched hand, he rises to his feet. He looks at the hand she's offered but doesn't take it. If I didn't know any better, I'd say he was intimidated.

"I've heard a lot about you, Wayne," Busara says. "I thought it was about time you and I met."

Wayne glances back at Kat and me. I look over at Kat. No one but Busara and Elvis seems to know what's going on.

"Busara—" I start to say.

"It's okay, Simon. Remember what I told you in the ice cave. None of this is real."

"But apparently I'm smarter than I thought," Elvis says with a grimace. "She says I hacked the simulation."

I'm starting to put the pieces together when I see Wayne Gibson's body go stiff for a moment and a new look appear on his face. It's as if another version of Wayne has taken over his body. This one isn't confused. He's furious. Kat grabs my hand and squeezes it tightly. Something has just happened, and I have no idea what it could be.

"What the hell is this?" Wayne demands. He's talking to Busara. "You're not supposed to be here."

"I'm not?" she asks. "Are you sure about that? Where am I supposed to be?"

Wayne doesn't answer. He storms past us all to the suite's second bedroom. We hear the door bang against the wall. A few seconds later, he's back. "Where is it?" he shouts.

"Where's what?" Busara asks with a satisfied smirk.

"Where is it, you little asshole?" he shouts at me.

"I honestly have no idea what you're talking about," I say as I wipe his spittle off my face.

"What the hell is going on?" Wayne shouts at the top of his lungs.

"Maybe there's something wrong with the tech," Busara says. She's clearly enjoying this.

"We'll just run the simulation again," he snarls. The *simulation*. There's that word again.

Oh my God. I think I know what's happening.

"Go for it," Busara tells him. "This run bought us more than enough time."

Wayne marches over to one of his men and grabs the gun out of his hand. In a single swift movement, he aims it at Busara's temple and fires. There's a bright flash, and I hear Kat scream.

Immediately afterward, there's a second flash. Wayne has disappeared, but Busara is still here. There's no way that Wayne's bullet could have missed her, but she appears completely unin-jured.

I remember what she told me back in the ice cave.

She turns to Elvis and wraps her arms around him. He's just as surprised as I am when her lips meet his. But despite everything that's just taken place, he still manages to kiss her back. You'd think the two of them had been together for ages. "I love you," Busara tells him. "I'll see you soon."

"Busara—" I say.

She looks over at me with pity in her eyes. "I'm sorry you've suffered so much this time. I wasn't expecting it to be so hard on you. You went back and forth to Otherworld so many times, the worlds got mixed up. I promise, things haven't been as hard for you back in the real world."

"Real world?" Kat asks. Then she turns to me. "Simon, what's going on?"

"None of this is real," I tell her.

REALITY IS ONLY A
STATE OF MIND.

OTHERLIFE

Fall 2019

ABOUT THE AUTHORS

JASON SEGEL is an actor, a writer, and an author. Segel wrote and starred in *Forgetting Sarah Marshall,* and also cowrote Disney's *The Muppets,* which won an Academy Award for Best Original Song. Segel's other film credits include *The End of the Tour; I Love You, Man; Jeff Who Lives at Home; Knocked Up;* and *The Five-Year Engagement.* On television, Segel starred in *How I Met Your Mother,* as well as *Freaks and Geeks.* He is the coauthor of the *New York Times* bestselling Nightmares! series—*Nightmares!; Nightmares! The Sleepwalker Tonic; Nightmares! The Lost Lullaby;* and *Everything You Need to Know About Nightmares! and How to Defeat Them. OtherEarth* is his second novel for young adults.

KIRSTEN MILLER lives and writes in New York City. She is the author of the acclaimed Kiki Strike books, the *New York Times* bestseller *The Eternal Ones,* and *How to Lead a Life of Crime. OtherEarth* is the sixth novel Kirsten has written with Jason Segel. You can visit Kirsten at kirstenmillerbooks.com or follow @bankstirregular on Twitter.